THE MONGOOSE AND THE COBRA

MIKE KINGDOM THRILLERS
BOOK 4

DAVID JARVIS

This edition produced in Great Britain in 2025

by Hobeck Books Limited, Unit 14, Sugnall Business Centre, Sugnall, Stafford, Staffordshire, ST21 6NF

www.hobeck.net

Copyright © David Jarvis 2025

This book is entirely a work of fiction. The names, characters and incidents portrayed in this novel are the work of the author's imagination. Any resemblance to actual persons (living or dead), events or localities is entirely coincidental.

David Jarvis has asserted his right under the Copyright, Design and Patents Act 1988 to be identified as the author of this work.

All rights reserved. No parts of this book may be used or reproduced by any means, graphic, electronic, or mechanical, including photocopying, recording, taping or by any information storage retrieval system without the written permission of the copyright holder.

A CIP catalogue for this book is available from the British Library.

ISBN 978-1-915-817-72-3 (pbk)

ISBN 978-1-915-817-71-6 (ebook)

Cover design by Jem Butcher

www.jembutcherdesign.co.uk

Printed and bound in Great Britain

ARE YOU A THRILLER SEEKER?

Hobeck Books is an independent publisher of crime, thrillers and suspense fiction and we have one aim – to bring you the books you want to read.

For more details about our books, our authors and our plans, plus the chance to download free novellas, sign up for our newsletter at **www.hobeck.net**.

You can also find us on Bluesky @**hobeckbooks**, Twitter/X **@hobeckbooks** or Facebook **www.facebook.com/hobeckbooks10**.

CHAPTER ONE

"C'mon, Michaela, make up your mind," she was talking to herself in the mirror, mimicking her mother's voice.

Mike, as she was known, had changed her wig from the black one to the bright red one and back again. "I don't know why you are so nervous. He has seen you in both of them before."

She settled on the jet-black Cleopatra wig and straightened the collar of her white cotton blouse. Some face cream to disguise the pitted skin caused by the accident was the only item of make-up. Rubbing her hands down her jeans, she gave the cabin a final check. This did not take long as it was essentially a single room, lined with tongue and groove pine boarding. The few pieces of furniture were all second-hand and definitely at the shabbier end of shabby chic. A scruffy hat took her eye. It was on the floor where it had been dropped. She quickly transferred it onto a peg by the front door.

Her cabin was almost a mile along a track in the middle of a wood. Living an isolated life above a forester's garage suited her very well as people, in general, tended to get on her nerves.

Her phone rang.

"Leonard, what a pleasant surprise." He was pretty much near the top of the list of people who got on her nerves.

"Are you in the office today?"

"It's Saturday or haven't you noticed. Why do you need me in the office, anyway?"

"I don't need you, but Chuck has gone missing. Have you seen him?" He was speaking in a restricted way as they always needed to do on an open line.

"Why would I have seen him?"

"I thought that he might have headed your way."

"Don't be stupid, Leonard!" she said in a stern voice. "Why would you think that?"

"Hey, look, the troops here think that he might be headed your way." By 'troops', he meant the CIA team that Mike had rejoined in London under his directorship.

In the several years since the ambush in the Netherlands in which her husband, Dylan, had been killed and Mike had been severely injured, she had been tempted by Leonard, her CIA Director, to freelance for him on several projects, all of these had not gone entirely to plan. After the last one in the Middle East, she had accepted his offer to rejoin the team in London as an operative.

The title 'operative' had been a major sticking point; she was trained as an analyst and did not want to go into the field. He, however, had convinced her that if her new contract specified 'operative', she could have more freedom and mostly work from her cabin, if she was an analyst, she would be office-based and have to travel into central London every day. Leonard had promised her that he would ensure that in reality she only did desk-based analysis, at which she excelled.

"What? What do you mean by 'headed my way'?"

"Well, he likes you."

"Leonard!"

"OK, what do you want me to say? That he's a loser and you are his last hope?"

"What? ... I've only talked to him a dozen times by the coffee machine about meaningless crap. I've had closer relationships with squirrels on my bird feeder."

"He's a great analyst, sorry, operative."

"You couldn't tell an analyst or operative from a block of cheese," although she instantly regretted mentioning food, a subject dear to his heart.

"I think that he might be feeling the stress, you know, he might need some time out."

"He can join the club. I've had a lousy couple of weeks, as you know."

"If you see him, get him to phone home."

"Talking of phones, haven't the troops tracked his?"

"That's why I am calling, he is somewhere near you."

"Shit, Leonard!"

"You operatives need to look after one another."

She didn't bother to respond because she heard a car outside – a rare occurrence when you live a mile up a track in a forest.

―――

Over the previous year, Mike Kingdom had been back in contact with someone whom she had met in Spain while working on a job for Leonard; his name was Waldemar Wasielewski.

Wazz, as most people called him, had been a postman in London but had given this up after a spell in prison to become the paid security to rich expats living along the Costa del Sol, this was mostly escorting wealthy wives around expensive shops and on overseas trips. A year earlier, he had been appointed to provide security to Charles Yelland, the oil magnate. Mike had suggested to Charles that he needed some serious protection, and this had turned out to be a good idea; Wazz, and some of his Spanish ex-military friends, had proved to be very necessary.

He had decided to return to his home in West London to finish his Degree in International Studies at the Open University. The main reason for going to Spain in the first place had been to be near his son who was there with his mother. Times had moved on, and his son was now more interested in the local girls than in his father who was often away for days or weeks on jobs.

Although their lives had only crossed for a week or two, Mike and Wazz had developed a mutual respect. He was the mongoose to her cobra – Wazz seemed unfazed by her sharp tongue and immune to her bite. Events and timings had meant that their relationship had never progressed beyond platonic despite the obvious chemistry.

Now, on a hot and steamy August morning, he was visiting Mike in her cabin deep in the woods of Oxfordshire for the first time.

After turning off the tarmac onto an un-metalled track, he was not sure what to expect. The Volkswagen hire car rocked and bumped its way over the ruts, ridges and potholes. A short distance later, a small estate cottage appeared, but there was no sign of life. The coniferous trees and waist-high bracken closed in around the track and the sunlight became filtered through the canopy. Rabbits, surprised to see any human activity, scampered away between the fronds – their eating disturbed. A buzzard glided directly towards him but swerved upwards over the treetops, its meal also disturbed. After a mile, a second cottage came into view near a two-storey building which was partly open underneath but with external steps that led up to a door.

He parked in front of the garage, disappointed that Mike's Italian motorbike was not visible. He had heard so much about her pride and joy. Sadly, it was a tractor and trailer that took up most of the open area under the upstairs accommodation. Feeling nervous, he began to climb the stairs.

Mike opened the door, and he kissed her on both cheeks, the awkwardness inevitable. He was wearing faded jeans and a white tee shirt, which he comprehensively filled. All of the tattoos on his forearms were on display. A small, brown leather man-bag was slung over his shoulders, unremarkable in Marbella but worthy of comment in Marlow.

"I finally get to see you in your castle," he said.

"I'm not Rapunzel and I wouldn't grab my hair if you need to escape."

It was as if they were continuing where they had left off next to the bins outside of the Yelland villa near Málaga.

"It's just as I imagined it."

"Then you have a warped imagination. Would you like something to drink?"

"Tea would be great. It's never the same in Spain even using the same brand of teabags." He walked over to the floor-to-ceiling window that formed the end wall, peered down at a neatly stacked pile of logs and turned back into the room. "Is that log-burning stove your only form of heating?"

"That and cigarettes. You still vaping?"

"No, I have quit completely."

"That would make me ratty," she said. Very wisely he said nothing but sat on a chair and rested his elbows on her small kitchen table, "Are you still freelancing for the CIA?"

"No, I have gone back full-time. I know, I know …" she paused to acknowledge his faux shocked expression, "… and Leonard is my boss again, but I can work from here most of the time. I go into the office once a week."

"Into Central London?"

"Yes, he and I are no longer seconded to Five Eyes," by which she meant the grouping of English-speaking spy agencies, "we are back working for the Agency. So, where are you living?"

"I've got a flat that I've been buying in Ickenham. I've moved back in. It's handy for Heathrow or the other London airports, not that I use them anymore. My son doesn't need me ... or, so he thinks."

"Have you got a job?"

"Yes, but my main aim this year is to complete my bloody degree. It has been disrupted for reasons that you know all about." He stared directly at her, and she was struck by how good-looking he was. His face was chiselled, OK she would accept that it had been a blunt chisel, and his nose had been broken, but his blue Slavic eyes were something special, intelligent and kind.

"So, what's your job?"

"A lap dancing and strip club in Paddington. I'm the bouncer," he paused before mimicking her soft American accent, "I know, I know ..." after she had looked skyward, he continued, "Look, it pays the mortgage and does not involve much thought. The only downside is that I have to work until 3.00 in the morning, but I get to lie in the next day until I do my coursework."

"You're weird."

"You're weird," he repeated.

She stared at the teabag in his mug as if it was about to do something new to science. However that it was meant to taste, she had ruined it by splashing in a generous amount of milk. Wazz, who had been excited about his drink, now handled it as if it was hemlock.

"What?" she asked, "It's a mug of tea. Get over it. What's wrong with you British ... or Polish ... or whatever you are?"

"Do you ever take any prisoners?"

"I never get to that stage. The enemy has normally retreated."

She leant back against her kitchen cabinets, arms folded, and legs crossed at the ankles. He looked up at her with a broad smile but said nothing.

"What? And you are judging me? You're the one who works in a strip club."

"I think the key word is 'in'. I don't work 'in' a strip club. I am outside of the front door."

"That's the argument the SS Guards used at the concentration camps, isn't it?"

"God, I've missed you. Why are you so angry?"

"I'm a square peg in a round hole."

"You could buy a lathe?"

"Huh! Do I look like I do DIY? I need a cigarette," she walked to the door and stepped out onto the external landing. He joined her in the doorway having picked up the baseball bat she kept leant against the frame in anticipation of unwanted visitors. He was gently rubbing it.

"Did you make this? I knew that you had a lathe," he smiled, leaning on the handrail while she lit up. A couple of deep inhalations seemed to calm her.

It was 11.30am and the day was beginning to really heat up; there was a smell of pine resin and a background hum of insects.

"This is a beautiful spot. I can see why you live here."

At that moment, it was 12.30pm in the Aare valley, 500 miles southwest from Oxfordshire in Switzerland. A man in a green hunting jacket and peaked cap was leaning against the white peeling bark of a birch tree. He was standing above a very high concrete retaining wall at the edge of the forest on a mountainside. A tinder fungus that was growing on the tree, resembling an elephant's foot, provided a handy place to rest his left hand to steady his binoculars. He was, apparently, birdwatching and absorbed by the black kites circling above him.

What was about to happen had taken months of planning

and the target, or, specifically, the mother of the target, was notoriously protective of her private life.

His location had been chosen so that he could coordinate operations and because he could approach along a little used road that wound along the contours of the mountain whilst hidden by the birch canopy, this route avoided the small group of houses down to his left. Even if someone one hundred yards away had spotted him, it would have taken them nearly thirty minutes to drive up the valley, through a town and a village before joining the winding forest road by which time he would be long gone.

Beneath the thirty feet high retaining wall and across some immaculately manicured lawns, a small, pale-grey industrial building complex had been built. It was the headquarters of CdP Chemicals AG, one of the Big Pharma and cosmetics conglomerates that had their research departments within a few miles of each other near Berne in Switzerland. Whether controlled ultimately by American, French or Jordanian owners, they all benefitted from the pool of scientists attracted to the area even if the loyalty of these individuals to any one company was less than a layer of skin cream deep.

In a few minutes, there was to be a rare visit by Valentina with her son Diego. She was American, of Puerto Rican extraction, and her family trust owned over 80% of the shares in CdP Chemicals AG, named after the highest point on her native island, Cerro de Punta. Where some of the money came from for her to buy the controlling stock in industries as diverse as cement or oil or pharmaceuticals was the subject of much speculation. Her visit today was to finalise a $135 million loan to the company from another of her enterprises, this one theoretically based in Bilbao, Spain. The German CEO and the Swiss board of directors of CdP Chemicals AG were less than enthusiastic about having their company saddled with an unnecessary debt with its burden of quarterly interest payments.

Valentina was fifty-five years old and for at least the last decade had been one of the largest political donors in the USA. Not one to attend balls or charity auctions, she managed to keep a separation between her public and private life. Political connections gave her some protection, but she knew that she had many enemies and that her life was in constant danger. One defence against this was to lead a peripatetic life, randomly staying at any of the many properties that she owned around the world. Her houses alone combined to create a real estate portfolio worth almost half a billion dollars.

She had flown into Berne airport from London that morning and was now heading for her meeting.

A graphite grey 7 Series BMW, driven by a chauffeur, slowed as it approached the research building. It pulled up right in front of the main entrance where someone was already waiting to open the rear doors. Valentina stepped out first, her thick black hair framing her face, not a strand moved. Her eldest son did not get out of the limousine but instead was holding his phone to his left ear not wishing to interrupt a call.

There was a sudden roar as the BMW's engine was re-started and it roared off, throwing Diego back into his seat. His mother's screams were drowned out and there was nothing she could do apart from watch the car disappear from view. She ran into the building shouting for someone to call the police and screaming that Diego had been kidnapped.

High above, the man in the green jacket and cap was happy that everything had gone so smoothly. He turned and scrambled the hundred yards back up to his small 4 x 4 and drove off not to Berne but to Geneva where he would fly back to his farmhouse outside of Biarritz in France looking forward to tending his bee hives.

CHAPTER TWO

Their couple of hours together had passed quickly.

"I'm not going until I have seen your new bike," Wazz was halfway down the external stairs.

"Really? It's black and got two wheels like the last one," Mike said dismissively as she followed him, enjoying the warm sunshine.

At the bottom, he stopped and savoured the smells and sounds of a coniferous forest at the height of summer which was a new world to him; it had only taken one week in a prison cell, unable to see a single living plant, animal or bird, before his perception of nature had changed forever. He was absorbing the heat from the wall of bracken that surrounded the track, forming its own microclimate as they had both stepped onto the greyish ash surface, the product of natural fires over the centuries. At their feet, ants were attempting to devour a slow worm that had oddly died out in the open.

Something else took his eye, "What are they?"

"Fire beaters," she had answered. He had been fascinated by the rack of ash poles with squares of black rubber attached, standing erect like soldiers on parade, ready to be used to dampen down any outbreak of fire.

He walked across the sandy track thinking that they were a ridiculous first line of defence. He knew better than mention this opinion.

"It's in here," she said, "and, no, you're not riding it."

They entered the relative cool of the undercroft and navigated their way around an old blue tractor and trailer. Swallows were flying in and out, having wisely chosen a nest site away from anything belonging to Mike. An Italian motorcycle took pride of place at the back of the storage space. Every surface of the bike shone, whether it was the chrome or the glossy black paint. He was dumbstruck by the power and the beauty. It was a machine designed to be equally at home over the fields as on the open road. He could not resist gripping one end of the handlebars but was overly careful, not wanting to knock it off its stand.

"It's beautiful. Maybe one day you'll give in and let me have a go?"

Mike let out a sort of snort and turned to leave. Clearly this would not be happening any time soon, he abandoned hope and followed her. As she was about to step into the daylight, something caught her eye, and she bent down.

"What is it?" he asked.

"Blood, I think. What do you think?"

"Yes, looks like drops of blood to me and reasonably fresh." He looked around the rough, dusty concrete floor but couldn't find any more.

"That's a bit creepy." Mike was standing at the entrance, looking up and down the track.

Wazz did a more thorough search, peering under the trailer, opening two bins and investigating anywhere that could conceal a human being. "Perhaps, it was a wounded animal looking for a bit of shelter?" he was trying to sound reassuring, "Do you want me to have a look around outside, before I go?"

"No, I'm fine," she said attempting bravado but just failing.

"Sure?"

"I've lived here for five years, and a wounded badger or deer is not going to frighten me."

"In that case, I'll make a move. Great to finally meet up again and glad to see that you haven't changed."

"Are you sure about that?"

"Was there ever a risk?"

"No."

"Hopefully, you'll come and see me in London?"

"At home rather than at work, I assume?"

"Well, actually, you would be ..." but he never finished his sentence.

She walked with him to the Volkswagen.

"It's a hire car before you say anything," he was learning to get his defence in early.

"I am sure it will get you back to Ickenham."

He opened the car door ready to leave and walked back over to her with open arms. She was not in full 'repel boarders' mode but most men would probably have sailed back to their home port, even the Vikings.

He hugged her but did not attempt to kiss her, even a peck on the cheek.

"Any trouble, you phone me."

"I can cope with a dying roe deer but thanks for the offer."

"I meant that if you have trouble cutting up the meat, I can help. I love venison. I'm happy to bring the Merlot".

She folded her arms and crossed her legs trying to look uninterested; in this she also failed. He had seen this many times before.

"Stay safe." He slid into the driver's seat and started the car.

———

"Leonard, I would really like to call you one day when we can have a long, fun talk about basketball, but it seems we only speak when the proverbial is hitting the fan," Thomas, the US Director of National Intelligence, was on the screen looking surprisingly calm with his white hair combed back, serving only to emphasize his big forehead.

Leonard let him speak. They were on a secure line.

"Diego Ortiz has been kidnapped," he allowed Leonard to digest this, "The President is not happy, as you can imagine".

"Is Valentina safe?"

"Yes, but up the wall and angry, as you would also expect – you know that she's a control freak," there was a second before he said," Is Chuck safe?"

"He's gone walkabout, but I think I know where he is."

"What? Well find him fast. If they get him as well, you and I might as well pack our bags."

"No problem, I have a whole team on it, trust me," Leonard was unrecognisable, almost sounding grown up.

"Leonard, I am up against it. The President is ... let's say, concerned about his good friend and her sons. Valentina is not only his biggest financial supporter, but he is also a little too close to her, if you get my drift. He wouldn't be in the White House without her. Find Chuck and get him somewhere safe, real safe. You understand?" the last two words were spoken softly and slowly but not leaving any room for misinterpretation.

"Where was Diego when he was kidnapped?"

"Val was at a factory in Switzerland with him."

"I thought they might try in London."

A few seconds elapsed before Thomas said, "You're continuing to track them, right?"

"Of course, we're working with the Brits via Pathfinder. We are following their phones wherever we can and there are surveillance crews in place. Don't worry, we'll find Chuck ... the idiot."

Mike screamed.

She was halfway up the steps when someone came around the building below her.

"God, you frightened me."

"Oh, sorry, Mike" the forester, in his grubby dark blue overalls, was carrying four dead rabbits by the back legs, "I've been trapping."

"That explains the drops of blood under the cabin?"

He didn't reply directly but simply said, "Sorry." He averted his gaze.

"No problem."

"Your visitor gone?"

"Yes, I was showing him the bike when I saw the blood."

"Sorry, I'll get these rabbits home," he wandered off back towards his cottage. As they were the only two people who lived within a mile, it was surprising that their paths crossed so infrequently but then, his responsibilities did extend across five thousand acres of Oxfordshire.

Relieved, Mike opened the door and stepped back inside her cabin unaware that a pair of eyes had been watching her from behind the rack of fire beaters.

She was not entirely relaxed, and this had taken the edge off the visit by Wazz. Needing a drink, she walked over to her fridge, pulling off her black wig as she went and placing it on its brass stand between the blonde and red ones. Rubbing her bald scalp was always a relief and on a hot day she did not want to wear anything on her head inside the cabin.

The cool beer from the bottle had its desired effect. She calmed down and reflected on Wazz. The last time that she had seen him was in the Yelland's villa in Spain a year or so previously. Seeing him on her home turf was a risk. Would she still like him? Would she still fancy him? The answer was yes. *But is this what you want in your life right now?* She mulled over her situation.

The accident seemed to have made worse all of the quirks and personality flaws that she had before it. Her lack of social skills and inability to read emotion had increased to the point where she was better off living alone. Even though most people, young and old, found her attractive, she thought that she was ... well, she didn't actually care what anyone thought. The three stark wigs on their brass stands, blonde on the left, black in the middle and red on the right, were more about order than vanity; she would happily walk down the street bald-headed.

Although she had started it, Wazz had said to her, "You are weird," and this had surprisingly affected her.

She slumped into her threadbare armchair and stroked the head of the Giacometti bronze statue that sat on the floor beside her, a ridiculous present from some thankful, very wealthy friends. If she had sold it, she could have retired to a very happy existence that most of the population could not even imagine – she was not most of the population. She fitted into no pigeonhole. Who else shopped in Aldi once a fortnight and, afterwards, sat eating pasta next to something that any burglar would have missed but was worth a million dollars.

With all of the distractions over the last few hours, Mike was frustrated that she could not get back to pursuing a breakthrough that she had achieved at work on a longstanding project. Two and a half weeks ago, she had suffered a major setback; it had knocked her already low confidence. Although she had been told unequivocally that the project was now dead and she should move onto new work, she had not given up and part of her could not wait to return to the office on Monday and to try a new line of enquiry.

There was a hammering at her door that jolted her out of her downward spiral.

She jumped but it was probably Graham, the forester; he had

been very embarrassed earlier. This really was not a typical day in her cabin. Speaking to two people at home was more than she normally did in a month. Her interaction with the planet was more likely to consist of her shouting at a wood pigeon or rescuing a red admiral butterfly, fluttering at the large window.

With a wig back on her head, she opened the door to be faced by a tall, young man with bushy black eyebrows, long nose and a gap between his front teeth, looking dishevelled.

"Mike," was all he said but it expressed so much relief.

"Chuck, what are you doing here?"

"Can I come in?" he said in his mid-Atlantic accent.

"Of course."

His clothes were dirty, and he smelt of ... what was that smell, horses? His eyes were bloodshot.

"Sit down and tell me what's happened."

"No, I'm covered in shit from the stable."

"Don't worry, sit here," she pulled out a wooden dining chair, "Are you OK? Do you want a drink ... some food?"

"I'm fine," was what he said but this was as far from reality as one could imagine.

Mike could never in anybody's wildest dreams be described as 'maternal', but even she could see someone in meltdown. It took one who had been through this to recognise it in someone else.

She said nothing until she had opened a bottle of beer, taken a slice of pizza wrapped in foil from the fridge and put it in front of her visitor.

"Eat."

Drinking from her bottle, she looked across at someone that she had seen in the office over a period of about nine months but with whom she had barely spoken. It was a little strange to find a person that you occasionally passed at work on their way to get a coffee, sitting in your living room. He did not tear into the food like she expected but took a very slow look around the room, "Your clock's fast," he said before biting into the cold pizza.

"It gains a minute a day. Every ten days I adjust it; I can do the math." There was no sharpness in her tone, she was speaking his language.

"No problem but remember to do it in two days' time." He took another bite of the pizza, and it became his focus.

While he ate and drank, she watched and tried to work out what was happening. Why had he come to her home?

All that she knew, and it was more than most thanks to her relationship with Leonard, her boss, was that he was genuinely an analyst but that Chuck Kilminster, was not his real name. He was under some Agency witness protection program or similar. He had not really appeared on her radar and, yet here he was in her cabin. He was American like her, probably thirty years old, tall, hairy and, without doubt, scared shitless, beyond that she knew nothing.

"Would you like some more food?" Mike wanted him to relax before she asked him the million-dollar questions.

"No, that was great, thanks. Actually, do you have any ice cream?"

"Does this look like a Dairy Queen?"

"It might if you put a counter in front of that big window," he had taken her literally.

"I have a slice of cheesecake."

His face lit up, "Yes, please."

She cleared the table and went over to her refrigerator. With a piece of blueberry cheesecake transferred onto his plate, she carried it back towards the table.

"While you are eating, how about you tell me why you are here?"

He took a mouthful, "Blueberry is my favourite."

Under the table, Mike was wiggling her fingers and hearing the voice of her aunt, Jana, who had taught her this technique to release stress. Wiggle, wiggle, wiggle. To keep quiet at this moment took all of her control.

He was eating with his mouth open when he said, "Do you ever think that this might be your last meal? It's gotta happen sometime, right?"

"That's a bit morbid."

"I – I have this feeling. Do you get these feelings? I think you do. That's why I came here."

There were times when Mike wanted to go back to being a ratty teenager again, being an adult had serious drawbacks.

"Are you in danger?" She sounded like her father.

"I've always been in danger. I was born in danger."

Mike for some odd reason thought about those people specially trained in talking potential suicides down from window ledges, a profession probably not likely to have featured in her career's adviser's notes.

"I'm not Chuck. Who wants to be called Chuck?" he was now rambling.

"Whoever you are, something has gone wrong ... obviously. What do you want me to do? How can I help you?"

"My mother is crazy. She cannot hide me anymore. They know who I really am. I'm dead."

"... and you came here?" it suddenly occurred to Mike that he had found her home, an address not readily available.

"You're not like the others."

"Well, that's true. Probably the red wigs."

He smiled, "I enjoy being an analyst, like you do. I only wish I had a different mother."

"Would you like another beer because I sure need one?"

"Thank you, I'm ... I'm on edge."

She stood up and began walking to the refrigerator, "who are 'they'?"

"You're an analyst. It's obvious, isn't it? But if I don't tell you anything, you won't get hurt as well."

"That's kind. What are you going to do next?" she knocked the top off two beer bottles.

"I'm going to see the tulips. Is that a Giacometti?" he nodded at the bronze statue of *The Running Man* on the floor behind him.

"It is. Excuse me, I need the restroom," she turned and began to walk the few short steps to the slightly damp-smelling cubicle with its shower, basin and toilet.

"I had nowhere to go, it was either you, Jim or my brother, Diego, and he lives in Europe."

"And I lost out?" she kept walking but later regretted what she had said. When she came out Chuck, or whatever he was called, was gone.

CHAPTER THREE

Mike had, in fact, been asking Chuck a question as she came out of the restroom, rubbing her hands but she had been met with silence. Her living room was empty.

"Shit!" she walked over to the table and then over to the front door that was ajar, a shaft of bright sunlight stretching across the floor. On the outside landing, she scanned the area but could not see him.

"Shit!" she said again, running down the stairs to look underneath the cabin. She called out his name but there was no sign of him, she retraced her steps and went to go back inside.

On her threshold were drips of blood.

She did not swear again but, instead, walked inside and flopped into an armchair. Why her? Why come to her cabin? Why run off? Why was he bleeding? Mike moved to pick up her bottle from the table. His phone was next to his plate. Perhaps this meant that he had popped outside and would return. She tried to calm down, but a mouthful of beer did nothing to settle her or provide any answers. In fact, more questions formed.

Had he been hiding under her cabin when Wazz arrived? Was

it his blood on the concrete floor? She felt that the answer to both these questions was yes.

For weeks, Mike had been looking forward to today, it was meant to be so special but all of the excitement that had been building in anticipation of seeing Wazz again had proved to be a waste of energy, it was all now history. For no apparent reason, Leonard's face came into her mind.

"Shit!" she said for a third time.

A large swig left in her bottle of beer gave enough time to dial Leonard's number. He picked up immediately.

"Chuck was here a few minutes ago."

"Great. Where's he now?"

"No idea. He just left the cabin and has disappeared. He's dripping blood."

"Give me ten seconds while I give the team an update. They are about five miles away from you. I'm told that Chuck turned off his phone or it ran out of battery, so they lost track of him." There was a click on the line and silence. She stared at the wall clock which was eight minutes fast and waited until Leonard came back, "Hi, the team are on their way, they will let you know when they arrive at your cabin. Please play nice."

"Leonard, my Saturday's been ruined, and you want me to play nice?"

"Hey, I'll give you a day off in lieu, tell me what happened, what he said, what he looked like."

"Chuck turned up at the door half an hour ago looking rough, he stank of ... I don't know, a farmyard. He was starving. I fed him and gave him a beer. He had started to calm down, I thought, but while I was in the restroom, he simply disappeared."

"Tell me what he said, don't leave anything out."

She repeated the conversation as best she could remember it. He asked her only to repeat the bit about the tulips.

"What does that mean?"

"No idea, he was rambling most of the time. Leonard, he was disorientated and scared. For some reason, he said that he could only trust me and his brother, Diego and someone called Jim. Perhaps, that's where he's headed next?" Mike was unaware of what she was saying.

"Oh, crap! You stay in the cabin in case he comes back. I will come over to you. I'll be an hour. I need to fill you in."

Her Saturday, already ruined, was getting worse.

———

In a way that only someone used to living on their own might appreciate, Mike had been looking forward to the last piece of pizza that she had put in the fridge, but it had been consumed by Chuck. She was starving. With her whole day turned upside down, she had opened a can and was microwaving a bowl of soup when there was yet another knock on the door. This was the most visitors in one day she could ever remember since moving in, having selected the cabin purposely to avoid the human race. Something inside made her pay attention; it could be Chuck returning. This was very possible as he was following his own line of logic that would test every supercomputer on earth unless, of course, he had stepped outside for a pee or forgotten his phone.

Ignoring the microwave, she headed to the door.

"Hi, I'm Zack, I hope that Leonard de Vries has told you that we would be calling?" He was perhaps from Texas and had a respectful tone to his voice.

She was confronted by a man who was fit in the sinewy sense of the word, like an Olympic sprinter, perhaps.

"He did. How can I help?" she stared down at one other man who had stepped out from a BMW four-wheel drive. Only the driver stayed at the wheel. They were US Special Forces in tee shirts and jeans unless she was seriously mistaken.

"Where is Chuck?"

"He was here," she looked at her phone, "eighteen minutes ago. He left the cabin, and I haven't heard or seen him since. That's his blood, by the way," she pointed at the dark red drips in front of her.

"Which way did he go? Did he have a vehicle?"

"I didn't see him leave but I don't think he had a vehicle, I never heard one."

"Ma'am, are these tyre tracks his or do you recognise them?"

She leant over the handrail and began to go down. They did not look like they belonged to Wazz's Volkswagen, and she couldn't think who could have created them.

"No idea." She descended to the track looking at what appeared to be fresh tyre tracks, but they were nowhere near where Wazz had parked. Zack and Mike walked over to the BMW to include the others in the conversation. This was lucky.

The cabin exploded in every direction. The noise was deafening, and it echoed around the forest. Dust and smoke instantly obscured the sun and continued to eddy and swirl around; a pair of jays screamed as they flew away through the trees.

Immediately afterwards, there was a stillness, a long silence broken only by the shouting of a team trained for such eventualities checking on each other.

Mike had lost consciousness and was face down in the grey ashy sand. Her arms were spread, and her black wig was a couple of yards away. The tyre tracks that she had been attempting to examine no longer existed.

Zack, while dazed, had grabbed her and was hauling her towards the open door of the BMW. His mate had helped to push her onto the back seat; they both jumped in. The car's engine was roaring as the driver span the vehicle on the sand creating shapes worthy of a Speedway rider before they roared off back towards the main road.

It bucked and barrelled along the track as the team took stock.

Mike, hanging strangely across the back seat with one arm down in the footwell, started to recover consciousness and began speaking garbage. "Bronze melts at 913°C," she mumbled. This meant nothing to the search team who could have no concept that a million dollars' worth of art may have been exposed to extreme heat, that's if it had not been blown to smithereens. Zack, with his fingers bleeding needed to wipe them on his jeans before he could dial on his phone.

It took a few minutes until he was patched through by his controller to Leonard de Vries who was already in a car being driven out of London.

"Zack, I'll be at the cabin in ... thirty-seven minutes," Leonard said after checking his ETA.

"Sir, there is not much of the cabin left. It's been blown up. We are all safe, including Miss Kingdom. She's concussed."

"Jeez, where are you all now?"

"At the end of the track where it joins the main road."

"Does she need medical attention?"

He didn't answer but asked Mike, "You OK?"

"I'm fine!" she had regained consciousness and was piecing things together but not necessarily in the correct order.

"She says that she's fine. Where shall we meet you? I think we need to get away from the area before someone calls the fire department. There's a lot of smoke that people are going to see."

"Did you find Chuck?"

"No, Sir. No sign of him."

There was a long pause while Leonard spoke to somebody. Eventually he came back on the line, "Meet us at Bavant Manor Cottage" he gave the address and postcode, "We will be there in thirty minutes. It's a safe house in Buckinghamshire." He broke the word down into four very distinct syllables.

Zack's colleague at the wheel had already put the postcode

into the satnav as he was repeating it back to Leonard. They bumped onto the tarmac and set off eastwards at speed. Mike swivelled to look out of the rear window; in the distance a plume of black smoke was clearly visible above the forest.

Built in the 1890s, Bavant Manor was a small brick-built country house with stone-mullioned windows. It had been substantially extended post-war in a less than attractive way and since this time had been used by the British military as a training college. It was set in two hundred acres of oak woodland that had looked beautiful in April when the rhododendrons were in flower. On the perimeter, with its own access track, there was a well-hidden property that was used by the CIA as a safe house. It had originally been two estate cottages that had been knocked into one.

Leonard arrived first and his driver parked the car next to a wooden garage whose roof could not be seen under rampant ivy. Joseph, the house manager, had opened the gates remotely for his visitors and was now stood at the front door awaiting their arrival.

"Hi, Joseph. Anyone around at the moment?"

"No, a few days before my next guests arrive. The place is yours. What do you need?"

"A meeting room and a snack later would be good. Zack and his team will be here very soon." Leonard entered the cool of the hallway and followed Joseph to the door of what had originally been a dining room. The dark furniture could almost have been original as could the pale green patterned wallpaper. He pulled out a chair from under the table, sat down and began checking the messages on his two phones. In the hallway he could hear Joseph speaking to the team who had arrived at the gate.

Leonard was reading messages from the Director of National Intelligence and from the President's Chief of Staff. They were both in coded ways asking the same thing – have you found Chuck? He scrolled on through his phone looking for a reply from his own deputy in London who was liaising with the UK authorities, now aware that the fire at a forester's cabin in Oxfordshire was a bomb blast and an attack on a CIA staff member.

Somebody entered the room.

"What have you done?!" Mike did not bother with any pleasantries.

"Jeez," this had come out more in the form of a whisper than a cry as a bald woman covered in grey dust, dressed in a dirty white shirt and torn denims, came into the room. Her cheeks were streaked where tears had washed away the dust.

"What the … just happened?" her tone of voice was at that level where the listener is left in no doubt of the importance of the question.

"Mike, I'm sorry," he had never seen her without her wigs or her own hair.

Zack, a veteran of Iraq and Afghanistan, who was entering behind her, retreated back through the doorway but stayed in the corridor to listen; he more than most understood the meaning of the expression 'collateral damage'.

"Who is Chuck?" she had moved forward, resting one hand on the dining table for support.

Leonard stood up and walked to the door, "Zack, can you and your team go and clean yourself up and walk around outside? Shit is happening and we are all a bit twitchy?"

"Yes, sir."

Returning to his chair, Leonard asked Mike to take a seat. Knowing her and with the knowledge that the chair could be used as a blunt instrument, this was, perhaps, a bold move.

But there was no more aggression. Rather, silent tears streamed down her face. Leonard for all of his superficial buffoonery was not CIA Director in London without good reason and not without some humanity. He was blindsided. The barbs and abuse from Mike, he could take – she was his favourite analyst, operative, whatever she was, but the tears, he could not.

"Mike, I'm sorry. Let's get you some medical help."

"Don't worry about me. Apart from a ringing in my ears, I'm fine. Who blew up my cabin?" she did not look or sound fine.

"Let's not rule out a gas cylinder blowing up or something stored by the forester guy."

"Really? You came out here at a minute's notice because you think it was a gas cylinder? Let's get real, who's Chuck and why did he come out to the cabin?"

"Chuck is the son of someone famous and important to the US. He and his brother, Diego, have been a major target. Diego stays mostly with his mother, but Chuck has been hidden away in London working for me under a false name."

Mike took this in, and the tears started to dry up.

"Why did he say that he only trusted me and Diego ... and someone called Jim?"

"He's not a normal kid ... he has issues," and Leonard wanted to add '... like you' but knew that now was not the time and if he did say it even Zack and his entire year's intake at Fort Liberty couldn't save him.

"Well, he's not going to hang around here now my cabin's been blown up, is he?" and the tears began to well up again.

"Don't worry about your cabin. It will be rebuilt and everything in it'll be replaced, I promise you ...," he was about to add 'I swear on my mother's grave' but he had tried that once before.

"He hasn't got a phone ... or anything. How's he going to contact his brother or this Jim?"

"Diego was kidnapped this morning in Switzerland."

"Jesus Christ! Leonard."

"I know, trust me, my phone is red hot from you know who."

"Damn it!" she pulled out her own phone from her pocket and checked it was working, "This is all I have in the world. I don't even have any other clothes, Leonard!" The implications began to sink in.

"Joseph!" and a few seconds later, a face appeared around the door, "Can you ask Sally to come in. Mike has lost everything, so we need Sally to sort out Mike with the essentials. She needs to sleep here tonight."

"No problem." He disappeared.

"What? Oh, yes, thank you," she had not even thought about where she was going to live, "But who has kidnapped Diego and put a bomb under my cabin to kill Chuck?"

"Mike, I thought that I knew but now I'm not so sure," he paused, "I'm sorry this has happened to you. Why don't you let Sally sort you out with the basics and you get a good night's sleep here? Together with the Brits, I have several teams looking for Chuck. By morning, I hope that we have found him."

"And if you haven't?"

"I will need you."

CHAPTER FOUR

Given what had happened the day before, it was a surprise that Mike had slept through the night without waking; to her intense relief, there were no nightmares, no replays. The bed was king size and very comfortable which may have helped. That evening a couple of hours after Leonard had left, she had relaxed under a steaming hot shower, put on a pair of soft pyjamas and crawled under the duvet. She had felt safe; there was something reassuring from knowing that Zack and some other teams were on the case, and her last thought had been that if you weren't safe in a CIA safe house, where would you be?

Joseph and Sally had made her feel welcome. They were calm and experienced such that nothing was too much trouble. It was as if she had turned up at a friend's house after her car had broken down a mile away in the pouring rain.

Sally had said that after breakfast she would take Mike into High Wycombe where she could buy clothes and essentials. There was a retail park that would be open on a Sunday morning at 10.00. Someone called Ray would drive them, but his main purpose, clearly, was to provide security. Mike was wearing a silk paisley scarf tied around her scalp that Sally had offered until she could buy a replacement wig.

Later, walking around the superstores, Mike felt no effects from the blast except that her hearing was defective and there was a ringing deep inside her head. They had made two trips from the shops to the car made necessary by the piles of bags and boxes that they had acquired. With the boot full, Mike asked if they could go to Every Three Weeks, a shop that she had found earlier using her phone while eating her eggs and bacon. She had made an appointment.

Accessed through a narrow gap between a cottage and a chapel in a village outside High Wycombe, the driver avoided the largest of the potholes and parked outside of a 1960s bungalow. Mike, accompanied by Sally, walked up the concrete path and rang the bell on the porch. Someone materialised through the opaque glass panel and opened the front door while trying to control a black and white spaniel.

"Hi, I'm Carla … and this is Wally. Come on in."

"Thanks for seeing me on a Sunday. I won't delay you for long," Mike entered and patted the dog.

They chatted, following her through to the back door and out into the garden at the end of which they could see a large shed or, perhaps, a sunroom.

"Welcome to Every Three Weeks."

Inside, they were confronted by shelves and shelves of wigs on polystyrene heads. In the middle there were two small sofas, and, on the walls, several ornate mirrors surrounded by hanging fairy lights. Mike, of course, was attracted to the most vivid colours and outrageous styles. Carla told her to take her time and to try on as many as she wanted, "Nobody is watching and there are no cameras."

Carla was used to coaxing nervous women undergoing chemotherapy into relaxing and exploring. This was not the case with her new customer who pulled off her scarf and began trying on everything, admiring her reflection whether looking like a pantomime dame or Roxie Hart from Chicago. Sally sat on a mini chesterfield and enjoyed the show; Mike was not the usual type of person she and Joe were expected to look after.

It was ten minutes before Mike settled on bright red and blonde Cleopatra wigs as replacements for those that had been lost and on one that was long, wavy and black that changed her appearance completely; she hadn't had flowing, curly dark hair since she was twelve. Something, however, was disturbing her. She put the red wig back on its polystyrene head and tried on a khaki forage cap with a red star in the centre. She tilted it and, in that moment, accepted that her world had changed forever and that she must move on; it would no longer be her accident or the explosion that defined her life. She stared at her reflection and adjusted the cap to wear on the return journey. Despite buying two wigs, she wondered if she would ever wear them. Sally paid the bill and, with their shopping complete, Ray drove them back to Bavant Manor Cottage.

Mike put most of her purchases straight into her bedroom unopened and took the three remaining boxes down to the dining room. When Sally brought her some lunch, she had not noticed that it was well after two o'clock. Mike needed to clear a space on the dining table which was a mess covered in cables, opened cardboard boxes, polystyrene packing and pristine computer equipment. For almost two hours Mike had been setting up her new laptop having lost her hardware and, more importantly, software in the explosion. The majority of her effort had been expended on the dark web, downloading all that she would need in the future to enable her to search where she should not be searching. This was her life.

Not having noticed what she had consumed apart from the fact that it was meat in a tomato sauce, she began to search online for the explosion yesterday; what were the official and unofficial theories?

Early that Sunday morning, several teams had assembled at the scene of the explosion. Mike's living accommodation had been destroyed but the garage and storage area beneath had survived – mostly. The tractor, trailer and her motorbike were intact, if covered in mud and debris. The external stairs were in place but only leading up to a pile of smoking black timber and shattered glass. Four concrete pillars projected up to the sky like teeth, without any roof or side walls to support. Fire had destroyed Mike's furniture and belongings as the dry pine cladding had proved to be the perfect flammable material.

The Running Man was no longer in full flight; he had survived but had been knocked over and thrown against the remains of the kitchen sink. Five fire engines, pumping thousands of litres of water, had taken an hour to put out all of the flames by which time the dust and black ashes had been turned to liquid mud dripping down onto the pale, sandy track and flowing towards the trees like lava. The hoses from one engine had been trained on a small fire that had broken out in the bracken nearby. Ironically, it was the row of fire beaters that had been seriously burnt. Finally, satisfied that there was no longer a danger to life or to the forest, they had left mid-evening.

In the morning, the site was still a busy scene. Zack and his team had returned, and he was being debriefed by a Commander Trevelyan, a policeman from the Counter Terrorism section. A Forensic team was upstairs in the remains of the cabin looking for the cause of the explosion and fire. Local police were preventing access anywhere near the site whether down the track or from a public footpath, now temporarily closed.

Another police team, accompanied by the other two members of Zack's team, were over a mile away following two tracker dogs. They had not been able to start until someone from Leonard's office had retrieved a hoodie that Chuck kept on the back of his chair in the office; it had been rushed across to the team by police motorcycle. Out of its sealed bag, it had provided the excited dogs with the necessary scent. They had immediately charged around the base of the building and set off through the bracken.

Their handlers in black overalls, caps and protective glasses crashed through the green fronds following the dogs who left the relative safety of the ferns and raced into the dark of the pine forest with its soft floor of orange needles and treacherous spear-like branches at eye level. Emerging onto a rutted track, the two Belgian Shepherds lost the trail or rather, ran up and down the track confused by where Chuck himself had probably wavered. For no reason apparent to the human mind, they settled on a northerly direction and set off again at pace.

They had all eventually reached the forest edge where the landscape changed to fields which were full of horses, spooked by the sudden appearance of the dogs and men; the mares charged around the boundaries neighing, only to suddenly stop and turn towards the cause of their fear. It looked as though Chuck had followed the vehicle track bounded by fences until he had reached a wooden field shelter in the corner. Perhaps, this is where he had slept on the Friday night before visiting Mike. Had he returned here when he had vanished before the explosion?

The handlers brought the dogs under control with difficulty, while the Americans called out Chuck's name approaching the shed with caution. Was he frightened? Was he alone or armed? Peering around an upright they could see that the shelter was completely empty and there was no sign that he had spent time there yet the excitement from the dogs indicated that he probably had.

Knowing that Chuck had a whole night's start on them, they needed to move on. Leonard had made it clear to his team that Chuck's mental state may be delicate. Of course, Leonard had put it in a much blunter un-PC way. The dogs raced around the next fields, along the access tracks and back into the forest but could not pick up a definitive scent.

"Did he have a vehicle?" one of the Americans asked and they all examined the ruts in the track and the surrounding area, but the ground was hard and dry. No tyre tracks looked recent, those that existed were temporarily fossilised awaiting the autumn rain.

"Well, it looks like he had a car or bike ... unless he stole a horse. He didn't walk from here. The dogs would not lose the trail now that they are locked on."

They seemed to have reached a dead end. In one hundred yards this is exactly what happened as the track was barred by a substantial wooden gate chained up with an industrial scale padlock.

Chuck had vanished.

―――――

Later, back at the cabin, Commander Trevelyan had finished with Zack going over the exact positions of everyone at the times that the explosion had happened and the actions of everyone following it. As Zack walked off speaking to one of his team who was with the dogs, the estate manager, Rory, arrived to see the Commander. Not surprisingly, the estate was being kept in the dark about the CIA connection via Mike and Chuck, but Rory was suspicious that so much urgent activity was happening because a gas cylinder had blown up and had destroyed a small building in the middle of a wood.

Rory was responsible for a very valuable five thousand acres of the best mixed farmland and woodland in Oxfordshire and his employer, a Lord whose grandfather had made his money from cigarette papers and, later, packaging, was more than inquisitive.

"Why is our tenant of such interest to you? Is it drugs?"

"No," Commander Trevelyan had said, taking another ten

minutes to prevaricate, neither confirming nor denying anything. He called Mike 'a person of interest' and asked Rory to suppress discussion about the incident for twenty-four hours while the various teams finished their investigations.

When the estate manager mentioned that his employer knew the Home Secretary, Bob Trevelyan had heard enough.

He brought the conversation to an end by asking whether there had been any break-ins or suspicious activity over the last few weeks. When Rory confirmed that nothing of note had happened, the commander took his leave saying that he needed to go and interview Michaela Kingdom. Rory likewise said that he needed to go and see his forester, Graham, who had been traumatised by the incident.

―――――

Valentina Ortiz was emotionally drained and had also reached her limit.

As she had said to Conrad, the American President, when one of your two children has just been kidnapped, how can you not question the value and importance of one thousand, one million, one billion dollars? Her other child was now the prime target and in danger; she would give it all away to save him. She had told Conrad that it was the fact that she could not get hold of her youngest that was driving her crazy. His real name was Eduardo, and he had suffered with problems from birth but had ended up doing something he loved in a very safe place. Now, when she needed to hear his voice, he was not answering his phone. This frustrated her. Why was he not answering his phone? Conrad had tried to assuage her.

While Diego was worldly-wise and gradually taking over the family business interests, Eduardo had been different. On top of this, she knew that her family was under constant threat. Diego was travelling with her and sharing the same protection. Eduardo had no real idea of the threats he was under.

Years before, Conrad had asked her what she wanted in return for being his biggest supporter. She had said that she had no interest in being the Ambassador in London or anything similar, but could her son be found a job – a safe job under an assumed name. She had hidden him away for years in London, but he was getting frustrated. Within the last year 'Chuck Kilminster' was doing what he loved, playing at computers all day as an analyst in the secure environment of the CIA office in London under Leonard de Vries.

Of course, Eduardo had a house in Kensington that no member of the public could even begin to imagine with a staff of seven, including a driver and security. Most people would brag about this at work, but this was never a risk with Eduardo, he could care less. Every weekday morning he was dropped around the corner from his office where he walked along in a dream followed a few yards behind by a thick-necked ex-Marine who watched until he entered the security of a boring-looking London building.

Apart from her, there were only eight people who knew who 'Chuck' was, and one of these was the President of the United States, as well as his National Security Director and the Head of the CIA in London.

After several interviews with the Swiss police and the public prosecutor, she had answered every question about the abduction of Diego. She told them that she had got out of the car after her security had opened her door while Diego was concentrating on a call. Suddenly, the car had roared off across the tarmac.

In the aftermath, she had telephoned several important people, but it had taken a few hours for all of the connections to be made. It was not until the US Ambassador in Berne had made some telephone calls that the Swiss authorities fully understood who they were dealing with. The Swiss President had now been informed.

She was about to board her plane when she answered a call from Conrad.

"Val, I am so, so sorry. There are no words."

"Conrad, they've kidnapped him," there was a short silence while she dismissed someone talking to her, "and I can't get hold of Eduardo. I think I know what this is all about, but do you know what is happening?"

"I don't know but, trust me, I have everyone at my disposal on the case – and that's the State Department, CIA, FBI, Homeland Security and everyone you can think of."

"What am I supposed to do? Diego is ... I don't know where and I can't be in two places at once. I need to be with Eduardo. Why can't the CIA find Eduardo?"

"Val, isn't it better to stay in Switzerland? We will find Eduardo. Where are you now? Are you safe?"

"Yes, I am flying to London in a few minutes. I need to find Eduardo. There is nothing more I can do for Diego until I hear from the kidnappers. I will keep the plane on standby and fly back. It's only just over an hour."

"By the time you are in London, I will have made some more calls."

Valentina, with her face set in a scowl, walked up the steps into her aircraft and flopped into a comfortable, grey leather seat.

CHAPTER FIVE

It had rained overnight, and the sky outside was still dark but improving.

Mike was feeling human again, wearing her khaki cap and having eaten a breakfast of poached eggs. It was a little after 9.00am on Monday morning and she was using her new laptop on the dining room table in Bavant Manor Cottage. The strange silver wall lights in the form of candlesticks were not adding much cheer to the dull interior.

Unbeknownst to her, during the previous afternoon a series of communications had taken place between the British and Americans that had culminated in Commander Bob Trevelyan speaking with Leonard de Vries. The fact that the home of a CIA employee may have been bombed in the UK had raised several security and legal issues that needed to be ironed out. Eventually, everything had been settled.

Leonard had used Sally to communicate to Mike that she should stay at the safe house for a few days and that Bob Trevelyan would visit her at 9.30am for an informal interview. Using the harmless Sally to communicate all of this to Mike was clever and demonstrated a skill most people did not realise that

Leonard possessed. However, even though Mike was reasonably polite with the very experienced Sally, she still managed to send Leonard a message that expressed that, firstly, she was frustrated at having to stay in the cottage and that, secondly, she wanted to go back to the cabin to see for herself what had happened and to collect anything retrievable.

His first reply had not satisfied her, so they had finally agreed that she would do the interview and go back to the cabin immediately afterwards, but this would be with Zack and his team. Leonard had a few theories about what had happened but was very unsure as to why someone had placed a bomb under Mike's cabin, and he wanted her under CIA protection at all times.

It was Joseph who brought Bob Trevelyan into the dining room having met him at the front door while his driver reversed a dark blue Jaguar against a rotten wooden fence ready for their departure.

Mike looked up from her screen to see a tall man in his late forties with swarthy skin, greying hair and high cheekbones enter the room. With the most innocent-looking hazel eyes, he was as far away from her concept of a police Commander as she could imagine. He looked like an actor playing a policeman.

"Miss Kingdom, so sorry for what happened to you," he said nothing else but let the silence express the disgust he felt for the situation in which she found herself.

She started with, "You must be the policeman who is going to take me back to my cabin?" and, ended with, "I am Mike, by the way."

"I am, indeed, going to do that ... and I am Bob Trevelyan. Please relax, Mike, I only have a few questions before we can set off back there."

She tried to work out what was odd about this man and settled on the fact that he was simply incredibly good-looking, this was only enhanced by his uniform. He pulled out a chair and looked around the dimly lit room located on the west side of the cottage. With a reassuring smile, he started to ask questions.

The interview had mostly been her describing what had happened that Saturday lunchtime. She answered truthfully bearing in mind that Leonard had made it quite clear that she could mention that Chuck had visited but not to give any other details except that he was a work colleague; everything else was up for discussion.

Perhaps lulled into a false sense of security by his general disinterest and his gentle encouragement, she began to chatter away. While talking about the drops of blood on the concrete floor she had inferred to him that she was not alone when she saw them. A minute later she was explaining that Wazz had come to see her that morning.

"Tell me about Wazz."

She instantly regretted mentioning him and tried to backtrack, dismissing his visit.

"He's a friend ... nothing to do with any of this."

"What do you mean by 'any of this'?"

She flipped and gave him one of her looks that usually prompted people to remember that they had something urgent to do elsewhere.

"How many of your houses have been blown up?" she asked.

"Well, it's not a long list."

"He is a distant friend who came to see me. It had been arranged for weeks, ask Leonard."

"Does Leonard have a telephone number or contact details for Wazz?"

She glared at him, "Wazz has nothing to do with this!"

"I am sure that you are right, but he was there immediately before the explosion happened and may have seen some trivial detail that you may have missed." The last few words were a mistake, and he instantly regretted them.

"I missed nothing. There was nothing to miss."

He took a mental step back, looked around and asked, "How long are you intending to remain here? Do you have somewhere else to stay?"

"When I've seen what's happened to the cabin, I might ask you to drop me at The Dorchester, I keep a suite there."

He put the tips of his fingers together, rested his elbows on the table and tilted his head forward, "Who would bomb your cabin?" This was said in the most neutral tone possible.

"I don't know. You're the policeman. Who do you think?"

"I think that you are one of the smartest people I have met in a very long time," he rubbed under his left eye and asked again, "Who would bomb your cabin?"

"Who says it's a bomb? My gas cylinder for cooking is under the cabin. Perhaps, it blew up?"

"I'm afraid that the gas cylinder has been eliminated by Forensics. It is there intact next to your motorbike."

"Really? Is the bike OK?" she was suddenly animated.

"It looked alright to me. It was on its side, but I didn't see any damage."

She breathed out with a sigh of relief. This was good news but, despite this, Mike drifted away for a moment. Deep down, she had been clinging to the hope that it wasn't a bomb, and that Chuck was not the target.

He asked her some more general questions before returning to the question of Wazz. Reluctantly, she gave him contact details and, after the Commander had declined tea from Sally, suggested that they headed off for the cabin; it would take them over a half an hour.

Under a sky of broken cloud, they drove off in convoy. The Commander being chauffeured in his Jaguar and Mike in the BMW with Zack and a driver in the front.

———

How could she be anything other than devastated?

There was little left of the upstairs living accommodation even if the undercroft and garage were relatively intact. There was a strange, sweet smell from the warm rain overnight that had fallen on the burnt remains; this was intermixed with the scent of the pine forest. Bob Trevelyan stayed at the bottom while Zack accompanied her up the stairs to where her front door had stood. The floor was concrete so there was no danger of her falling if she kept away from the edges. There seemed to be no logic to what had happened with most things burnt to black ash and others nearby merely severely smoke damaged.

She lifted the Giacometti sculpture of *The Running Man* until it was upright and walked it back to its original position, which was no longer next to an armchair but, instead, next to a pile of burnt coiled springs which was all that remained. This was a pointless act, but she needed to begin restoring order to her life.

One of the important reasons for coming back had been to retrieve any bits of her secret hardware that might still be operational or recoverable; she need not have worried, it had all been burnt and distorted in the extreme temperatures.

There was no sign of her wigs or their brass stands, and her framed photographs of Dylan were nowhere to be seen. Her past had been obliterated.

There was no point staying any longer. It would only be distressing.

She asked Zack to carry the statue downstairs and went, herself, to collect her motorbike. Her hands were black, and she had nothing to clean off the muck. In a horrible lightbulb moment, it dawned on her that she did not have the keys. She left the bike on its stand and walked back outside.

"That's it," she said to the Commander. "Those are all I have from my previous life – a motorbike and a sculpture." The Giacometti looked ridiculous on the track between the Jaguar and BMW.

"I'm sorry." He took out a folded white handkerchief from his trouser pocket and handed it to her. She looked at it but declined it, shaking her head. Instead, she rubbed her hands together to remove some of the black mud. Like after the disaster in Holland, she was mentally moving on. This was a coping mechanism that had worked before – well, sort of.

"Mike, I think that Zack should escort you back to the cottage. Leave the investigation of what happened here to me."

She was standing with her hands by her sides, taking a final look at her cabin.

"Zack, can we take the sculpture back with us?" her eyes were moist.

"No problem. I'll arrange for the bike to be picked up later, as well."

"Thank you." Everyone was being so understanding.

Something, however, wasn't right. Something was bugging her. It was jarring some pattern in her tidy mind. She turned to the Commander.

"Why is everything underneath intact? There can't have been a bomb underneath, it must have actually been in my cabin, mustn't it?"

"Forensics are still checking, I'll let you know what they find out" he replied but her questions had simply confirmed what he had already decided. Mike Kingdom was very smart.

———

As she was being driven back to the cottage, Leonard de Vries was being chauffeured to a hotel in Park Lane for an important appointment at 11.30am.

The uniformed doorman in a top hat welcomed him at the top of the steps before Leonard disappeared inside through the solid revolving doors. He was about to ask for directions to a specific meeting room when he spotted a helpful sign pointing along a corridor. Walking on the extremely luxurious carpet with its loud, swirling pattern, he passed by some other small meeting rooms named Harlech, Corfe and Pembroke until he read the illuminated brass plate outside of Ludlow. The fact that these were named after castles passed him by. He wiped his brow, tucked in his shirt and knocked firmly.

A man in a dark suit and black tie, at least a foot taller than Leonard, opened the door. He took a pace back to let the visitor enter before stepping outside himself and shutting it.

"Valentina, I am so sorry," Leonard held out his hand which was lightly shaken by the woman sitting in a high armchair. She did not get up.

"Thank you, Leonard. Have you found Eduardo?." Her eyes were puffy behind lightly tinted glasses, the helmet of black hair immaculate, as always. She physically resembled Imelda Marcos; they were also both mega-rich with similar sized shoe collections.

"No, we haven't but I have teams on the case, and we have a lead."

"He hasn't been home, and his phone is dead."

"I know, he went to see a work colleague in Oxfordshire on Saturday. He left his phone there."

"Are the British police involved yet?"

Here, Leonard was in some difficulty, and he was teetering on a tightrope. If he said no, she would wonder why not? If he said yes, she would want direct access to the investigating officer. On his way over to the hotel, Leonard had decided that he wanted to keep Chuck's true identity, he couldn't think of him as Eduardo, away from the police for as long as possible or until they discovered it, which assumed that there was a chance that they could stumble across it. This meant that he had to lie to Bob Trevelyan or, at least, not tell the whole truth.

Leonard was not playing this game for the fun of it. He, genuinely, believed that it was in Chuck's best interests (and his mother's) that he was found by Leonard's team and not by the British police which would almost certainly blow Chuck's cover and put his life even more at risk. Unfortunately, Zack or the police tracker team had lost the trail at some stable a mile or so away from the cabin. Zack knew that they were following somebody important, but the police had thought that it was only a work colleague of Mike's.

Apart from his mother and brother, Chuck seemed to only trust two people – Mike Kingdom and someone called Jim. Leonard decided that he would set Mike the task of finding Chuck; there was nobody better at this sort of thing. First, he needed to appease Valentina and reassure her that all was being done. He did not want her using any of her vast wealth to appoint her own investigation. He knew Valentina a little from when he was asked to take Chuck under his wing and look after him. She was grateful and he believed that she would trust him, although with both sons missing, she was very likely to be at breaking point.

"No, not directly. We are in contact and using their staff and databases. Hopefully, we will not need to involve them formally."

"Why did Eduardo go to visit a colleague in Oxfordshire? That doesn't sound like him. Who is he?"

"It's a 'she'."

"What? Don't tell me he has a girlfriend. He never told me." This was clearly a very over-protective mother.

"No, no, she is a friend, a work colleague."

"Where did he go after he left her? Does she know?"

Leonard did not like the way this was going, "No, he didn't tell her."

"What's her name?"

Checkmate. Leonard had made all of his moves. "Mike, Mike Kingdom. She's an analyst like Eduardo. She's part of the team looking for him."

"They haven't run off with each other or anything stupid like that, I couldn't handle it."

"No, no, Valentina, I spoke to her yesterday, she is fine ... and she's trustworthy." Leonard felt that now was not the moment to mention the explosion.

There was a moment's reflection.

"Why has he run away, Leonard?"

"Everyone tells me that he was happy at work ... well, you know, as happy as Eduardo ever was."

"This has nothing to do with what has just happened to Diego, does it?"

"I've no idea but I doubt it. Have the Swiss made any progress tracking his kidnappers?"

"Progress? In Switzerland? Of course not."

CHAPTER SIX

On that hot, humid and threatening morning in August while Leonard was in the hotel speaking to Valentina, two brothers named Emmanuel and Henri were driving in a black van, a Vauxhall Vivaro belonging to their uncle, near Slough in Buckinghamshire; they had been shopping and had been to a car wash. They were at a loose end and were removing all traces of the dust and dirt from the wheels and underside of the vehicle. Henri was smiling while driving, happy that they would soon be back home to France, not all jobs went so well. Emmanuel's face was blank, but this was his normal expression; he was not big on emotion.

As far as they were concerned, they had completed their task. The cabin had been completely destroyed, of that there was no doubt. The noise had been deafening and the smoke could be seen for miles. Enough explosive had been used to obliterate the cabin. They had returned on that Saturday afternoon to their uncle Alain's restaurant. He was serving at a table when they appeared from the kitchen door and Henri had smiled broadly at him, a sign that it had been a successful trip. He followed them out of the eating area and, when alone, they filled him in on the details. He clasped them both and they knew that they had made him very happy.

Two weeks earlier they had arrived on an EasyJet flight from Montpellier to London Gatwick where they were met by friends and driven to meet their uncle. Looking out of a car window at the blue road signs, they had seen that they were on the M25 motorway; this meant nothing to them but less than an hour later they had established that they were on the M4 and finally saw signs mentioning Slough. They were not sure how to pronounce it but soon formed an unfavourable opinion of the place. Sadly for the late Sir John Betjeman, the bomb they were to make in Slough was not used there but on a cabin a few miles away in the next county.

Time had dragged as, for almost a fortnight, the two nephews had been placed on standby by their uncle who, in turn, was waiting for instructions on who was the target and where they could be found.

Finally, he was given a mobile phone number and an address. On that fateful Saturday, they had found the location which turned out to be a cabin somewhere in Oxfordshire.

The bomb would have killed anyone inside.

―――

The storms on that Monday morning eventually developed to their full potential and the rain for an hour was intense. While Leonard de Vries was being driven back from the Park Lane hotel, Wazz had been woken by the thunder and lightning; he had been exhausted after an extra-long Sunday shift.

Nursing a hot mug of tea in both hands, he was sitting at his kitchen table barely awake, listening to the radio. After a song by Becky Hill that he loved, an advert came on air that he found truly irritating; it degenerated into a tsunami of terms and conditions. He eventually stood up to turn off the radio but hesitated.

A news update was explaining that an explosion in a cabin deep in an Oxfordshire wood on Saturday had still not been explained nor had the blocking of the public footpaths nearby or the need for two helicopters and fire engines from two neighbouring brigades. The excited reporter was speculating widely as to what had happened.

Wazz grabbed his phone and began searching the backstory. His tiring weekend had meant that he had seen no news as he could do without the world's problems; a drunk punter at one o'clock in the morning who was complaining to him that two of the lap dancers had stretch marks and stank of cigarettes, was enough irritation for one day.

How many cabins were there in the woods of Oxfordshire? He had no idea but if anyone was going to attract trouble, who would he possibly pick?

He dialled Mike's number.

"You drove off and missed all of the action," was how she began.

"Are you in one piece?" he sounded very concerned but had worked out that she wasn't dying in some hospital.

"Physically or mentally?"

"Let's start with physically. Mentally, I'll make assumptions."

"I'm good apart from my hearing which is fucked so I might miss all of your words of sympathy."

There was silence.

"Are you there?" she asked.

There was silence.

"Haha! I take it that I just missed your kind words of sympathy."

"You crazy woman, where are you?"

"At a cottage in Buckinghamshire. I lost everything apart from the Giacometti sculpture and the bike … and I don't have the keys to it any longer either, but I should pick up a spare pair this afternoon." She was speaking rapidly and finally able to release some tension.

"Let me come over and see you."

"How about I come over and see you tomorrow? By which I mean, do you have a sofa I could use for a few days; I can't stay here much longer?"

"What? Of course ... and I have a spare bedroom, OK, it's a boxroom but your ego should just about fit. What happened, tell me."

"After you left on Saturday, someone took a dislike to my cabin and blew it up. The good news is ... I was outside at the time."

"You're OK? I mean *really* OK?"

"I'm fine; a bit deaf but still breathing."

"... and the cabin? Have you really lost all of your stuff?"

"Yep, apart from the statue and the bike, the rest is pretty much all charcoal."

"But why?"

"Trust me, that's all I am thinking about. It's not like I've ever upset anyone, is it?" she paused and before he could think of an acceptable answer she said, "You do have good internet connection, don't you?"

"Yes, but, thinking about it, with you around, do I need to increase my house insurance, only my credit rating is at rock bottom already?"

"I'm fully house-trained."

"Yeah, right."

"Is there somewhere for me to put my bike?"

"Yes."

"Then, no problem, I will leave the statue here. It will be fine." She didn't bother to explain about the CIA safe house.

There was a natural break in the conversation when the consequences began to sink in.

"I wish I had been there with you," he was rebuking himself.

"I was with three ex-Marines when it happened, so don't beat yourself up ... that's my job. I will tell you the details tomorrow. What time do you get up? 11.00am?"

"Yes, but any time you want to arrive is OK."

"Let's say tomorrow at 11.00am."

"Do you want me to get anything in for you?"

"Peroni and pizza. I don't do champagne and flowers."

"I'll send them back."

She almost forgot. "You might get a call from the police asking about your visit here. I had to give them your name, sorry, I told them it was nothing to do with you."

"Oh great. Something else on my record."

"Sorry."

He finished the call and stared out of his window at the driving range next to a damp-looking golf course and an old people's home. What had happened? He made a coffee and sat quietly in his small kitchen wondering where his life was about to go next. He could never have guessed.

———

Leonard was eating undisturbed on his desk.

Avoiding the dining room available to him and his senior colleagues, he had a tray delivered to his room. His order from the lunchtime menu of a steak with salad had long been interpreted as a very large steak with a very small salad garnish that, if pressed, could be left off and replaced with fries.

He was punch-drunk from the phone calls and messages starting with the President's Office downwards.

Not a dicky bird had been heard from Chuck. There were no new leads, and he had not gone home, withdrawn money from his accounts or contacted anyone from his family or work. At 5.00pm London time, Leonard was to call his effective boss, Thomas, the Director of National Intelligence and give him an update. As the last piece of steak went down, he had precisely nothing new to report to Washington.

What would I do next, if I was Chuck? He asked himself but struggled to get into the mind of a thirty-something with an overbearing billionaire mother like Valentina and a life of armed guards and lonely nights watching movies. It would help to know why he had run away in the first place and why he had chosen to visit Mike Kingdom.

Chuck probably had a second phone or would get one soon. The police and Leonard's CIA colleagues had searched all phone numbers and calls made from near Mike's cabin in the woods on Friday and Saturday; unsurprisingly, this had not taken long, and every number had been accounted for. In all likelihood, he would have taken the battery out of any second phone so that no one could discover it until he was well away from the cabin.

Leonard wondered about this person named Jim, whom he had no idea about. Who would Chuck contact next? This Jim? Would he contact Mike again, perhaps frightened by the explosion and worried that he had brought this upon her by turning up at her home? Or Diego? Surely, this was more likely, but he would get no reply from his brother. Then, what would he do? Chuck had not been home since, perhaps, Friday morning and had probably been living rough. This meant that he may not have seen the press coverage about Diego's kidnap in Switzerland. It had barely made the British newspapers but was now across the major American television networks and social media. Leonard came back to the question of whether Chuck had a second phone and whether he was keeping up with world news. Or this mysterious Jim? A quick check by his staff of his phones, laptop and work computer had not thrown up any mention of a Jim.

He pushed his empty plate away and dialled a member of his team, "Hi, can you update the list of numbers that have tried to call Diego Ortiz's phone since, say, Thursday and bring it into me? That's ASAP." He pronounced ASAP as 'A-sap', one of his favourite expressions.

He dialled Mike's number. "How you doing?"

"I'm doing fine, thank you. Any news of Chuck?"

"No. When you coming into the office?"

"I think *that* is what you asked me on Saturday morning and a couple of hours later my cabin exploded."

"It won't happen again. Lightning doesn't strike twice and all that baloney."

"What's so urgent? I am still deaf, by the way."

"I wish I was. You can't even believe the earache I'm getting. I need you to find Chuck."

"Leonard, I could ask HR for six month's paid sick time after what just happened, you know that. I will get onto it soon but at the moment I am sorting out accommodation, replacement bike keys ... you know, boring crap like that."

There was no one on the planet who could talk to a CIA Director like this but then, they had been through the wars together and he needed his best analyst on this ... and now.

"If you need anything domestic sorted, I'll get someone on it ... and stay at the cottage for as long as you like. Whatever. All I want you to do is find Chuck."

"OK, OK, I'll come into the office tomorrow at 2.00pm. I want to get back onto my project where I'm close to a big breakthrough, I can feel it ... but please send me anything new about Chuck before that so I don't waste time."

"Great, I will." Now was not the time to remind her that, after six months work and a disastrous intervention, her project was dead, totally dead.

"Leonard, what do you think this is about? Is this about who he is and his family or is it what he was working on?"

"No idea but that's two lines of inquiry for you. There's nothing else for you to worry about."

"I can check the first one but what was he working on?"

Leonard went quiet. He was at the point where she needed to know.

"Art fraud?"

"What?!"

"Money laundering using paintings and stuff."

"Why didn't you give me that job? That's right up my street."

"He speaks Spanish. We think that it is based in Spain ... and New York and London."

"What? I spend years following Colombian and Mexican drug money for you and you have forgotten that I speak Spanish? Whatever ... I need to get back to my work, I'm at a critical moment, as you know."

He needed to keep her on side.

"Well, you can take it over. His cover's obviously blown."

"Damn! Send me the stuff via the normal link and I will look at it whenever I can. Are you in the office tomorrow?

"Yes, but I might be in the bunker. It depends how the phone calls go this afternoon."

"I'm off shopping and to pick up some bike keys."

They ended the conversation.

Immediately, Leonard's PA put through Commander Bob Trevelyan.

"Good afternoon, have you found out what happened?" Leonard asked.

"No, Leonard, sadly not and I'm guessing you haven't either?"

"No, there has been radio silence. What can I do for you?"

"Forensics have got back to me. They have found some interesting pieces at the cabin. They are parts of an unusual IED, you know, a home-made improvised device." He waited for Leonard to respond.

"So, it was a bomb? Sheesh."

"Leonard, whoever is after Chuck, they are serious and have done this sort of thing before."

CHAPTER SEVEN

"You are kidding me?" Leonard could not believe his ears, "That's a sophisticated IED? Sheesh! I was hoping that it was a gas bottle."

He was continuing the call with the Commander.

"It had been attached to the back of the cabin at first floor level; that's the best guess at the moment." Bob Trevelyan was filling in the details.

"Was this home-made? You know what I mean, British?"

"Probably, and by experienced people but it's early days. I wanted you to know. I don't think this is a personal vendetta, it's professional with someone powerful behind it."

"Great. This is all I need." Leonard was thinking of the call to his boss in a few hours.

"Who were they after? At the moment, I have only four names: Chuck Kilminster, Mike Kingdom, someone called Wazz who had visited Mike earlier and a forester on the estate called Graham who lives nearby and keeps his equipment under the cabin. Anyone else? We are talking about the middle of the countryside, there was no one else anywhere near."

"Can't believe it's the forester. It's an OTT way to get cheap timber. Never heard of this Wazz, who is he?" Leonard's mind was in overdrive.

"I'm off to see him next. Mike is certain that he is not involved and not the target, but he has been in prison and lost his parole through boxing with another inmate, so he stays on the list."

"Is he a boyfriend?"

"No idea, I went easy on Mike immediately after the event, but I will press her harder after I've interviewed him."

"Good luck with her, I wouldn't use a sharp stick unless you want it blunted."

"I know that you cannot tell me what Chuck and Mike were working on but surely one or both must have been the target? It's all too much of a coincidence. Were they working on something together?"

"No, not together. They never have to my knowledge. They sit in the same room occasionally but at opposite ends. I'd be surprised if they have spoken twenty times." Leonard wanted to help. "Hey, please don't write this down but Chuck was working on fraud in the art world and Mike was checking out the drug trade between the Caribbean and Europe, that's her specialty but her main project is dead."

"The second one sounds more likely to attract professional retribution, don't you think?"

"Possibly, but she works anonymously on all of this, like everyone else. Her name appears nowhere. You'd need to gain access to the Agency network to find her name ... and that is not going to happen." Leonard didn't want to mention that Diego had just been kidnapped so it was almost certainly Chuck that they were after.

"Unless someone spoke out of turn down the pub? If you know what I mean?"

Leonard did not reply but his thoughts wandered off to Chuck. What might he have said or done? "I will investigate internally but I need to tell you that Chuck had ... issues. He was a nerd with family issues back home. He may have had some sort of breakdown."

"We need to visit his address; it might give us a clue. We don't have an address for him, do we?"

There was a pregnant pause that would have had most obstetricians reaching for the gas and air themselves.

"Bob, we have known each other for years. I need to tell you something else about Chuck ... in absolute confidence. The address that you will have been given will have come via the FCO; it is one of our accommodation blocks. Chuck will never have stayed there. He comes from a very wealthy family back home. They've put him in a big house with security here in London. He's working under me to keep him out of trouble."

It was Bob's turn to take in all of the nuances. "Thanks, Leonard, I know that you didn't have to tell me that and we both know that, at the moment, you don't need to say anything more but I'm guessing that this family is," he paused, 'well-connected', am I right?"

"Bob, don't even speculate."

"OK, we both have jobs to do. He is clearly the target, for whatever reason. At the moment he is not a 'missing person' and is only a 'person of interest' in the destruction of an unimportant cabin in some woods, which is no big deal ... or, at least, as far as the public is concerned. I will go and see this Wazz and, perhaps, someone from your office could check out his ... house."

"That's a plan."

"... and maybe you can find him before we speak tomorrow, and we can put this all to bed?"

"Even better plan."

Bob put down the phone as he continued to speculate which family was powerful enough that the head of the CIA in London had to take one of its nerdy sons under his wing. He stopped running through names and concentrated on the task in hand. He needed to speak to Wazz.

On the previous Saturday evening after the explosion, Emmanuel and Henri had faced an inquisition from their uncle Alain when they had returned to his house near Slough. They had both said that, unequivocally, the cabin had been destroyed by the IED; no one inside could have survived. Partially hidden by pine trees, they had positioned themselves no more than 600 metres away and could see the plume of dust and smoke as well as hear the blast.

Emmanuel and Henri were experienced bombers having undertaken many sorties in Europe and Africa, often using drones …… they flew under the radar … literally. While neither of them could be described as stable, it was Henri who kept some sort of control on his psychopathic brother, a man devoid of feeling and with an emptiness behind his eyes. There was never any doubt who their uncle would choose to take out the target when asked by a man that he knew only as Xavier.

On the Monday, while Leonard and Bob were speaking to each other on the phone, the uncle was, himself, being grilled by Xavier about what had happened. They were not in the main house on his estate in Hertfordshire but in a tithe barn that had been converted into a swimming pool and spa. It had palm trees in pots and murals on the walls of blue tropical sea and skies. Being hot and steamy may not have been conducive to a calm appraisal of what had occurred. They were sat on white metal chairs at a small round table. Alain was on the back foot describing in English, their common language, what had happened. When he had finished, Xavier was asking him why there were no reports of deaths in the media?

"Perhaps, the secret services have prevented them from

revealing anything about this and who they really work for?" Alain said, referring to a person causing Xavier real problems and about to blow the lid on his most lucrative and important business venture.

"Couldn't they have checked if the bomb had been successful?"

"No, that was not possible; they had to get away from the area. The cabin was completely destroyed, no one could have survived, and they know who was inside seconds before the explosion. I am sure that this is simply the media being gagged. This will have spooked the CIA."

"You may be happy to irritate the CIA, I am not. I want the subject buried and forgotten. I don't want fallout."

Alain frowned not understanding the word fallout.

"I don't want any consequences. I don't want anybody paying any attention, you understand?"

Alain was sweating on his brow despite growing up outside of Montpellier, the capital of Hérault département in southern France, only seven miles from the Mediterranean coast, "The mission was successful, I'm sure. The cabin is destroyed and everything in it. My nephews are back with me and there is nothing for the police or anybody else to trace."

"They need to stay here in the UK. They may be needed again."

"That is no problem. They won't leave until you are completely happy."

"I will quietly check behind the scenes, but I don't want to open up links back to me or you. Can you check very discreetly as well. Until there is confirmation in the press, I will not be happy."

"As always, I will make sure that you are happy."

―――

Chuck was staring out of the bay window at a field criss-crossed with white tape; each subdivision was occupied by a bored looking horse. It was midday and the flies on such a hot August day were beginning to bother them. He was eating a crudely constructed ham and cheese sandwich, this being almost the sum total of his culinary skills having spent his entire life never having to worry where his next meal would come from or the need to cook it. A bottle of something orange was fizzing quietly on the small fold-down table before him. Reading the contents on the label, he was feeling the calmest he had felt for weeks which was surprising given the sugar content and the long list of E-numbers.

He had a roof over his head (OK, it was a static caravan in a holiday park and not the mansions he was used to) and he had an old Land Rover Freelander parked outside under a beech tree. It was Monday lunchtime, and he needed some quiet time to reflect on what had happened.

In Mike's cabin, he panicked; it was a mistake to go there in the first place. He was not thinking straight. In his confusion, Mike seemed to be one of the only people he thought that he could trust other than his brother, Diego, who was not answering his phone or replying to messages. Sitting at the kitchen table in the cabin with Mike, Chuck realised that he must do this alone. He ran away into the forest and made his way to meet Jim.

When the explosion happened, he was stunned and frightened. He was no more than a mile away. Guilt washed over him. He hadn't bothered to pick up his phone from her kitchen table as it was virtually dead, but he knew that he had a second in his bag. Had the people chasing him and his family, used the first one to locate him? Had this meant that someone he regarded as his friend, Mike, had been killed in his place? He had hurried back through the trees to the horse shelter at the corner of the field to retrieve the bag he had left, hidden behind it. Inside was everything that he thought he needed including plenty of cash and his second phone with its battery removed; the planning had taken weeks. There had been no time to think, his attackers were probably not far away.

Now sat in his rented caravan, he was reliving how he climbed up onto the second rail of the wooden fence, making his way around the field at this level before jumping down and disappearing into a stand of poplars. Twenty minutes later, a group of barns and sheds had appeared in the distance. There had been no sign of activity, and he had approached the biggest building from the rear, its walls were constructed with concrete blocks up to about six feet with wooden slats above. Tucked around a corner, he had looked through the window into a lean-to office; the solitary desk was covered in untidy piles of paperwork on top of which there had been a set of car keys.

He had found a log and had smashed the small window, waiting to see if any alarm sounded or if there was any sign of human activity. There had been no sound which was not surprising as it was a Saturday, and the barn complex was miles from the nearest village. He had clambered inside and taken the keys; a tag helpfully showing the registration number. Before leaving, he had grabbed a waterproof jacket and a cap from a peg on the door.

It had not taken him long to find the vehicle; there had been only one – a dirty, dark green Land Rover Freelander unhelpfully attached to a horse box trailer but helpfully an automatic. Chuck had not driven for several years, in fact, ever since his mother had become convinced that he needed to be protected by chauffeurs and security. Unhooking the trailer and disconnecting the electrics had not been difficult. He had thrown his bag, the jacket and cap into the car and looked around. He had found a dog-eared road atlas in the pocket behind the passenger seat which would be useless as he had no idea where he was exactly.

He had started the engine and driven nervously down a track expecting to be stopped at any moment.

At the junction with a narrow lane, he had made a random decision and turned left. His intention had been to avoid any major roads and settlements until he was about ten miles away, at which point he would turn on his second phone and navigate his way to his intended destination. The plan had worked, and he had driven westwards using minor roads until he was in the Cotswolds and Burford had appeared on the road signs. He had stopped at a village shop and bought a bagful of basic food.

He needed somewhere to stay for a few days and had kept a look out for an appropriate place. Chalfont Valley Static Caravan Park had caught his eye.

In a layby, he had googled the site and thought that it looked as if it fitted the bill, and it had a vacancy. With a story prepared about being on his way to look at horses near Cirencester, he had put on the cap and driven down the access road. The lady at reception was used to horsey types on their way to Cheltenham or Badminton and had not batted an eyelid as Chuck offered to pay cash upfront for a week.

She had showed him around the thirty-five feet long caravan; this had not taken long.

In the strangest of ways, the complete and utter contrast with his lifestyle and that of his mega rich family, made it special. He loved the scale of the caravan – everything within ten paces. It felt like it was his – a concept that would be understandably lost on the rest of the population. He had chosen it without influence from his mother. For a week it was his world.

He had parked the Freelander under a mature tree in case there was any surveillance from above, but he felt safe. As far as he could see, there had not been any security cameras along his route. Yes, they would eventually get to know the Freelander's number, but he would only need it for one journey of fifteen miles after which the car would be abandoned.

Later and before he checked what had been said about the explosion, about his disappearance or before he even looked for replies from Diego, he allowed himself to relax while reheating a pie in the microwave. He turned on the television to watch Saturday's offering from a very restricted range of channels – he didn't care.

With the pie smothered in ketchup, he clicked the lock on the door and settled in for a quiet couple of days.

CHAPTER EIGHT

Mike, wearing a new matt black helmet, black leathers and with a very large rucksack, was riding her bike along the M40 motorway towards London. How strange to have all of your belongings on your back or in two paniers, if you exclude *The Running Man* sculpture that she had left at Bavant Manor Cottage. It felt disconcerting and incredibly free in equal measure.

Hitting the junction with the M25 at 10.30am on a Tuesday morning was not as bad as she had expected and she rode along the A40 towards RAF Northolt, an airport from which she had once flown in Charles Yellands' private jet. Long before reaching the airport, she turned off in a northerly direction towards, what was described on a decorative Olde Worlde sign as, the village of Ickenham. She was headed for Pinn Green House which proved to be a huge architectural disappointment. The Planning Inspectorate was probably still getting letters complaining about this three storey, brick-built block of flats resembling a 1960s telephone exchange squeezed between two attractive pairs of Victorian semis that had once stood in reasonable sized gardens.

Pulling up at the rear of the apartment block next to the

communal wastebins, she dismounted and took off her helmet replacing it with her new cap.

"Do you need help with anything?" a voice from a balcony, the size of a handkerchief, floated down to her.

"Relationships," she shouted back.

"Sorry, can't help you. Did you have any trouble finding the place?" Wazz was relieved to see her alive.

"Hard to miss it, I think. When does the architect get out of prison?"

"That's a bit harsh," he replied, "he won Best Young Architect in 1978."

"So not for a few more years, then?"

He shook his head and raised his arms skyward, which was difficult on such a small balcony, and disappeared back inside.

After climbing the stairs, she could see him standing at the door to his flat.

"Glad you made it." He leant forward in his loose shirt to kiss her on the cheek.

"Nice place you've got here."

"You have had all of your jabs, haven't you?"

She raised one eyebrow as he took her rucksack pointing to his right.

"Let me show you to your suite." He stepped one pace and opened a white-painted door to a box room. "Before you say anything, it is deceptively large."

"About the same size as the cell that the architect's in?"

"Yes but he's got a television and a friendly screw."

She frowned at him and peered inside the room. If she stretched across the single bed, her feet and outstretched arms would touch three of the walls. "Perfect," she said.

"Do you need help carrying the rest of your stuff?"

"No, only one more panier to empty."

"I'll finish making the chili con carne, I didn't get pizza, but I do have some beer for you," and with that, he left her to settle in.

Ten minutes later she came into the kitchen.

He was stirring a saucepan while a noisy extractor hood failed to remove all of the pungent steam.

"I've heard of living out of a suitcase, but I never thought that I'd end up living out of a rucksack," she said and began to relax. "Thanks for letting me stay."

"No problem."

"Are you working later?"

"No, Monday and Tuesday are my days ... well, nights off."

"I'm going into work for an hour later to see Leonard and catch up."

"Any developments?"

"Not since we spoke yesterday. Have the police been in touch?"

"I am going to see a Commander Trevelyan in an hour. His office called. They stressed that I was not under suspicion, but he wanted me to go over what I had seen at your place and make a witness statement."

"Really? But I think that he's OK. I'm guessing that he doesn't have much to go on?"

"I know but you have to look at it through my eyes, with my record."

She nodded while deciding that she wouldn't tell him anything about Chuck's visit; what he didn't know couldn't compromise him.

He gave her a door key and they agreed to compare notes in the evening over the chili con carne and beers.

———

Swiping her card felt oddly strange to Mike as she entered the CIA building where she had worked on and off for six years.

She handed over her phone to the lady in security wearing a beige and dark grey uniform; Mike walked through the scanner with her arms held aloft as if surrendering. It looked all the more strange as she was bald-headed and attracting looks from the staff. The building was old but had undergone a renovation that had removed any character – it could have been any nondescript office in London. At the elevator, there was no one waiting, and she went up to her floor not engaging with a single person.

Mike had dismissed what had just happened at the cabin and, despite explicit instructions to let it drop, wanted to get back to her main project where she had previously made a connection between where drugs were coming from and how they were concealed to enter at Southampton docks; unfortunately, a search undertaken on her recommendation had not had the intended result.

In a large open plan room, she sat down at her desk after a few cursory greetings and commiserations from four other colleagues; Chuck's workspace was noticeably unoccupied.

Logging into her computer, she checked her emails and messages; there were hundreds mostly related to her drug smuggling and shipping research. She was reading the most important of them when a woman entered the room carrying a bouquet of pink roses. "Mike, these are for you. Sorry to hear what happened."

"Um, thanks."

Receiving such things at work was entirely against protocol but, given the circumstances, had been allowed by someone senior in Security.

There was a note with the flowers, it read: *I never meant you to be involved. Sorry. They didn't have any tulips.*

Mike's mind was all over the place. What did Chuck mean? Where was the florist? Did Chuck visit in person or phone in the order? Did he pay by credit card? Did he want to be found?

"Nice flowers. So, you've got an admirer? Men are suckers for women in distress. And it's not even Valentine's Day." Leonard was at the door having been told that she was at her station.

"I'm not in distress ... and are you talking about the massacre?"

Leonard was about to say something about her cabin but thought better of it, "Come to my office and update me." He disappeared and the other analysts visibly relaxed. Mike finished what she was reading on her screen and logged off.

"Shall I put those in water for you?" a woman with short ginger hair offered.

"Thanks," Mike took the card with her and walked up to Leonard's office, where she knocked and waited to be called inside.

He was sitting in a black leather chair behind a wide wooden desk. There was a Stars and Stripes flag furled and propped in the corner. Apart from a framed basketball shirt, there was nothing of a personal nature on display anywhere in the room.

She handed Leonard the note that came with the flowers and sat down opposite him. He read it, tapped it a few times on his desktop and stared into the middle ground, thinking things through.

"Involved in what? And what's with the damn tulips again?" is what he eventually asked.

"No idea. I will get onto it."

"Your priority is to find the clown."

"I will try. The florist label will lead me to him, I'm hoping," she changed tack, "You are not going to tell me who he really is, are you? It would help."

"Mike, I'm sworn to secrecy. I'm sorry." He was smiling as he spoke, very well aware that it would not take her long to search, "Hell, when have I ever stuck to the rules. His mother is Valentina Ortiz, his real name's Eduardo."

"Wow," she couldn't wait to search Eduardo's history, "Can

you fill me in more on what he was working on – that really would help, I think."

"Sure ... but keep it to yourself. As I said, he was working on art fraud. We're talking about a major ring dealing in stolen religious paintings and sculptures. I cannot get excited about it, but I'm told that the sums are now off the scale. We are talking hundreds of millions of dollars and it's funding the bad guys."

"Had he made progress?"

"Not much. He is here so I could keep him safe ... not to save America and the free world from art theft."

"Can I have access? There may be something in it that leads me to him."

"Fine. I'll give you access."

"What's your gut feeling?"

"Hunger, I only had a burger and salad for lunch."

"Leonard! You know what I meant, and you've never eaten a salad in your life."

"OK, OK, I don't think that it involves stolen paintings of Jesus on the cross. I think he may have lost it, you know, mentally. Whoever has kidnapped his brother Diego is probably after him as well ... and he may not have all of his brain cells firing at once, if you know what I mean?"

"Who's this Jim?"

"No idea and no one here knows. It's a good place to start."

"I'm going to stay here in the office for a couple of hours before I head back. Any news on my cabin?"

He smiled but this might have been caused by gas as talk of food had made him think about what he would eat later. "It was a professional hit."

"What?!"

"It was a specific type of IED."

"Leonard! What is this all about?"

"They might have been after any of four people, including Chuck."

"What are you talking about? It was either me or Chuck."

"... or your boyfriend or this forester guy."

"I don't have a boyfriend and as to Graham the forester, he's not that bright, he can barely string two rabbits together."

"Well, it must be one of you four."

"Damn!" she wanted to be annoyed with Leonard, yet again, but something made her conserve her energy and use it once she was back at her desk; the quicker she got back onto her project, the better.

She walked down to her office with her fingernails pressing into her palms.

The pink roses were on her desk in an emptied plastic container that had once held anti-bacterial wipes; it ruined the effect.

She flopped back down into her chair and went into professional mode. A couple of things needed to be checked. She started with the first.

The florist was easy. It was a one-shop enterprise in Burford, Gloucestershire called The Darling Buds of May but how to get the next level of information from them? Did Chuck come in personally? Ring up? Pay cash? She could hack into several places that would give her all of these answers, but it would take hours. She parked this line of enquiry but made a mental note that he had gone half an hour west of her cabin to order the flowers. He had a vehicle or an accomplice.

Secondly, she wanted to know every detail about Eduardo Ortiz. He was from one of America's wealthiest families and one that the CIA needed to protect. The only thing she knew about this family so far was that Eduardo's brother was called Diego and he had been kidnapped in Switzerland.

Mike never whistled but when she saw that Valentina was the largest political donor in the USA, she let out a stream of air from her pursed lips, "Wow!"

She didn't get a chance to look any further into the Ortiz family, Leonard re-appeared at the door.

"Grab your coat. We are going to look at Chuck's place."

"Now?"

"It's not far. It will take an hour. Tops."

Mike logged out and shut down her system and, as she left the room, glanced back at the pink roses on her desk wondering why he had wanted to buy her tulips now so obviously out of season.

———

The first thing that Mike noticed when sitting in the back of the car with Leonard was that there was a thick-necked man in the front passenger seat alongside the driver. Leonard was always so casual that she had never thought that he would even think about protection being driven across central London. This made her worry.

"This is exciting?" she said rather provocatively.

He said nothing but was gently perspiring while holding onto his seatbelt, something she could not believe he wore regularly.

"Is this what it is like to be an operative?" she poked further.

"No idea. It's so long since I was one. Now I'm a punchbag for people above and below me. I manage managers. Who sets out in life with the objective of managing managers?"

"Are you expecting trouble?"

"When somebody attempts to kill an Agency operative on my watch and on my patch, it's time to wake up and smell the coffee."

"Have you ever been to," she paused, "Chuck's house?"

"No, why would I? He has more staff at his disposal than me."

"Will his mother be there?"

"Jeez, I hope not. She gave me permission and has given instructions that we should be let in."

"I realise why Chuck is important."

He turned towards her, "Good. Let's continue this conversation when we get inside."

It was only after about ten minutes further driving that the car stopped outside of a Regency house with imposing cream pillars and a black metal boot scraper at the top of the flight of grey limestone steps.

The security in the front seat jumped out and opened Leonard's door in one movement while scanning the street. Mike was not offered this courtesy. She opened her own door and stood looking at a seriously impressive London townhouse.

A large, glossy black door opened to let them inside to another world; busy London seemed far away. They did not need to say anything, they were both thinking the same thing – *How could Eduardo live in such opulence and still come to work at the Agency office every day?* The house was as if prepared for a photo-shoot in Tatler magazine; nothing was out of place, there was no clutter and no sign that anyone was living there. It was a beautiful museum or, perhaps, art gallery. Mike was already mesmerised by the impressionist and other paintings in the hall and on the walls up the sweeping staircase.

Someone called Max, who had introduced himself as the house manager, explained that he had been briefed by Valentina and that he was to give Leonard access to everywhere. "Would you like me to accompany you, or would you like to explore alone? If so, where would you like to start?"

"Which rooms did he spend the most time in?" Leonard asked.

"Chuck only really used three rooms; his bedroom, his study and the lounge where he ate his meals and watched the television."

"Can you take us to the lounge first, please Max?" Leonard's voice was echoing around the hall.

He walked down the side of the staircase and opened a white panelled door.

Like the rest of the house, this did not show any signs of occupation, it looked like a film set. Mike and Leonard walked around pulling out books from shelves and discreetly exploring down the sides of chesterfields and armchairs. They found nothing relevant.

Mike moved a table lamp on a side table to reveal a small painting, perhaps eighteen inches square in a thin frame. It was black with a red smudge across the bottom half.

"Oh my God," she put her hands over her mouth, "is that a Rothko ... Max?

"I believe so," he said, "although this is not my expertise".

She bent forward, "It's wonderful."

"How do you know it's the right way up?" Leonard was not impressed.

"The signature is at the bottom," Max also did not sound like he was a fan.

"Can we see his study?"

"Of course," and he led them across to a cosy room that would be described by an estate agent as a library.

"Is there a safe hidden in here?" Leonard asked while Mike sat at the desk opening each drawer.

"I'm not aware of a safe."

Leonard was now shuffling around the room, "If there was a safe, would you know about it?"

"Um, well, I'm not sure. No one has told me about any safe."

"Can we see his bedroom?"

Mike followed the two men up the stairs beneath the glass cupola that cast a gentle, comforting light. On a landing, she stopped to look at a Ford Madox Brown painting that could have delayed her for hours.

"Here," Max opened the door to a large room that was the master bedroom.

"Thank you, Max, can you leave us here and we will make our way back downstairs. Could we meet you in the lounge downstairs in fifteen minutes?"

"No problem."

They stood in silence, looking around. There was too much to take in.

CHAPTER NINE

The visit with Leonard had raised so many questions and the relatively short ride on her motorbike back from the office to Ickenham had not given Mike much chance to process anything.

Eduardo's bedroom was weird, seriously weird; it was a cross between a church and an upmarket hotel suite. This is not where any nerdy thirty-year-old would choose to sleep, surely?

The room was dominated by a four-poster bed with a dark green velvet canopy that faced a religious shrine on the opposite wall. There were several oil paintings on the walls including one that Mike thought looked like an El Greco but can't have been. A glass-topped display cabinet intrigued her, however it turned out to be full of seashells.

They had opened wardrobes but there was nothing of interest. His bedside drawers were full of the usual detritus – a dollar bill, Vick's inhalers, an old passport, a bunch of keys, a Spanish dictionary and an eye mask from some airline.

In his study, they were even more disappointed. There was no computer, no laptop and there wasn't even a printer. On the walls were modern black and white photos of Spanish cathedrals and next to the desk was a red metal trolley on wheels that displayed every type of pencil, pen, ruler and writing aid. Mike was playing with the pens when she saw a memory stick which she put in her pocket.

After cursorily checking underneath drawers, chairs and tables, they left the room unsure how often he used it. Leonard and Mike had gone downstairs where they had joined Max in a lounge giving them the opportunity to raise the important issues.

"Did any girlfriends or boyfriends visit much?" Leonard had asked. This could only sound creepy coming from an overweight man with thinning ginger hair above a sweating forehead.

"Eduardo did not have many visitors, in fact, really only one. A young man called Jim."

"Could you describe him please, Max."

"About thirty, dark hair in a ponytail, big ears and long nose. He came half a dozen times over the last year."

"Did he stay over?" Leonard was in full flow and trying to get a fix on Jim.

"No, he usually came early evening. They ate dinner off trays in the study watching films or playing computer games, I think. They would often talk about art. He left about 10.00pm."

"British?"

"Well, not sure but, yes, I think so."

"Did you speak to him about anything? His job, where he lived? You know, general stuff?"

"No, he was quiet and polite, but he never really said anything to me."

"Did he arrive on foot, bike, taxi?"

"On foot."

"Max, can I cut to the chase? Chuck is missing and we need to get a break. Is there anything about Jim or anybody else that might be of interest? Don't worry about what it is, if you think of it, please just say it out loud."

"Sorry, I would love to help, if I could. I have looked after

Chuck for a long time, and I like him," he stopped, looking genuinely reflective, "Jim was good for Chuck, I think."

"What did this Jim wear?"

"He often wore jogging bottoms and the same grey hoodie with a big badge that had '37' on it."

"Do you have any contact details for Jim?"

"No, sorry."

"Max, you've been great. You know the drill, if you think of anything, call me. I'll tell Valentina that you've been most helpful," Leonard gave him one of his cards.

During this whole exchange, Mike had been silent, staring at a Jeff Koons sculpture of a bunch of tulips in vibrant, bright metallic colours on a sideboard.

———

Having parked the bike and jogged up the stairs in the echoing hallway, she was about to use the front door key that Wazz had given her. Not knowing if he was back yet, she hesitated; it felt like she should ring the doorbell. The compromise was to knock while turning the key and shouting "Honey, I'm home!".

Wazz, wearing a green polo shirt, dark blue shorts and flip-flops, was in the kitchen stirring the pot of chili con carne he had made earlier. He had been quietly fuming about the police interview, but his mood instantly lightened as her presence filled the flat.

"Good day at the office?" he asked.

"Is this where I tell you about the three-mile tailback at Hangar Lane and that Sandra from Accounts is pregnant?"

"No idea."

"You were married. You should know these things."

"Sandra and I never got married and we always used protection."

"Glad to hear it. How was your day?"

"Well, I got stuck in the traffic at Hangar Lane and Sandra is leaving me for a body builder from Ongar," he put the lid on the pot and continued, "Actually, my day was awful. I keep trying to tell you that you haven't got a criminal record, so you won't understand how it changes everything."

She took off her rucksack and slumped onto a chair; he joined her at the kitchen table.

"I was interviewed by that nice Commander Trevelyan and ended up giving a formal witness statement. They clearly suspect me given their line of questioning."

"But why?"

"You will probably never understand that police investigations are like flowing water, they take the line of least resistance. I have been in prison so I'm the obvious suspect."

"That's crazy! I will kill that Commander. I told him that you had nothing at all to do with it. I'm so sorry. I will call him tomorrow," she was getting very animated.

"No, no, please don't. I know that it will only make things worse."

"They haven't arrested you or charged you or whatever the procedure is?"

"No, nothing like that ... and please don't mention what we were involved in at the Yelland's villa in Spain, if they contact you." He was referring to the job on which they had first met.

"Hmm, OK."

"Would you like a beer? We can eat in half an hour, if you like."

"I'd love one. I feel awful intruding on you like this. Where can I work later so I don't disturb you? I will probably be up all night."

"Anywhere. I normally lie in on Wednesdays before I go to work late afternoon."

He walked the two paces to the fridge and took out the beer.

He opened them both and put one in front of her. They clinked bottles. "Let's start again, good day at the office?"

In a millisecond she weighed up the consequences for and against telling him anything about what actually happened at her cabin. She came down on the side of being open ... to a degree.

"Yes, thank you. Someone sent me a dozen pink roses with a note. It was an apology for making me the target of the bomb attack on my cabin. How was your day, honey?"

The police had spent Tuesday looking for a Land Rover Freelander that Rory, the estate manager, had discovered missing on Monday afternoon. He also reported the break-in and the theft of a jacket and some other small items. The police were frustrated because, outside of the estate, there was limited CCTV coverage along so many of the country lanes nearby. Even on the estate's own security cameras, they could not make out the driver or if there were any passengers. It was not until the car was spotted on a farm shop's camera travelling westward along the A40 that they had begun to make progress.

It had been short-lived. Somewhere near Burford in the Cotswolds, they had lost the trail. They checked the A40 traffic cameras all the way to Cheltenham without spotting the car. They visited numerous shops and garages in the area, but their CCTV footage showed nothing; the Freelander had disappeared.

Leonard had been given this information on Tuesday late afternoon after he had parted from Mike, but had it forwarded on to her.

Through that evening and into the early hours of Wednesday, Mike was sitting at her laptop in the kitchen while Wazz was on a sofa in the lounge surrounded by his Open University course notes on Sovereignty and Security and several books. It was a scene of domestic harmony broken only when Mike screamed some expletive or walked to the kitchen door to vent her spleen. At 2.00am Wazz had gone to bed intending to get up at 10.30.

Mike had said "Goodnight" and put on her headphones, promising not to shout out when something went very well or very badly.

She had not bothered tracking the Freelander, the police would do this anyway. If they found Chuck, all well and good. Instead, she had started with the premise that this whole escapade had been comprehensively thought through by Chuck. She assumed that the bomb attack was not part of any plan. If this was the case, how did he get from his mansion in Central London to her cabin? No one had found a car or motorbike, and realistically he could not have reached there using public transport.

What would she do in that situation? Chuck, or Eduardo Ortiz as she needed to think of him, was very clever even if he was having some sort of breakdown. He obviously did not want to be traced so would this mean that he would not use his credit cards? He would know that he needed to hide this all from his mother and family. Her best guess was that he had built up a pot of cash and purchased several phones to be used and disposed of. If it was her, she would have booked a taxi and asked to be dropped a few miles away from her cabin. She parked the questions of why he came and what he intended to do after he had left her cabin alone in the forest.

Whatever his thoughts, he had stolen a Freelander from the estate and had headed west to somewhere near Burford. Why?

At a point in the night, perhaps 3.30am, she stood up, walked away from the screen and made a cup of coffee. She had learnt that being an analyst could tear your mind apart. There were so many dead ends, so many questions that led to more questions and so much to do in so short a time. When she was suitably refreshed and with her lines of thought broken, she made lists of subject matters giving each a priority rating. She always did this using a pen and paper, starting with the most important.

After this, she scribbled another dozen minor questions and thoughts down on the paper to be considered later; it was too easy to get distracted. This whole exercise was cathartic and released the tension that inevitably built up after hours and days of searching.

Holding the coffee mug in both hands, she sat back in her chair to consider the most important pair of questions: Who was Eduardo Ortiz and who are the Ortiz family?

The first thing that Mike discovered was that the public perception they were Puerto Rican and American, while this was true at one level, had been manipulated and emphasised over decades. Yes, Valentina was Puerto Rican and in 2002 had married Paco Ortiz, a second generation American of Spanish stock, but he was not the father of her sons, and they had divorced in 2010 after eight years. Valentina, Diego and Eduardo had all taken the surname Ortiz.

She discovered that the father of the two boys and creator of the initial family wealth was Agustin Vergara whom Valentina had married in 1992 but who had died when the sons were aged two and four in 1998. He had built up the wealth investing heavily in undersea cabling as well as the pharmaceutical and chemical industries from his businesses based in New York and Bilbao in northern Spain. Valentina had taken over the reins of the companies and they had grown exponentially; timing was everything. The boom in the internet made the demand for undersea cables unquenchable as diet fads and pandemics similarly created a massive opportunity for the pharmaceutical sector.

Diego had joined Valentina in the running of the companies after he had completed an MBA at Harvard. The family wealth was almost inestimable.

Yet so many rumours persisted that somehow Valentina was

the front for Caribbean and Central American drug and gang money. No prosecutors could land anything that would stick despite several money laundering charges. She carried on regardless, shielded by the best lawyers in every jurisdiction within which she traded. However, her best guarantee clearly came from her eye-watering donations to the President's party and subsequently to his personal campaign.

So many of the stories in the media returned to the fact that if she was innocent of all the allegations, why did she live such a nomadic life with so much secrecy and security?

Mike shouted out aloud and quickly suppressed her excitement so as not to wake Wazz. There on her screen were the details of the death in 2014 of Valentina's beloved son Eduardo and his interment in a private ceremony in New York.

This was a major step forward. Mike took time out, leant back and took a swig of her coffee now absolutely stone cold.

Knowing that Eduardo was vulnerable and a target, it had been a clever strategy to 'kill him off'. He could then enjoy a privileged and protected life in London under a new name. It was some years later that his mother had pulled political strings that went all the way to the top, securing her younger son gainful employment in the safe environment of the CIA office in London under the name of Chuck Kilminster. Valentina was either a very careful or a very neurotic mother ... or both.

No wonder he is messed up Mike was trying to imagine how as a young man Eduardo had coped with his fake death and a new life under a new name in a foreign city while his mother and brother flew around the world running businesses and dodging bullets. Or in Diego's case, perhaps not dodging bullets. This all helped Mike build a picture of Eduardo that she knew would help her find him before his attackers did, whoever they were. She had the memory stick from his bedroom, but that was a task for tomorrow, now she needed bed.

CHAPTER TEN

Two people had independently been given a kick up the butt by their respective Minister or Director of Homeland Security.

Bob Trevelyan had been pressured over whether the bombing of the cabin was a terrorist attack and if the perpetrators were still out there and active. He had been told to speak to Leonard who had also been put under pressure. It was suggested that the Commander make contact with Valentina Ortiz whom he had been told was the mother of the missing suspected target, and he was wondering who she really was and why he should need to call this woman. He needed an update from Leonard first.

After speaking to his own boss, Leonard felt like he was a polar bear on a very small melting iceberg; there really were not many places left to go.

"Good morning, Bob," and, after the usual pleasantries, went on to explain, "she's the mother with the connections ... as in strings to the top. I've met her several times."

"Have you found her son, Chuck?"

"No, Bob, and his real name is Eduardo Ortiz," it was time to come clean, "she is the largest private political donor in the USA and close friends with the President. She is a billionairess with a lot of connections and her eldest son was kidnapped, probably murdered, a few days ago in Switzerland. There have been no ransom demands. Unsurprisingly, she is a bit nervous about where her youngest son is ... as is the President."

"Oh great. No wonder I am being kicked by the great and the good ... especially those up for re-election. Have you been to his house yet?"

"Yeah, I went yesterday afternoon with Mike Kingdom. We didn't find anything of use. The place is weird but a nerdy lad living in a $20 million mansion with seven staff isn't exactly normal, is it?"

"No new leads?"

"Nothing except he had no friends beyond his brother, his work colleagues and someone called Jim with whom he played computer games. Mike is searching Eduardo's phone records and history to discover who this Jim is."

"I'm in an odd position. No one has reported him missing so he's just a person of interest. He might have had a breakdown, gone to see his mate and is sitting at this moment playing Grand Theft Auto on a sofa."

"That's quite possible."

"As far as I'm concerned, currently, it is a random bomb attack on a cabin in a wood with nobody injured." He paused, "Except, you and I suspect that it isn't as simple as that."

"Not when linked to what's happened to his brother. Oh, by the way, the family faked Eduardo's death some years back and sent him over here for me to look after. Theoretically, no one should know that he's alive let alone his new identity and where he works."

"This just gets stranger and stranger. I'll call the mother now."

―――

Ten minutes later, Bob Trevelyan was on the phone to Valentina Ortiz. She was in an aggressive mood and had chastised him for not finding Eduardo and not making any progress.

"Mrs Ortiz we are making progress with our friends at the American Embassy. Only a few minutes ago, I was informed by my team that we have discovered and interviewed the taxi driver who drove your son out to the area of the cabin in Oxfordshire."

"Really? What did he say? Did he think that Eduardo was, you know, mentally in a good place?"

"He said that your son either slept or looked out of the window for the whole journey and did not want to engage in conversation. He dropped Eduardo at a crossroads not far from the area of where Mike Kingdom lived as agreed and was handed £500 in cash, also as agreed. That was it."

"What did he have with him?"

"Nothing much. Well, just a rucksack. He was wearing a hoodie."

"What? Poor Eduardo. What was he thinking?" She was struggling and her voice trailed off. Bob, for his part, decided not to mention that it looked like he had stolen a Freelander that was last tracked to somewhere near Burford.

"Mrs Ortiz, there may well be an innocent explanation to all this. He is probably staying with a friend called Jim with whom it looks like he played computer games."

"Who is Jim? He has never mentioned a Jim, but then he wouldn't," she conceded.

"We are looking for Jim now. When we have spoken to him, I will call you back and update you. May I ask a favour from you and please forgive me for asking this way. May I visit his house? Leonard de Vries has filled me in on some of Eduardo's background."

"Of course. Whatever helps you to find my son."

"I wanted to ask this informally. I think that it is better if you don't report him as missing just yet given his ... complicated past and status."

"I think that I understand."

"Please be assured that we and the American Embassy are working flat out."

"Good. Good." She gave the Commander the address of Eduardo's house and said that she would phone Max, the house manager, immediately.

———

Across London on that Wednesday morning, Mike was approaching the mansion at that address in Kensington on her way to work. Late into the night she had sat at Wazz's kitchen table searching Eduardo's memory card and phone records. There was no mention of a Jim, James or, indeed, anyone relevant beginning with the letter J. There were also no conversations with anyone that could not be explained; they were mostly with his mother and brother. She was stuck.

After a chat with Leonard, she had spoken to Max and arranged that she call back in at 10.00am while riding to the office. There must be more clues that they had missed. She rode the short distance to Kensington on what was a dry, airless day that promised blistering heat later; there was not a cloud in the sky. It was the hottest August on record and trees and areas of grass were all turning brown. Locking up her motorbike in the mews behind the imposing house, she walked around to the front steps and stood under the portico. Max let her in and offered her coffee which she accepted.

Mike followed him into the kitchen and asked if it was OK while they were alone for her to pick his brains for a few minutes.

"Where do you think he's gone, Max?"

"I've genuinely no idea. He did not give much away. He was

so introverted that it was difficult to know if he was happy or sad."

"Had he ever run off before?"

"Once he stayed away for a night, but his mother read the riot act to him. He never did it again."

"When was that?"

"A couple of years ago."

"Since then, there has been nothing strange?"

"No, he likes routine. The staff stick to the same menu, same mealtimes, same clothes put out for him in the same place ... you can guess."

"Actually, I can ... although my mother is not a billionaire. When I came yesterday with Leonard we didn't search thoroughly but we never found his phone or laptop or anything much to do with computers. Where did he keep them or use them?"

"His phone he always carried with him. I'll show you where he used to sit either on his own or with Jim to play his games."

"Tell me about Jim again. What was he like?"

"They were similar, they even looked a bit like each other. They got on well. He was polite."

"I know what you said yesterday but were they, as you British put it, an item?"

Max furrowed his brow and broke into a smile, "No, nothing like that."

"I need to find Jim. Eduardo may have gone to his place, or they may have gone somewhere together. Which reminds me, do you know where his passport is?"

"Yes, I know where it is. Mrs Ortiz's PA keeps it in a drawer upstairs. She has to organise any visas, tickets, private planes. Eduardo doesn't do any of that."

"One more thing," she finished her coffee, "did Jim have an accent?"

"There was a hint of something foreign but mild west country, I would say, but not strong."

"Anything else about him?"

"Actually, I haven't mentioned that he had one small earring. It was a silver shell," he added as an afterthought.

"What's with all of those shells in the display case in Eduardo's bedroom?"

"He gets a bit obsessed with things. If he starts collecting something, he can't seem to stop."

"Fair enough." She stood up and they walked through the house.

In a lounge that doubled as a study, she spent a little longer this time opening every cupboard and drawer while Max went off to retrieve the passport. While lifting the red velvet cushion on an ottoman box, she found his laptop, game console and all of the computer peripherals. There was no mobile but that didn't really matter as she had access to his call records.

Max returned to say that the passport was gone.

"He must have taken it with him," she said, "Can I take this laptop and this unit?"

"Of course, I've been told to let you do anything that helps to find him."

"Can I have another quick look in his bedroom?"

"No problem," Max replied.

They made their way up the ornate stairs under the stained-glass cupola. Mike stopped at a painting that took her eye. She could not resist.

"Jim used to like that painting as well," he said, and they entered the bedroom.

"This is all a bit weird, isn't it? This is not a normal young man's bedroom, is it?"

"No, I've got used to it, I suppose."

"What's with the shrine or whatever it is?"

"He loved it."

"Was he religious?"

"He was a lapsed Catholic, he told me, but he liked to decorate the shrine and light a candle on certain days like the 25th of July, a few weeks back."

She walked over to the large carved wooden unit attached to the wall with its stone sculpture of some saint or religious figure. She made out the word *Iago* chiselled into the base of the statue behind a pot with holes for flowers.

"I have only recently thrown away the flowers from this July 25th. He always wanted tulips."

Twenty miles to the west, Xavier was having a WhatsApp conversation with Alain asking for an update. He was not happy. "Your nephews missed the target. This must be nipped in the bud ... now. Time is critical. There is too much at stake." He never heard the reply as there was a ring from his doorbell. With the call abruptly ended, Xavier quickly walked out of the room. He was hoping for a delivery.

He was not disappointed; it was his courier and not your usual white van man delivering cardboard boxes and plastic bags. Together, they stepped into the dining room having closed the outside door. The courier placed an attaché case on the table and waited. Xavier took out a key and entered a combination. He flicked the locks. Inside was a single brown A4 envelope bulging at the seams.

Xavier opened it and took out wads of dollar bills cut in half and bound in red elastic bands. Each bundle had an identifying number on a piece of yellow paper. He did not need to count, there would be no mistakes. He took out the top bill from the first wad marked 'One'. As with all of the others, there was only half of the note cut randomly through George Washington's image beginning somewhere in the words ONE DOLLAR at the bottom and cutting through the words FEDERAL RESERVE NOTE at the top. The other halves of each of these notes were in Mexico at the other end of the operation.

He took out his phone and filmed himself with the half of the first note. He sent it to Saltillo, Coahuila, in northern Mexico as proof that the package had been delivered. His phone rang and he said only one word. The verification process was complete. He thanked the courier in their native Spanish and after a couple of words about the weather across the Atlantic, allowed him to return to London Heathrow for the evening plane back to Mexico City.

Now he would resume his WhatsApp with Alain.

———

Commander Bob Trevelyan had turned up at the Kensington address only about twenty minutes after Mike had left. She now headed to her office where she had taken Eduardo's laptop and some other computer bits out of her rucksack and handed them over to be examined by a specialist department in the basement at the Agency headquarters in London. She had gone straight to Leonard's office.

"Hit me with all of the good news, I cannot take any more crap." Leonard was looking tired with heavy dark bags under his eyes and thinning ginger hair that had not seen a comb for some days.

"Well, let's start with his phone records and a memory card that I checked overnight. There's no Jim or anything like that name."

"And this is good news?"

"No, but when I went to the house, I found his laptop and some computer stuff that I've sent downstairs to be checked out."

"Great, I'll give them an hour and chase them."

"Also, his passport is missing."

"Your and my definition of good news varies considerably."

"I learnt some more details about this Jim from Max, the house manager."

"His name, address and phone number, I'm guessing?"

"No."

"Sheesh."

"Look, I need a couple of hours at my desk to check out a few theories, but I think that they might be related. It's just a feeling."

"That's crazy but, hey, check it out." Leonard was not impressed.

"He's also obsessed with some Catholic saints. That's what the shrine in his bedroom is all about. It's dedicated to St Iago who is celebrated on July 25th ... which has just passed."

"Oh, great," Leonard put his head in his hands, "he's joined a fucking bunch of religious nutters and is about to give away Valentina's billions."

"Maybe but I don't think so. I believe he has gone to see this Jim in the west country somewhere. I'm not sure why but I will get onto it."

"Mike, I've got POTUS flying into London in less than a week on his way to Bilbao. I need you to find Chuck, alive and well by then otherwise he will use my butt for kicking practice." Here Leonard was referring to the President of the United States by acronym. Conrad was up for re-election in November. The happiness of the principal contributor to his war chest, Valentina, would be very high on his agenda.

"Leave me to it. So, there's nothing new I need to know before I start ... from the British police, for example?"

"No, they are six yards behind you ... and the rest. Actually, they have spoken to the taxi driver who drove Chuck out your way and they have tracked the Freelander to somewhere near Burford, wherever that is."

"Leonard!" she sounded like an exasperated mother, "Were you going to update me?"

"I've only just heard. I've got a lot on my plate."

"Funny, that's how I will always remember you ... with a lot on your plate."

CHAPTER ELEVEN

When Eduardo had pulled up at the caravan site, he had sent Jim the briefest of messages before turning off his second burner phone and removing the batteries. They had agreed to meet at midday on Wednesday. Jim was to bring lunch.

Time had dragged for Eduardo as he couldn't drive anywhere or use a phone. He did have a new laptop on which he could watch movies and play games that he had previously downloaded.

Outside it was another stifling August day and he was glad that his caravan (and the Freelander) were hidden and shaded beneath the spreading branches of the trees. He had every window open and even the narrow front door. He searched around for cutlery, plates and glasses to lay the table. Having to do so many menial tasks for himself, his appreciation for Max and the staff in Kensington had gone through the roof. He had never taken them for granted but you only truly appreciated something when it was gone.

At noon precisely, he heard the approach of a vehicle and walked to the door to watch Jim park his silver Audi, open the passenger door to retrieve two overfilled supermarket bags and waddle towards the caravan and up the aluminium steps. His visitor had his black hair tied back in a ponytail and was wearing a pale checked shirt and khaki chinos.

Eduardo took the bags and put them on the table with relief and excitement in his eyes. They hugged and closed the door.

Sat opposite each other in such an enclosed space was so different to when they had met at Eduardo's house. Neither could form a meaningful sentence and instead they broke out into fits of laughter and giggles.

"You made it," Jim said.

"By the skin of my teeth."

"It smells like a farmyard in here."

"It's a long story."

"Shall we have a drink? I will pour it." Jim got up enthusiastically and, rifling through his bags, found two bottles of cold cider. He put some others into the miniscule fridge and found a bottle opener. He was patently more used to catering for himself than his friend.

"To the future!" Eduardo proposed.

"Txotx!" came the reply.

"Txotx! I have so much to learn." They both swigged at the refreshing drink.

"What is the long story?" Jim asked in a well-educated Gloucestershire accent.

"Um, I took a detour on my way here to see a work colleague. She lives in the woods in Oxfordshire," he started rambling, "I had a bad night before, you know what I mean, and ended up sleeping in a horse shelter. Don't worry, my phones were off and the batteries out. When I went to see her, I lost it and ran away but her cabin exploded."

"What do you mean 'exploded'? Wait a minute, is that the one in the news?"

"Yes, probably. It's the one in Oxfordshire. I'm sorry. I don't know what is happening or who is after me."

"Eduardo, we need to be really, really careful."

"I know, sorry."

"Did you manage to bring everything?"

"Yes, it's all on a memory stick. My phones and laptop are brand new."

"How did you get here? Were you followed?"

"I had a taxi to Oxfordshire and ... I borrowed a car. It's out there under a tree."

"Eduardo," Jim sounded reassuring and chastising in equal measure.

"I know, I know. I am not cut out for any of this. I'm losing it."

"Don't worry. I'll deal with it. I'll move the car to a barn behind my house. Relax. Is it that green Freelander?"

"I don't know what it is."

"Take a deep breath." They drank and got used to their new surroundings. "You remembered your passports and some dollars?"

"Yes, I've got my passports and $20,000 dollars ... that took me a while to get all of that cash out so that nobody noticed."

"Let's relax. It looks like they failed to kill you on Saturday, so they missed their chance. Tomorrow, the car will be in our barn, and you can sleep at my place. Our plans have changed slightly, we can now fly out on Friday. Let's book the flights this afternoon."

"How far away is your place?"

"Twenty minutes. It's in a village called Barrington. You'll be able to chill out. Trust me."

"And your family live there?"

"Yes, my parents live there, and my sister and her husband farm the area around about. You will be among friends."

"And your shop? I really want to see your shop."

It's on the High Street in Burford. You will like it."

"I so want to get an earring like yours. Do you have some?"

"Of course, you take your pick."

"Is business good?"

"Very good, thank you. Hand-made jewelry in Burford sells well. At the moment, the High Street is full of tourists, mostly Japanese."

"This is a new world to me. It's like being reborn."

"Which you have been once."

"That is so true, but Chuck Kilminster has almost gone for good. I am going back to my roots."

"It will help you make sense of your life. I hope that it is all good news from here on."

The pink roses on her desk at work looked incongruous.

This did not bother Mike who, with mind racing ahead, was checking out so many new lines of enquiry. At moments like this, distractions would not interfere with her focus. It was as if every cell in her body was suddenly reprogrammed to perform a single function. This is what made her tick and, if she was honest with herself, the only thing in life that really gave her pleasure. Her task had been reduced to *Identify Jim. Find Jim. Find Eduardo*.

Until the computer guys downstairs cracked Eduardo's laptop and gizmos, she would work with what she had gleaned from her two visits to his house.

Mike always started any new search by eliminating as much as possible, even if this was only by small amounts. Most people would be completely daunted, Mike was not. There are seven billion people in the world but how many speak with a west country accent and, perhaps, live near Burford? This would mean Jim was likely to have been born or raised locally and stayed in the area. She had just reduced that initial mind-blowing number to, say, a million people. He was male. This had halved it again. He was called Jim or, most probably at birth, James. This had reduced it to a few thousand individuals in the Wiltshire/Gloucestershire/Oxfordshire area.

This remained a frightening number, but it was beginning to be manageable.

She used her specialist search programmes to look for any James, aged 30 to 35, in each of the three counties. She saved this information but there were too many. Knowing that her 'Jim' was very likely to be on this list gave her a buzz. She reduced the search area to a few miles centred on Burford and the number was reduced to eighty-four. She fully accepted that the list was not exhaustive but was her 'Jim' among these?

At this early stage, she would concentrate on this small number, widening and refining her search if she failed to find him.

What else did she know about him? She searched among this list for those that played computer games. This was very inconclusive, but seven names were identified, and she called up their photographs from the internet, mostly Instagram, Facebook, Twitter/X and TikTok. They did not fit Max's description of Jim so were removed from her list. She was down to a possible seventy-seven individuals, on the assumption that he lived broadly near Burford.

He wore a small, silver seashell earring; what did this mean? She tried some more searches, but they were all meaningless or, at best, unreliable.

It would be quicker to call up photographs of each of the seventy-seven and see which ones matched her idea of 'Jim'. This took almost an hour. With three left to check, she was beginning to feel tense. The last person's face came onto her screen – a blue-eyed cherub with curly blond hair and no earrings. Damn!

Her annoyance came both from having high hopes that she would find him and from not having time to pursue her new ideas on, what was meant to be, her main project.

She logged off, shut down her system and left the room without saying goodbye to any of her colleagues.

On her bike journey home, she took particular pleasure in speeding past the queuing traffic and had calmed down at least one per cent by the time that she used her key to open the front door of Wazz's flat.

"Hi, how was your day at the office?" Wazz was wearing a white tee shirt hanging over his dark blue shorts, the tattoos on his forearms particularly prominent.

"If I had hair, I would tear it out!" she dropped her rucksack onto the floor.

"That's lucky, then."

She glowered but said nothing.

"Tell me about your terrible day while I get you a beer."

"I went back to Eduardo's house and had a second look around. I told you that the place was weird. I found his laptop, but his passport is missing."

"Anything on the laptop?"

"They're busy checking. Hopefully, I'll hear tomorrow. I am worried, though, that he took his passport."

"Are they watching all of the ports and airports?"

"I expect so. Not my problem."

He handed her a bottle and took a swig from his glass of water. "Tell me why you think the place is weird?" His voice was calm.

"There's a load of religious bits and pieces around, especially in his bedroom. He has a stone statue in a big wooden shrine to some saint. He lights candles and has flowers put there on feast days. Always tulips ... I've no idea why he loves tulips so much. I need to get onto that, but I got distracted trying to find this Jim."

"With no success, I'm guessing?"

"It's another needle and haystack job. Why is he called Jim? Why not Aloysius or something rare?"

Wazz took a breath and changed the subject, "I was mulling something over all morning ... well, OK, I didn't get up 'til eleven but, even so, are you sure that it was Eduardo that they were after with this bomb?"

"Well, it's either me, Eduardo, you or Graham, the forester. Let's dismiss Graham, I cannot believe it's him and it's too much of a coincidence that Eduardo was at my place seconds before the explosion ... and just after his brother had been kidnapped and probably killed by now."

"That's all true but they might have been after you or me."

"Sure, I'm working on trying to put some dubious characters behind bars, but they don't know who I am; I am anonymous at the Agency."

Wazz said nothing.

"Do you actually mean that you think that they were after you?" she asked.

"It has crossed my mind. Eduardo's visit wasn't planned but mine was. OK, they could have followed him, I know."

She put the empty bottle in the recycling box and sat down at the kitchen table, "That begs the question of who wants you dead? Any ideas?"

"I can think of a few."

"But it would be easier to get you here in your apartment rather than at my place."

"True but I couldn't help thinking that we should both be a bit more careful just in case the intended target was you or me."

"Great. You have just made a shitty day worse."

"Sorry."

She looked up at him, "Please tell me that you are not involved in anything criminal."

"Apart from delivering a couple of kilos of coke to Graham at your place? No, nothing."

Fortunately, there was nothing within reach that she could throw at him.

"Sorry, to disturb your evening but I have some good news."

At this point, Mike would normally have said something abusive to Leonard, but she was intrigued to know what he had discovered and was glad he had phoned.

"No problem."

"The supergeeks have gained access to the things you brought into the office. I will send you access via the usual way. I haven't looked yet myself. If you find anything important, send me a message. Don't wait 'til morning. I am getting a lot of grief right now."

"No problem. Sorry about the grief."

"It comes with the job. Check everything out … and find the knucklehead … fast."

The call ended and, before she had pulled up a chair, her laptop pinged. All of her encryption devices were in place as she had been searching for people called Jim near Burford with a Roman Catholic connection.

Wazz had gone to work, and she wouldn't see him until she returned from the office tomorrow; it was all a bit odd and different. They were like ships that passed in the night. For a millisecond, she missed her cabin.

By late evening, she had eaten, washed up and spent several hours following leads and ideas. Each time, irrespective of the outcome, she saved her results. Later, much later, she would cross reference and check everything she had explored and discovered; this was joining up the dots. She rubbed her sweating scalp; it was oppressive and close in the flat. She was enjoying being bald with her cap resting in front of her on a plastic bottle of water. The kitchen window was open despite Wazz's warning that she should be careful.

Having access to Eduardo's laptop and hardware did not instantly give Mike any answers, nobody had analysed it and provided a succinct summary. Instead, she faced another few hours rummaging around, looking for a bargain.

She started with the various contact lists and directories looking for a Jim or James. Unfortunately, this produced nothing and, immediately, she smelled a rat. Eduardo was an analyst who knew how anyone would try to find his contacts, his diary or his plans. This laptop was always going to be searched and dissected. He had left it in his house and knew that it would be interrogated.

Was there disinformation on it? Mike began to suspect that anything she found was compromised. If she now found a 'Jim' hidden away, was she meant to find this connection?

After an hour, she felt as if she had sucked all of the meat from the bones. There was nothing useful.

Mike swapped from *What is on this computer?* to *What is obviously not on this computer?*

What was missing? Firstly, there was no Jim, or James. Secondly, there was no reference to gaming. Thirdly, there was no reference to Catholicism and the feast days of saints. She concluded that this was not his laptop used for his day-to-day communications and interactions or, indeed, anything important.

After several diversions and cul-de-sacs, she gave up searching the files, his Apps and his messages and instead looked at his search history. This was a lightbulb moment.

He had, from when he had bought it, been cautious using this laptop. However, some searches were revealing, she suspected, and she produced her own list. At the top of this was his interest in his birth father, Agustin Vergara.

CHAPTER TWELVE

Valentina had gone to bed early and was wide awake. Sleep was hard to find as there was too much happening in her life; the Swiss police were trying to find one son who had been kidnapped, and the CIA were trying to find the other who was missing. In Switzerland, they had confirmed that there had been absolutely no contact since the car had roared off from the factory; the 7 Series BMW had not been found and neither had the driver.

The bedroom was not large or lavishly furnished but it was one of her favourites from the many that she owned in London. It was in a neo-Gothic house in Holly Village in Highgate. Her friend Maria lived in it and was the owner to all intents and purposes but, in reality, it belonged to Valentina, and she kept a pair of bedrooms for herself and her security.

The village was built in the 1860s by the richest woman in England after Queen Victoria, Baroness Burdett-Coutts. Each house now looked as if it was from a horror filmset with the turrets and steep roofs; Valentina had always been attracted to Gomez in the Addams family, perhaps this had played a part in the purchase originally. However, the peace and space among the mature trees was very unusual in the centre of any major world city.

She drew some comfort from having her long-time security, Tadeo, in the room next door with Bud, one of her drivers. This was her life moving every few days from one beautiful place to another, always with the two of them next door and her doctor, PA, hairdresser and pilots not far away.

Her phone rang. It was 9.30pm on Wednesday evening in London and it was getting dark outside.

"Hello Valentina, are you prepared to withdraw?"

"What?"

"All that matters is that we know who Chuck Kilminster is, and ... we know where you are."

She had sat up and almost retched when she heard those words, "Who is this?"

"Valentina, you know full well. Unless you and your sons want to die, you will sell your cable business. To begin with, we want you tomorrow to announce everywhere that your company is withdrawing from the contract to lay the cable from Bilbao. You understand, that is on EVERY medium?" his English was perfect, who else would say *medium* and not *media*? Was he British? Her Puerto Rican ears thought so.

"What? What's so important about the cables? Selling and withdrawing doesn't make sense. Let's discuss it."

"Sorry, you are not stupid. Make the announcement."

He let her plead once more for more information. He finished with, "If you do not utterly and unreservedly withdraw from the tender and the consortium, you and your sons are dead ... then, we'll take over the business anyway."

Her nightdress was wet from sweat. After the call, she got out of bed purely to move around while she digested what had just happened. Caring about the financial consequences was only a small part of this thought process; her company had not even been officially given the $800 million contract yet, although it was near certain. What had gripped her was the request to drop out of the tender. Really? There was only one party that would gain from her doing that.

She had a hundred projects in planning and construction, therefore, withdrawing from one of them, even a large one, was not going to test her unduly ... but? The undersea cables had been at the heart of the family business from the beginning. She went to the bathroom and changed into fresh and dry night clothes.

"What can I do? This was not in the plan" she said out aloud to the Victorian lady pouring wine for her husband in a framed painting on the wall next to her.

For the first time in four days, she broke down, having no one in which to confide and finally having to accept that she could not control everything. She was a complete mess and the realisation that she had no close friends or family made it worse; her isolation had been the reason she had been so protective, perhaps over-protective, of her sons.

After an hour or two she calmed enough to accept that there was a way out and she felt herself beginning to swap from heart-broken mother to cold-hearted businesswoman. If Eduardo could also end his show of independence and return home, she would finally put an end to all this.

———

At the same time on that Wednesday night on the Gloucestershire/Oxfordshire border, it was a cloudy evening. Jim had driven over to the caravan park in his Audi and had joined Eduardo for a drink; they were waiting for nightfall. With dark clouds forming, this would not take long.

It took no time to transfer all of Eduardo's belongings into the Audi.

"Right, you have written the note and put it in the envelope

I brought you? And you have cleared out everything, haven't you? There's no point trying to wipe down any fingerprints, there will be too many. There's no reason for anybody to come here to check – you paid cash."

"OK, I've got the note. You want me to follow you in the stolen car?"

"Yes, stop at reception and put the keys with the note in the special letterbox. There's nobody there."

Eduardo, who was floating somewhere between reality, a dream and a computer games' nightmare, was again beginning to lose rational thought.

"OK, OK, let's go. Let's go," he was talking to himself.

They stepped out into the dark, locked the caravan and drove off slowly in convoy under the trees. As agreed, Eduardo dropped the envelope and keys through the big letterbox at the reception building. In the note he had explained that he needed to leave because of a family bereavement and that he would call back for the deposit in due course but that this might be a couple of weeks. This would never happen, of course. He was not interested in a few hundred pounds.

The traffic was not heavy at 10.00 in the evening around Burford. They were soon off the main roads and away from potential CCTV, although Jim was not aware of any from his frequent journeys along that route. The headlights illuminated the narrow lanes with their Cotswold stone walls and sporadic hawthorn bushes. As they approached the road sign at the start of the long village of Barrington, Jim slowed down partly because Eduardo was driving so close behind as if in fear of being separated. Perhaps, he had lived in London too long, not that he ever drove there, probably.

Halfway through the village where the houses and cottages were clustered around the pub, they turned down a sideroad that took them past the church and towards open countryside. This is where Jim lived in a sizeable brick and stone house behind a clipped yew hedge and where, a quarter of a mile further on, his sister and family had their farm. This was an even bigger and more rambling house covered in ivy surrounded by barns and outbuildings. At a sign for Willow Farm engraved on a stone pillar, Jim stopped and got out of his car.

"Well done. You get into the Audi. I will take the Freelander and put it in a barn around the back. I will be five minutes."

He made sure that Eduardo was sat in the front passenger seat of his car before driving the Freelander through a yard and out of sight. There were no lights on in the main farmhouse, and there was little for Eduardo to do except control his breathing and count the beads on the rosary in his pocket until Jim returned.

He still jumped when Jim opened the driver's door and slid onto his seat. "All done. Now we can relax."

Eduardo's eyes, however, had a distant look and he seemed to have stopped blinking. Jim reversed into the farm entrance and made his way back to his home a few yards away.

It was now a substantial property renamed Willow Tree Cottage, but it had begun life as a pair of pebble-dashed council houses built sixty years earlier. With the brick and stone now revealed, new wooden windows, reclaimed Cotswold stone roof tiles and a mature garden to the front, it was an attractive house.

"Welcome to my humble home."

While Jim helped with two plastic shopping bags, his guest was carrying his rucksack rather than wearing it. Eduardo had been travelling very light. They walked through to the modern kitchen in pale green wood where the clock above the Rayburn showed that it was almost 11.00pm.

"You look tired. You've done well. Let me get you a bottle of water and you go and get some sleep, and we'll all feel fresh in the morning."

He led Eduardo up the stairs and showed him into a

bedroom a tenth of the size of what he was used to in Kensington.

"I've put some new clothes in the wardrobe for you but worry about that in the morning."

"Thank you," and Eduardo was pulling off his hoodie before Jim had closed the door.

"Wait, Leonard." Mike was answering her phone, half-awake but immediately conscious that Wazz had probably only been home for a few hours. She pulled the phone under the duvet.

"I need to update you. The people who kidnapped Diego have made contact with Valentina late last night. They have instructed her to drop out of the consortium for some proposed undersea cable that one of her companies is going to fund and build."

"Leonard, do you remember?" she hissed, "I went through something similar with Charles Yelland a few years ago."

"Good for you," he wasn't in the mood for bleating, he had also been woken up at some god-forsaken hour, "Valentina is confused because she could care less about this demand. She absolutely doesn't get it."

"Let me catch up. You are ringing me to say that Diego's kidnappers have called her to ask for something that she doesn't give a shit about?"

"Well, she cares a bit but, yes."

"Well, Zippy do! Lucky her."

"I know, I know. Hopefully this will all end well and ... very soon but don't you get it? Something's not right. What is going on?"

"I've no idea but I am putting all of my effort into trying to find Eduardo not into finding Diego's kidnappers, although I see now that they are probably linked."

"Good ... and Eduardo won't know about this but what he will know by now is that his brother has been kidnapped and that fact is probably freaking out an already freaked-out kid."

"He's twenty-eight years old. He's not a kid."

"That's the trouble with you, you're not empathetic."

The call finished with a burst of exasperation; she threw back the covers to cool down.

It took her a few minutes to use the bathroom without flushing and to wash quietly in a few drops of water. She dressed and made her way to the kitchen table that now served as her work desk. There was something that had been bubbling deep in her subconscious overnight even before Leonard's call.

After making a tasteless cup of instant coffee that avoided the need to use the noisy little machine, she set up her office.

If searching for the elusive Jim and several other leads had got her nowhere, she settled on researching Eduardo's birth father who had featured so heavily in his search history. Before she could tap in his name, Wazz came out of his bedroom with his eyes barely open and made his way to the bathroom.

"You need to flush it."

"Whatever." He was wearing only a pair of dark blue boxers.

She jumped up, ever practical, and put a capsule in the coffee machine. It had almost finished as he retraced his steps back to his bedroom and shut the door.

It tasted wonderful and improved her mood considerably. Fired up and buzzing, she tapped in the name Agustin Vergara.

There was plenty for her to read. He had been so successful in business on so many fronts despite dying at thirty-six years old. He was a USA citizen but had not been born there; Agustin Vergara was British, and it was after his father had died that he had emigrated to New York where he developed his commercial interests in communications and pharmaceuticals. At heart, he appeared to have been a natural scientist with a flair for business.

THE MONGOOSE AND THE COBRA

Vergara did not sound a common English name to Mike; therefore she went further back in time.

The family were originally Basque, from the Spanish side of the border, in fact, named after a town, there. Agustin's father, Jon Vergara, had four Basque grandparents and had been born in the true Basque lands, known as Euskadi, with Euskera names and being Euskaldrun – speaking the Basque language. This was important. So how did Agustin end up being born in the UK?

Eduardo's grandfather, Jon Vergara, had been born in the foothills of the Pyrenees not far from San Sebastian in 1932. His parents were businesspeople like most Basques transporting goods between Spain and France, having bought whatever was for sale cheaply from the ships that docked at Bilbao from across the Atlantic. They were comfortably off. In the spring of 1937, their world was completely wrecked by the treachery of the young Franco and his Italian and German co-conspirators. The bombing by the Nazi Condor Legion of the Basque town of Guernica at 4.40pm on Monday April 27th, 1937, tore the heart from the Basque community. It was a busy market day. Guernica was crowded having already taken refugees from recently bombed towns and villages. The carnage was beyond words. There was an international outcry, no louder than from the United Kingdom.

A steamship, the SS Habana, assisted by the Royal Navy, took 3,862 Basque children aged 5 – 15 on 21st May 1937, across the Bay of Biscay to Southampton. They were accompanied by 120 helpers, 80 teachers together with Roman catholic priests and two doctors.

Each child had been given a cardboard hexagonal disk with an identification number and the words *'Expedición a Inglaterra'* printed on it. Conditions were awful. The ship was supposed to carry around 800 passengers making the journey across the stormy Bay of Biscay extremely unpleasant.

The steamer arrived at Southampton on 23rd May with the

bunting up from the celebrations for the coronation of King George VI which had taken place ten days earlier.

Jon Vergara, aged 5, found himself alone in a tented camp in North Stoneham in Hampshire cared for by the Salvation Army and the Catholic Church, who committed itself to take 1,200 children. By mid-September, all had been relocated to residential homes throughout Britain. After the fall of Bilbao and Franco's capture of the rest of northern Spain in the summer of 1937, the process of repatriation began. By the start of World War II in 1939, most of the children had returned to Spain.

About 250 children stayed in the UK. Among these was Jon who, at the age of eight, was adopted by a family from Oxfordshire.

Mike was completely engrossed but now began to stare at the coffee machine again. Its presence and her overwhelming need for caffeine took precedence. She unplugged it and, trying to make as little noise as possible, carried it into the lounge, returning to collect a capsule. Closing both doors quietly, she plugged it in down the side of the settee and made her second cup.

Completely unaware of the time, she returned to her reading, gripping the cup in both hands.

It was 9.00 in the morning and the door to Wazz's bedroom opened. He had managed five hours sleep. He said *Good Morning* and went straight to the bathroom. On his way back, Mike could not contain herself.

"Eduardo and Diego are Basques!" she said.

"Is that good?" he, too, needed a coffee having not had his full quota of sleep.

"I'm not sure but it's progress."

"Let me grab a coffee and get dressed."

"Here, you'll need the machine."

He carried it back into the kitchen without saying anything, made a cup and disappeared back into his bedroom.

Mike returned to her searches and found that Jon had a son, Agustin who was born in Oxford in 1962. Jon had died in 1978 and by age twenty, Agustin was in New York where he married Valentina, a Puerto Rican. In a very few years, his business interests flourished beyond imagination, and they had two children, Diego and Eduardo.

In 1998 Agustin, at the age of thirty-six, had died of complications after surgery for appendicitis.

CHAPTER THIRTEEN

Wazz re-emerged from his bedroom barefoot, dressed in a baggy shirt and stone-coloured shorts. He was getting used to sharing his small flat with another human being. Normally, he would be naked and, probably, unwashed and unshaven.

"You still here?" he asked.

"I ate some cornflakes," was the non-sequitur that came from Mike who was surfing on the crest of wave.

Wazz, with his arm on the back of a kitchen chair next to her, had to adjust his position because of the summer sun streaming in through the kitchen window. It highlighted his blond hair and blue eyes.

"You have been up all night, I'm guessing?"

Mike broke her train of thought and tried to remember anything about the last twelve hours.

"Did I disturb you? I tried to be quiet," she asked.

He folded his arms and tried to simulate annoyance. "You're a bloody fruitcake."

"And?" she asked aggressively.

"I love fruitcake," he said quietly.

For a second her mind left the secret squirrel world.

"Can I tell you what I have discovered while you make me breakfast?"

"That sounds like an offer that cannot be refused. What do you want?

"Can you boil an egg?"

He gave her a look that could have ... well, gone a long way to actually boiling one. She realised that she had been completely lost in her searches for the whole night and was being too rude. "Oh, don't look so hurt," she bent over sideways to pick up a pen that had fallen from the table.

"Shit!!" she screamed with the muscles next to her spine going into spasm, and she fell onto the floor.

"For fuck's sake!" he shouted running towards her as she lay on the kitchen tiles.

He hovered above, watching her slowly bend into an unnatural shape clutching her back.

"Mike," he shouted having no idea what to do.

She, eventually, lay still on his kitchen floor rubbing her slightly arched back that she, very reluctantly, was trying to relax.

"Mmm," she mumbled as she bit her lip and tried to find a position on the floor where the pain was even vaguely bearable.

"Mike."

"Don't touch me!"

He stopped and knelt next to her, his disturbed night somehow part of an irrelevant history.

"OK, OK, relax! Let's sort this out. I'll call for an ambulance. Yes?"

She hesitated for a second, "No, wait. Give me a few minutes."

He rearranged the furniture near her for no apparent reason.

"Where does it hurt?"

"My back."

The fact that there was no abuse attached to the short statement bothered him.

"You have been sat up all night on your laptop. You must have strained your back."

"Yeee ...!"

She had tried to turn but had realised very quickly that if she lay motionless, it barely hurt but if she moved, it was as if the world had just ended.

"I was making such good progress. No, really."

"It can wait a few days."

"What?! No, it can't! Ow!!" she had moved enough that the excruciating back pain shot through her like a lightning bolt.

"All right, relax," he paused, "Relax. Can you move?"

"No, you jerk!"

"Are you in pain? You're better off on the floor."

"Of course I'm in fucking pain! And if I had wanted to look at kitchen tiles up close, I'd have gone to effing B&Q."

He was hovering above her not knowing quite what was expected of him.

"Mike, I need you to tell me what to do."

"Right," she breathed in, and it hurt enough that she said through gritted teeth, "after you have got me back to bed, you need to retrieve the teaspoon I can see under this cabinet."

"You stupid woman." He lifted her so gently but still she screamed as he carried her into her bedroom. Holding Mike with both arms he lowered her onto the bed, and she continued to scream but not without pointing out the shortcomings in his first responder care.

"Now, what would you like?"

She needed to go to the toilet, but she parked this thought while she established a position on the bed that gave her the least pain; this was not easy.

"I need to tell you what I have found out."

"Later."

"Not later. I have been up all night."

"OK, if you really want to. Shoot." He was stood, silhouetted in the bedroom doorway.

She related what she had discovered up until the point that Agustin had died in New York when she forgot that she had twisted her back, moved on the bed and sat bolt upright. "Yowee!"

"Let me get you some painkillers." He returned quickly with some Ibuprofen and a glass of water.

After swallowing them, she tried to relax, and her breathing slowed down.

"Eduardo and his brother, Diego, were two and four when their father died. Valentina built up the businesses even more and re-married in 2002 to a Puerto Rican called Ortiz. He died eight years later by which time she was worth hundreds of millions of dollars. Since then, she has become a billionairess living all over the world and having the US President as a very close friend. Diego was earmarked to take over the empire while Eduardo has been living incognito in London watched over by Leonard."

"That's a great story but how does it help find Eduardo?"

"It won't immediately but it will help me find Jim."

While Mike was stretched awkwardly on the bed recounting her thoughts to Wazz, the US President, was on the phone to both Thomas, his Director of National Security and Wesley, the Deputy Head of the CIA. It was very early Thursday morning in Washington, and they were discussing the demands of Diego's killers with regard to the undersea cable business. Conrad wanted to understand the political implications and whether the demands had helped any of the agencies in the search for the perpetrators.

"I can only think of one group that gains from this. What do you think?" he had asked, pressing them both on whether, in addition, Eduardo had been found.

A half an hour later, Thomas was speaking to Leonard in London. The call was mostly about the arrangements for the President's trip arriving Monday at Heathrow before flying on to Bilbao two days later, but he took the opportunity to check up on progress finding Eduardo.

"He's disappeared. There has been absolutely no news from the Brit police, and we haven't located him either. He's not using his phone or cards; he is not contacting anyone that we are monitoring and this vehicle he stole hasn't been found. He's disappeared." Leonard was the bearer of no new information or leads. "Tom, can I be frank? The kid's all messed up. He could have changed sex and joined the Daughters of Charity for all I know. Nothing would surprise me."

"What do you make of the demands on Valentina?"

"They're more serious, I reckon. Chuck, sorry Eduardo, will turn up I'm sure but what happened to Diego ... I'm more worried. He was meant to take over a billion-dollar business empire. What's with the undersea cable business? Have our guys in Berne heard anything about the kidnapping?"

"Zilch."

"I'll give my team looking for Eduardo a kick up the butt."

The call ended and Leonard gave his 'team' a call, "Hi. How are things?" He left out any butt-kicking.

"I'm on a bed. I've really hurt my back."

"But you can still search?"

"Thanks for the sympathy. I'm in agony. I'm on my side with the phone on the pillow."

"Any progress?"

"Maybe. I'm zeroing in on this Jim who is Eduardo's only friend as far as I can tell. By the way, I'm totally convinced that Eduardo had this all planned. There is nothing on his laptop and he's using burner phones. I think that he has run away from home."

"I could care less that he has run away. Unfortunately, there may be other people chasing him, like those who tried to blow him up and who kidnapped his brother; they may not be friendly. We need to find him, and his mother needs to send him away somewhere safe ... preferably not in my neighbourhood."

"What have they learnt about Diego's kidnapping?"

"Nothing as far as I've been told. It's the Agency guys in Berne who have that headache, I'm sure relieved to say."

"Did Eduardo ever talk to you about being Basque?"

"He never talked to me about anything ... even work ... if he did any. I didn't care as long as he sat in the corner with a book doing some colouring and wasn't playing with matches," he hesitated, "Why? He wasn't Basque, he was American, well, Puerto Rican?"

"No, Leonard, his grandfather was a Basque who came over aged five to the UK after the bombing of Guernica in '37. His name was Jon Vergara and he had one son, Agustin, who was born in Oxford in 1962. Agustin emigrated to New York and married Valentina. He died and she remarried. Eduardo's mother is, and his stepfather was, Puerto Rican."

"Holy Moly," Leonard's mind was running ahead.

"Why Holy Moly?"

"Is Bilbao in the Basque part of Spain?"

"No idea."

"I think it is. We don't do coincidences, do we?"

The call came to a natural conclusion, and she suddenly screamed out aloud as she moved her body, having been in the same position for a few minutes. Wazz rushed in.

"You OK?"

"Do I ... yes, I'm fine."

"Good. I have to go to work in an hour," he stopped and looked her up and down as she gripped her phone limited by the length of the lead plugged into the wall that was keeping it charged. "Will you be all right?"

"I am always all right ... thank you."

"Would you like me to carry you to the bathroom before I go?"

"What? No, I'm fine."

"OK, no problem. Just asking." He retreated quickly.

She leant back provoking another seizure, "Shit!"

He reappeared at the door, "I don't need those specific details. Simply ask for the bathroom."

She laughed but it hurt enough that she spasmed and knocked her phone to the floor.

"I'll ring in sick. You need me here," he said.

"I'm fine," she said through teeth firmly clamped together.

"Has anybody ever told you that you are stubborn beyond words?"

"No, no one who's still breathing."

"Mike, Mike, please let me help. You are in a bad way."

"Thanks, but there's no need for you to stay. Please pick up my phone and give it to me."

"OK, but shall I get a bucket and some toilet roll?"

She laughed which caused her suddenly to scream, she called him something unrepeatable and rolled onto her back, "Will you stop making me laugh, it hurts so much."

"Sorry, I ... I was being a bit practical. That's what time in prison does for you."

She took stock. Always getting your defence in first had worked well for so many years but, perhaps, she needed to breathe. Actually, breathing hurt. "Wazz ..." she was conceding everything, "I'm fucked."

"I know, I know." He walked into the small bedroom, "Mike, please don't fight me. Just tell me what you want, and I will do it."

"If you want to be practical, a bucket and some kitchen roll would be great, although I'm not sure how I'll use it."

He smiled and left the room to get her requests. His time to leave for work was approaching; a night of dealing with men who wouldn't know what to do with a beautiful young woman at home if she actually stripped in front of them, beckoned. Wazz was having to force himself to leave her.

While he was wearing a dinner jacket a size too small and a black bow tie that was attached by a breakable string outside of the strip club, she was back searching, restricted to being on the bed and using her phone. The fact that Eduardo had taken his passport was bothering her; this felt pre-meditated and important. His obsession with tulips was preying on her mind. Having been to Holland, she put two and two together and got nowhere. Why would he go to Holland? An advert promoting Turkey popped up on her phone and she learnt that the tulip was its national symbol. Was this relevant? She cross referenced all of the other key words and found nothing of interest.

She ditched the passport/tulip ideas and went back to the infamous Jim. He was important, she felt this in her bones.

After taking another two Ibuprofen, she returned to her phone and opened her file on Jim. All of the little pieces of information she had gathered were in there including her notes from both visits to the Kensington house. Except it wasn't all there. For no apparent reason, her mind wandered back to Max's description of Jim and the fact that he wore a hoodie with a badge displaying the number thirty-seven. This had seemed strange to her at the time unless it was his age, but Max had thought that he was in his early thirties or younger.

It came to Mike in a flash.

She tapped the number '37' and 'Basque' into her phone and it all began to become clear. This meant that Jim, like Eduardo, was of Basque origin and that one of their grandparents or perhaps both had been on the SS Habana sailing to Southampton in 1937. Eduardo had discovered his heritage and somehow had met another grandson of that group of refugee children.

Now her task had been simplified or, at the very least, the areas of search had been heavily reduced. How many 'Jims' were there living within ten miles of Burford who had a Basque grandparent from the 1937 evacuation? She created a new list of 'Jims' using additional criteria and scanned their surnames. Of course, the grandparent might have been female and had married a Brit as could Jim's father or mother but here her luck was in. Amongst all of the surnames, she spotted a name that sounded Basque or Spanish. She had found a James Ibarra who lived in a village called Barrington near Burford.

It really looked as if Eduardo and Jim could be connected by their ancestry.

She so desperately wanted to get up and use the laptop at the kitchen table, but the pain was acute whenever she moved. It was nine o'clock in the evening and the frustration was overwhelming her. It was no good, she was trapped and however much she wanted to jump on her motorbike and ride for an hour to Barrington, this was not realistically going to happen. Reluctantly, she dialled Leonard's number.

"I think that I have found him."

"Great. Where is he?"

"He is probably visiting James Ibarra who lives at Willow Tree Cottage in Barrington," she gave him the postcode, "they are both of Basque heritage and must have discovered each other somehow."

"I'll get a team over there right away."

"You were probably going to ask if my back's better?"

"Nah, I know it's still bad or you would be halfway to Barrington by now."

"Let me know if you find him safe. I'm stuck here and winding myself up."

"I will send you a message ... and, thanks, I knew you would find him."

CHAPTER FOURTEEN

It was almost midnight when Zack and his colleagues arrived in Barrington having raced down the M40 out of London and along the A40 to Burford.

With no traffic at that time at night, they drove slowly through the village and turned down the side of the pub leaving behind the pool of light from the single streetlamp at the road junction. Zack had been briefed by Leonard that he should try to get Eduardo to return with him to London but that this might prove difficult given his fragile mental state. Leonard would be at the end of the phone, day or night, if Eduardo needed to speak to someone he recognised and trusted.

Zack had been reminded by his controller that this was not a 'Shock and Awe' mission. This was more about gently enticing a cat down from a tree – a very expensive and precious Persian cat. He made it quite clear that getting Eduardo back to London was as an important a mission as Zack would ever be involved in and his controller was someone who knew that Zack had been decorated to the highest level. For his part, Zack was beginning to wonder who this Eduardo actually was such that he and his team were chasing him all over Oxfordshire.

Having been there when the bomb exploded made this personal.

Leonard was also well aware that he probably should have immediately informed Bob Trevelyan and the British police but knew that Eduardo was not exactly a mass murderer. He was merely someone of interest who happened to be near where a bomb exploded ...in a wood. Leonard assumed that he was in for a long night so poured himself a Jack Daniels and sat in an armchair watching Mission Impossible on his television.

In Barrington, Zack was approaching Willow Tree Cottage. On the journey down, he had been looking at images of the place on his phone, but this was not to do with 'how do we break into the house'. Instead, this was to ensure that Eduardo did not run off across the fields or jump into a car out of fright.

All was dark. The driver turned the BMW around quietly outside of the house. Zack jumped out and walked along the front path while his colleague sneaked down the side of the building to the back. The doors to the car were left open. They were all ready.

The yew hedges and stone walls provided plenty of screening. Zack pressed the bell and stepped back. There was unlikely to be a rapid response, it was now after midnight but there was no switching on of lights, no barking of dogs. He tried again, this time more vigorously. Again, absolutely no response. He looked around the garden, up and down the road as best as he could and across to the farm in the near distance but there was no activity.

He peered into the lounge window and was surprised that the curtains were not closed but, then again, there was not likely to be anyone passing; they were down a cul-de-sac in a village. At the corner of the building, he looked down the side to where his mate was standing inside the opened rear gate looking around the back garden for any sign of movement. There was a shaking of heads that meant that no one was around.

Zack held up his small jemmy to indicate that he was about

to open the front door. There was no alarm box on the wall and there were no security cameras. He rang the doorbell once more without response.

The front door was opened silently, not requiring any sizeable effort. He stepped inside and called out Eduardo's name. This was not an assault. No one, especially Eduardo, was meant to be spooked by what was happening but Zack did not know whether other less friendly people were involved. There was only one pair of green boots by the front door. He turned on the light to reveal a small lounge with stairs to the right. The room was very tidy with no empty cups on the coffee table, no clothes thrown over sofas and nothing out of the ordinary; it looked as if it had just been cleaned.

He turned on the light at the bottom of the stairs and called out again – nothing.

At the top, he pushed open each bedroom and bathroom door, again shouting out Eduardo's name. The house was empty. He looked quickly for any sign that Eduardo or anyone had been there recently but found nothing except a glass by the bed in the spare room. He slipped it into a plastic bag and put it in his pocket. Returning downstairs, he walked outside and called out to his mate in a loud whisper. By the time that he had come back around to the front of the house, Zack was on the phone to Leonard.

"Damn! But thanks, Zack." Leonard had been hopeful that Eduardo could be brought home safely before the President's visit.

"The place was very tidy and there was no milk or salad in the refrigerator. I grabbed a water glass from the spare bedroom. No idea if that's useful?"

"Get it over to Henry ASAP. He'll check it out for fingerprints and DNA."

Leonard was treading a thin line by keeping important information from the British Police and, of course, the breaking and entering.

"Zack, any sign of the Freelander?"

"No, it's not here and there's no garage."

"Damn, and no sign which way he drove off?"

"No, sorry. We are up a dead-end in a village there is only one way out and the ground's hard. There are no tracks."

"Not having much luck, are we?"

"No, and we had better leave the area unless you want us to wait nearby?"

"No, you disappear. He's taken his belongings and the car, so I think that he's flown the nest."

The call ended and Leonard swallowed the last of his Jack Daniels. Despite being late, he did not feel that he would sleep. Where was Eduardo and what was he up to? In the morning, he would tell Bob Trevelyan about the connection to James Ibarra but not mentioning the visit to Willow Tree Cottage. He needed to update Mike.

Wazz opened the door to his flat at 3.40am expecting to find Mike asleep.

Instead, he was greeted by "A glass of water would be great."

He put down the small bag of shopping that he had picked up at an all-night store and peered in through her bedroom door.

"Do you ever sleep?"

"Not while I'm working."

"How's the pain?"

"Are you referring to me generally or just my back?" she

turned over on the bed with only a small grimace and no screaming, "I'm fine."

He looked at the bucket and the scrunched-up kitchen paper. "Let me get rid of that."

She was embarrassed, "You could have crept in while I was asleep and done that."

"I'm not bloody Father Christmas." He walked out and she heard the toilet flush. He returned with a wet flannel and a towel.

"Would you like a wash?"

Her face suggested otherwise.

"I meant did you want to wash yourself ... when I've gone to bed."

"Oh, sorry. Thank you."

He collected up the empty Ibuprofen box and a dirty side plate from the white bedside cabinet, "Would you like something else to eat?

"No, thanks. I'm fine. Really fine."

"Need to talk?" He was getting used to her.

She told him about James Ibarra, the Basque connection and Willow Tree Cottage, all of which was progress. Then, she relayed Leonard's message to her that Zack had found no one there.

"I'm sorry," Wazz could not imagine doing Mike's job. It seemed to be one disappointment after another, "What next?"

"Today, you drive me to Burford."

"You are a complete nutter. How can you do your ... searching on the computer yet be a complete idiot?"

"I've been researching the Vergaras and Ibarras on the SS Habana. The names are there. I want to go to Willow Farm which is close to Willow Tree Cottage. That's where James's sister lives."

"Whoa! Whoa. Engage brain. You cannot even sit up. What am I meant to do? Rent an ambulance? Which is relevant because I don't even own a car." He inhaled deeply and slowly, "You haven't told Leonard about this, have you?"

"It's four in the morning."

"Don't make excuses."

"You think so ... linearly."

"That's not even a word."

"It is if you don't think linearly."

"You drive me mad!" He had been standing up all night outside of the club and his own back was aching as well.

"I will be better tomorrow ... today, later today," she corrected herself.

There was silence when Mike rubbed her scalp and made a slight frown as there was a twinge in her back. She looked up at Wazz with as close to a puppy dog look as she was ever likely to achieve.

"Better than what?" He looked around the room to avoid her soft brown eyes, "Do you need anything before I go to sleep? And don't say a trip to the Cotswolds."

"You go and get your sleep and build up your strength. You'll need it later."

He shook his head and pulled the bedroom door behind him.

―――

A noise later that morning at 10.30 had disturbed his deep, contented sleep. He came out of his bedroom to find Mike sat, stiffly, at the kitchen table.

"Oh, for ... sake," he walked towards the kettle, "... and the award for Best Actress goes to ..." he mimed opening an envelope, "Michaela Kingdom for her role in Brokeback Mountain."

She had so obviously had a breakfast of painkillers.

"My back is not *broke*, and the Cotswolds are hills, I believe."

He clicked on the kettle having checked that it had enough water and threw a teabag into a cup. He stayed silent as he turned around to her, shaking his head and resting his substantial forearms on the work surface.

"You don't look well; you should ring in sick," she was looking directly at him.

He allowed his arms to bend so that his whole upper body collapsed onto the imitation marble surface in mock surrender. After several deep breaths, he raised his face and stared silently in disbelief at her.

"But not sick enough that you can't hire a car and drive," she quickly added, "and this company, here, does SUVs with big comfortable seats and a sidestep. I'll pay, so don't worry."

Resistance was futile.

"Fine. Fine. May I ask what you are going to do in the unlikely event that I get you to this farm without having to divert to the Radcliffe hospital?"

"Don't you see? Jim and Eduardo are up to something but if I talk to Jim's sister, she might reveal something useful."

"Do we know if she is even there? It's a lot of effort to drive there and find that she has gone on holiday for three weeks."

"She's there, I checked."

He didn't bother to ask how. "I need to eat and wake up properly."

"I'd offer to cook you eggs but my back's not good."

He turned around and opened a cupboard to take out a saucepan, "Could you not call this woman?"

"Yes, but she won't speak to me or, if she does, she won't say anything useful. I need to sit with her and have a chat."

"OK, resistance is over. I will book a car."

Two hours later, Wazz was closing his front door while watching Mike approach the stairs with an upright back gripping the handrail. She descended taking each step as if it was a new experience. Any pain she may have been suffering was almost being hidden behind a strange smile.

He was carrying her rucksack, although he had no idea what was in it other than a bottle of water and a box of pain killers. These, he had insisted, should be included.

Against her suggestion, he had not phoned in sick but had made clear that he wanted to be back by five that afternoon to go into work. It might be a welcome relief after a day with her, he had thought but had decided not to express this out aloud.

Getting into the SUV had been an eventful exercise in itself but, once she had manoeuvred herself into the passenger seat by a series of small heaves, she was enjoying her elevated view from the wide front windscreen.

"M40, A40 ... easy. Do you need the satnav?"

"When we get to Burford."

She pressed her body into the large, contoured seat that seemed to support her back in all the right places. "This is like going on holiday," she said avoiding turning to face him.

"We always went to Spain as kids."

"We went to Astoria on the coast of Oregon."

"I have a feeling that this is not going to be a holiday."

"It's rural, genteel England ... it's all morris dancing and tea parties."

"You have obviously not read any Jilly Cooper."

"We are going to talk to a woman about her brother who may, or may not, know our best friend. Relax."

He drove off wondering if he would ever finish the international studies degree that his prison sentence had so rudely interrupted. Fortunately, the traffic was light, and Mike managed to give the impression that she was in no pain, but the occasional unexpected pothole caused her to grab the armrest and grimace. Eventually, the female voice on her phone gave instructions to take the third exit at a roundabout and to follow signs for Barrington.

There were cows in the fields on either side as they drove along a limestone valley punctuated by occasional mature willow trees, once pollarded but now consisting of huge trunks and only a few branches of feathery, grey-green foliage. They entered the village and turned at the pub.

"Your destination is 800 yards ahead."

Wazz slowed to a crawl, and they passed Willow Tree Cottage behind its yew hedges; there was no sign of human activity, and no Land Rover Freelander parked outside.

They were approaching Willow Farm which was at the end of the lane before it changed into a track.

"Do you want me to drive in?" Wazz was wondering if she would even be able to get down out of the vehicle.

"Yes, we are not doing anything wrong. Just act naturally and leave me to ask the questions."

CHAPTER FIFTEEN

Stepping down from the car, Mike screwed up her face as her back went into a mild spasm. Putting on her cap, she walked towards the wooden porch of the farmhouse slightly on tiptoe which seemed to make it easier. Wazz brought up the rear. There was no need to ring the bell as at least two dogs could be heard barking from within.

The door opened to reveal a short, dark-featured woman in her early thirties wearing an apron and wielding a pair of very long scissors. To Mike she looked like the quintessential farmer's wife, to Wazz she looked threatening but that could have been the scissors.

"Hello," was all she said at first but, when she saw the look on Wazz's face, added, "... oh, forgive me, I'm in the middle of wallpapering the lounge."

"Hello, I'm Mike Kingdom. I'm wondering if you can help me. It's a long story but I'm looking for a work colleague of mine who has gone missing."

"What's their name?"

"Eduardo Vergara."

Mike watched for any recognition or reaction to the name.

"Sorry, I've never heard of anyone called Eduardo around here."

"Are you Rosa?" Mike asked, "Rosa Ibarra before you married?"

There was a pause.

"I am ... but I don't know an Eduardo. How do you know my maiden name?" Her voice was neutral, not revealing anything useful to Mike.

"Rosa, I believe that he is a friend of your brother, Jim. Eduardo told me about him at work," she lied.

"Why are you looking for this Eduardo?"

Here Mike had to make a choice: how much of a story should she spin? After all, she couldn't tell the truth that he was an American billionairess's son who works for the CIA and whose brother had been kidnapped in Switzerland. "He's done nothing wrong, in case you are wondering. It's ... well, he may have had a nervous breakdown, and I am worried about him."

"You'd better come in. Just give me a second to put a wet tea towel over the wallpaper paste. Come into the kitchen."

They walked through a narrow hall, past the lounge with its furniture covered in dust sheets, and into a kitchen with an unbelievably large central table. Mike, through her American eyes, was transfixed by the size of the cream Aga, the two deep Belfast sinks and the Welsh dresser with its display of blue and white plates. Wazz, for his part, was looking out through the window for a man who had peered in and quickly disappeared. Rosa came into the kitchen having put her wallpapering on hold.

"Pull out a chair."

"Do you mind if I stand? I have hurt my back." Mike leant back against the work surface.

Wazz sat in a chair having rotated it so that he was facing the door but, in truth, he was merely a spectator.

"Oh, I'm sorry. My husband has a bad back. Where have you come from?"

"London. Eduardo and I work in Central London. Rosa, I'm really worried about him. I think that he has had a sort of breakdown." The parts of the sentence were broken up into small, easily consumed segments. Wazz did not recognise the actress before him.

"I'm so sorry," Rosa's face creased at the eyes and her head bowed, "Let me make some tea."

"Rosa, I have done some research on the internet. Don't we all?" she added, "and that's how I discovered you and your brother. I read all about the SS Habana."

Speaking while she filled the kettle from the tap and put it on the hotplate, Rosa dried her hands on her apron and turned to face Mike. "Jim has not said anything to me about anyone called Eduardo. Again, I'm sorry. Yes, my brother and I are descended from someone who came across on the Habana, but we only meet the others from the community a couple of times a year."

"Is Jim around?"

"No, he has gone on holiday. He lives next door in the cottage."

"Where's he gone?"

"Spain," she replied and began to prepare the tea.

"Are Vergara and Ibarra common surnames?" Mike already knew the answer.

"No, in England they are not but I am no longer an Ibarra, I'm now a Roberts."

"If you wanted to find out if Eduardo and you and your brother are connected or related, is there someone you could ask?"

Wazz folded his arms and watched, in admiration, a woman leaning back against the kitchen work surface in some pain, extracting information as if she was a professional.

"Yes, we have relatives and Basque friends who are living in the UK. Would you like me to ask on our WhatsApp group? Someone will know who Eduardo is."

While Rosa moved the teapot onto the table, Mike had to make a decision as to whether this was the best way forward. Always good for Mike, she only had a millisecond to decide. "Yes, please do ... but may I ask you to be discreet? It's Eduardo's mental health that I am worried about. His father's name was Agustin."

"Of course, I will not put it on the main group. I will ask a couple of people I know well."

"That would be so helpful."

Wazz was distracted by the face that had reappeared and, just as quickly, disappeared from the window. Rosa began to pour the tea into cups after asking about milk and sugar.

"The names are so rare in England. I cannot believe that there is not some connection." She was moving cups and saucers on the table.

Mike accepted a cup of tea. "Do you know of other Ibarras in the UK?"

"In the UK? No, only Jim and me and our parents but a lot of that generation are either dead or back in the ... Basque lands."

"Gosh, this is a really good cup of tea. I lived abroad for a while, and it was the thing that I missed the most. Where has your brother gone on holiday?" Wazz spoke for the first time while leaning his head back to empty the cup.

"Santiago de Compostela with his friend, Jacob. They are walking part of the Pilgrim's Trail."

"That's Galicia?" Wazz had never been to this part of north-western Spain.

"Yes, I am not sure if he does it for the history or the beer along the way."

Mike was forming the view that Rosa may love her brother but did not really know what went on in his head. Had she married well and helped her brother to buy the cottage next door? Was Jim really on a boys' walking holiday or was this a convenient and believable cover story while he did something with Eduardo?

"Do you think Eduardo is with them?" Mike asked.

"I have no idea. Do you want me to ask him?"

There was only one credible answer to this, and that was 'Yes'. Mike, however, did not want to tip Eduardo off that she and others were after him. "Rosa, can you not ask yet while I search for Eduardo in the UK? He's not in a good state of mind, I think."

"Of course, let me know if you want me to ask."

"He was probably driving a dark green Land Rover Freelander. You haven't seen one, have you? Wazz was following his own thread.

"No, sorry. I could ask my husband. He's outside somewhere."

They chatted for another ten minutes before Mike pushed herself away from the support of the kitchen units and, together, they said their goodbyes and retraced their steps back to the hire car out front.

Before they had driven past Willow Tree Cottage, Mike had swallowed two painkillers with a swig of water from a bottle. "Looks like he's gone off to Galicia with his new friend."

As they left the village, Wazz turned to Mike, "You know that she will ask her aunt or one of the others who will tell her that there is no Eduardo Vergara in the UK; after all, he was born in New York and 'died' there. I suppose there's a chance that they heard about Agustin and that he had children but he's long dead as well."

"I know all of that. They will have heard of Agustin. I was only trying to establish a rapport so that she'll call me if Eduardo turns up or if she hears something."

———

"Leonard?" Mike was ringing from the car on their way back eastward to London.

"Are you on your way into work?"

"Is that your way of asking if my back is better?"

"You're in a car. It must be better."

"It could be an ambulance."

"I don't care how you get here."

"I've got some news. I have just been to meet Rosa Roberts at Willow Farm. She is Jim Ibarra's sister, now married to a farmer. She has never heard of Eduardo, or any Eduardo Vergara for that matter, but she is going to discreetly ask her relatives. However, she said that her brother has left for Spain with a friend, but she wasn't certain of the date or times. They are walking a stretch of the Pilgrim's Way in northern Spain."

"Is our Eduardo this 'friend'?"

"That's my guess. She thinks he is with a friend called Jacob, but I don't think she really knows. Can you check the ports and airports? He could be using a passport in the name of Chuck Kilminster or Eduardo Ortiz or Eduardo Vergara."

"Or a false passport. Talking of which, I have your new passport here. Sounds like you might need it."

"Leonard! I need to do some more searching. I'll have to work from home today."

"Sure. I'll get the team onto the ports and airports."

"Let me know what they find."

Wazz continued driving for a mile before speaking. "I'll take a few days off work. You are going to need me around, I think."

"No, that's not necessary," was her instant reply.

"You are stuck in the flat. You cannot ride your bike. You cannot go into work unless I drive you."

She mulled this over.

He did not wait for her to say anything. "I will keep this car for a week."

"Um, thank you, I don't know how all this has happened in

less than a week. I seem to always bring you problems and bad luck. Hopefully, things will get better from now. And I thought that the previous few weeks were a disaster."

Twenty-two days earlier, on Wednesday 31st July, Mike had ridden down under a blue sky streaked with cirrus cloud to Southampton docks; this was to be *her* day. She had woken early and could not get back to sleep.

After months of searching and analysis, she had pieced everything together and was convinced that she had cracked one of the largest drug smuggling operations ever. In particular, she had been looking for a specific ship with containers of soya bean curd that was used as cattle fodder coming from Cartagena in Colombia bound for Southampton. This was the *Carlos Sanguinem*, and it made the trip roughly every month, taking eleven or twelve days each way across the Atlantic Ocean.

It generally arrived on a Wednesday, and she had liaised with several authorities via Leonard such that up to one hundred and forty containers were to be scanned and physically searched over a two-day period.

Mike parked her motorbike next to the Harbourmaster's office and took off her black helmet; it had been a hot but enjoyable one-and-a-half-hour ride down the A34 towards the south coast. In a small office, she met John, a tall man with black glasses and a clipped beard; he worked for Border Force and would be part of the large team assembled to undertake what was to be a mammoth task. He displayed no surprise when introduced to a thirty-something woman in a blonde wig and motorcycle leathers who he had been told was the American liaison not only with Border Force but also the Ports Authority, the Port police, the Secret services and Special Branch. In all, there were to be fifteen individuals involved.

After a few hours, she had decided that she never wanted to smell soya bean curd in a hot shipping container ever again.

Time dragged and she enjoyed the break eating the sandwiches she had brought with her and chatting with John who told her all about the Neolithic sites in Thetford Forest in Norfolk where he grew up. She told him that she was not aware of any sites in her neck of the woods in Oxfordshire. They chatted easily with each other and soon struck up a bond. Then, it was back to the industrial-scale operation of making sure that every cattle fodder container was identified, diverted to the search area and both scanned and opened.

Any initial enthusiasm by the team for the project began to evaporate by 4 o'clock when the fiftieth container had been searched with no result.

"Relax, we'll find the stuff," John assumed that Mike was not used to this type of laborious search and, perhaps, was a little impatient.

"How do you do this every day? It would drive me nuts."

"Yes, it does, but when you find what you are looking for, you are over the moon."

Mike understood but failed to match it to her life which involved even longer periods of repetitive work that more often than not lead nowhere. This whole operation was happening because of her. Failure was not an option as Leonard had backed her unreservedly and she couldn't face him or, indeed, herself, if she failed.

Of course, she wouldn't fail. The pieces of intelligence that she had assembled were impressive and all led to this being the obvious way in which drugs might be brought to Europe. This was a cartel that the CIA in Washington had been after for a long time.

Her dogged research over years had correlated the various ways that drugs, in bulk, might be transported from South America to Europe. It was her analysis that had led to the discovery that containers could be built with a shallow hidden floor. Testing this in the field had led to her being in Holland with Dylan and the ambush that had killed him and wrecked her body and life.

She knew that the *Carlos Sanguinem* was the route by which the drugs were smuggled into Europe; this was a fact as far as she was concerned.

Except that, by late afternoon on that Wednesday, she was feeling something deep inside and it was not good.

"Relax," John had said in a comforting way as a mass of people and so much machinery had undertaken the arduous and repetitive process of searching the dark red containers.

"It's not your balls on the line," she had replied, having grown to like him and his simple, no-nonsense approach.

"I understand. Why not go and get a coffee. I'll shout if anything happens."

She had walked off, grabbed a drink and had stood gazing out at vessels the size of which appeared to defy her understanding of physics. How did they float?

At six o'clock, she had decided to ride home, as much to clear her head as to get a good night's sleep. John reassured her that she would be the first to get the phone call if they found anything; she gave him her number. They were already almost halfway through checking the containers but with so much to do tomorrow.

The ride home would normally have been a pleasure, and she was rarely presented with such a wonderful sweeping road across the chalk downlands of Hampshire, however she was too stressed. At her cabin, she had undressed, washed and flopped into bed, wondering why she did this for a living. Her last thought was that John was a lovely man of the type she never usually met.

She would ride back down the next day.

CHAPTER SIXTEEN

A good night's sleep had helped, and she had ridden along the A34 with renewed enthusiasm. Why had she assumed that the drugs would be found in the first container; this was wishful thinking and impatient even by her low tolerance to, well, anything. It was Thursday 1st August, and she felt that today would be a good day.

They had already resumed the moving, scanning and searching through containers when she had arrived. John had walked across to greet her wearing a Hi-Viz vest over his black overalls that would soon be unbearable on what promised to be yet another hot and humid summer's day. She had left her motorcycle helmet and jacket in John's office and replaced them with a white hard hat and another Hi-Viz vest. She had walked out onto the dock.

"Found anything yet?"

"No" John had replied, "We have only searched another twenty this morning so far.

"I think that I will take a walk to stretch my legs. Call me if you do." She had not bothered to explain her limp or the dull pain she experienced after a bike ride.

John had described to her where she could and could not walk. He then said, "I need to speak to the captain who is getting a bit nervous that we are going to prevent him sailing as scheduled."

"Do you think that he's involved?" she had not resolved this in her mind.

"No idea but unlikely. Why would he know what's in the thousands of units on board. Why should he care?"

With that she had wandered off along the dock, marvelling at the enormous scale of everything from the gantries to the vessels. Approaching the *Carlos Sanguinem*, she had taken photographs to remind her of the day; the ship had already been almost three quarters unloaded. It was registered in Panama, but this was a flag of convenience; all it ever did was sail back and forth from Colombia to Europe.

The day had dragged, and she had sought out an air-conditioned office and a cold bottle of water.

At 4.30pm, John had entered with a resigned look on his face.

"That's the last of the soya curd containers searched. They have found nothing. Sorry."

Mike bit her lip and tried to keep her emotions in check.

"Thank you," she said, "I'm so sorry, too."

"We'll have to let the *Carlos Sanguinem* sail back to Cartagena. She'll leave early the day after tomorrow, Saturday."

"John, thank you. This is all my fault. Sorry."

"Don't beat yourself up. This happens all the time. Wrong ship, wrong day."

"Hmm."

"Keep in touch," and with that, he had turned and left the office.

Mike had changed out of the safety gear and prepared herself for the long ride home. Before that, she needed to step outside and phone Leonard who would not be happy.

The conversation had not lasted long. He had not berated her too much considering what had happened but left her in no doubt that this project was dead. Absolutely dead.

———

"I put an aspirin in the water," one of Mike's work colleagues was explaining why the pink roses were looking perfect. It was three weeks after the dockside fiasco which now seemed a distant nightmare.

"Thank you, Morag."

"Is your back mending?"

"I am ten times better than yesterday."

Mike settled at her desk; she was feeling a sort of guilt that Wazz was having to find somewhere to park in central London, having dropped her at the nearest point possible to her building.

The phone on her desk buzzed and she picked it up and listened, "Sure, I'll come straight up."

She left the main office and, using the lift, made her way to see Leonard. She tapped the door and entered.

"I was expecting a walking stick at least," he said.

"Security were worried about your safety, so they took it away from me at the main entrance."

"I feel your pain." He was sat behind his desk as usual but with a new summer jacket over the chair back, unless Mike was mistaken. It had the look of beige linen or, perhaps, sackcloth. He was sweating but this was nothing new whether it was January or August.

"I like the jacket."

"They've just extended my contract by a year, so I went and bought it; I thought it was a concession to the UK summer."

"Perfect for Wimbledon."

"I get asked every year and I live so close but, really?" he let his face collapse into a disapproving grimace.

"Any news?" she couldn't wait to ask what really mattered to her.

"Yes, they drove to Bristol, stayed at a hotel and caught the lunchtime flight to Bilbao."

"Did they arrest him at Bristol?"

"For what? Being an idiot? They weren't officially looking for him."

"When do they land in Bilbao?"

He looked up at wall clock that showed the time in London and Washington, "They are landing about now."

"Which passport did he use?"

"Chuck Kilminster. Which reminds me," he leant sideways and opened a drawer, "here's your new passport." He handed it over in its pristine dark blue cover.

"Thank you," she opened it, looked shocked at the photograph and closed it quickly. "Are they being tailed?"

"No, not yet. I only just got the details ... so not yet."

"What do you mean by 'not yet'?"

"I will have someone on the case very soon." He reached a hand back to touch the lapel of the jacket, as if appreciating the texture.

"No, you're joking, I've hurt my back."

"It's very comfortable in business class."

"I don't care," she paused to consider this, "Do they have business class on European short haul? The flight must only be an hour and a half but I'm not going, anyway."

"Mike," she so very rarely heard him call her Mike, "Just find him," and he repeated, "Just find him."

She let out a deep breath and stared at him. Several seconds passed while she weighed up how this changed her negotiating position, "OK, I will, it's against my better judgement but I will, although you know that this week is so important for the drugs shipment."

He knew he had won so unexpectedly and easily that even he needed to make sure that nothing he said was offensive.

"No problem. If you need to go on checking the drugs shipment, that's OK. Let me know anything important but please make sure that you are on that plane tomorrow morning."

"Which plane?"

"To Bilbao. From Heathrow."

"What? What time's the flight?"

Leonard opened his desk drawer and took out a piece of paper, "8.30am, it says here. You are already checked in. Seat 2A in Business."

She retraced her steps down to her desk, resting a palm on her lower back occasionally for comfort. Sitting down in her chair was undertaken as if she would go into spasm at any time. Putting the piece of paper with the flight details next to her keyboard, she logged in and looked for new data on the drugs transportation.

There, before her, she could see so much displayed. She had been waiting for this level of detail for a couple of weeks.

Knowing that Wazz was going to be back outside the building in thirty-five minutes meant that she needed to be selective in her reading. To almost anyone else these reports and lists would be beyond tedious. They included the schedules of ships from South America to England. She spotted the name of the *Carlos Sanguinem*; it was on its way back to England from Cartagena. It would arrive Tuesday, a day earlier than planned.

Time flew and she looked at the clock on her screen and saw that she had only eight minutes to get downstairs, pick up her phone and bag from Security and get to the front of the building.

She made it.

As Wazz pulled into the bus stop, he could see her waiting in her cap, white blouse and dog tooth pattern trousers with her rucksack on her back. She managed to open the heavy front door and haul herself inside.

"Successful?" he looked into his wing mirror and pulled out into the traffic.

"That depends. Let's start with the positives. I read some critical updates on my project. Moving on to the negatives."

"So that's all of the positives?"

"You have high expectations of my job. That is more than I normally achieve."

"I am understanding you more every day."

"Good, when you have worked me out, let me know because I, sure as Hell, haven't."

The traffic leaving London was busy on a Friday at rush hour, therefore, he had to concentrate and couldn't turn his head.

She continued, "As to the negatives, Jim and Eduardo caught a plane to Bilbao and arrived not long ago."

"But your agency is meeting them off the plane?"

"Er, it doesn't work like that. We don't have people everywhere waiting for a job to do."

"But you know where Eduardo is and that's big progress, isn't it?"

"Sort of ... God, I sound like Leonard. Yes, it is."

"Well, not a bad day, I would say."

"I haven't finished with the bad news. I have my new passport." She waited for the inevitable question.

"That's not bad news, is it?"

"It is if you are using it tomorrow to fly at 8.30am to Bilbao."

"Oh, for Pity's sake."

They drove by famous London landmarks without registering any of them even though Mike was looking out of the side window; she was too busy trying to put today into perspective.

"What are you doing in Bilbao?" Wazz sounded eminently reasonable.

In fact, he sounded so reasonable that Mike, for once, was thrown, "I have no fricking idea. I cannot believe that you think that I do have any idea ... but thank you."

"This is Leonard's suggestion, I'm guessing?"

They had stopped at traffic lights and a Lycra-clad cyclist had pulled up next to Mike's window and had rested his arm against her door. She glared at him, and he immediately put both hands back onto his handlebars.

"Yes, isn't it always?"

"What are you meant to be doing?"

"Finding Eduardo. The problem is that he has not committed a crime. I accept that he probably stole an old Land Rover but that's not proven or likely to interest international governments. This is a problem that is deeply bothering the US President, consequently, the Agency is deeply bothered."

"But what about your main project? Is that derailed by this ... missing wealthy, spoilt ..." he searched for the words, "loser?"

"I can multi-task and stay flexible."

"Bully for you, I have taken a week off work and now you are going to Spain, and I face the lonely prospect of catching up on my university coursework."

"Possibly."

They began to pick up speed as they left the centre of London, following taxis, buses and delivery drivers as they changed lanes using some shared communal experience.

"Possibly?"

"Why not come to Spain?"

"You've spent too long with Leonard. Why would I come to Spain?"

"You know Spain."

He laughed, "And that's your best line? I also know the back streets of Warsaw, but I am not going back there either. What's your point?"

It dawned on her that Wazz had put up with more from her than, perhaps, even Dylan had, but he had his limits.

"I'd love you to see this through with me."

"Mike, I don't know Eduardo or your world."

"But what about my cabin?"

"Mike, it will only take one policeman who is down on his weekly target for me to be arrested as the easiest candidate for blowing up your cabin."

"Please."

With that single word their relationship changed. From that first moment where they had met next to the waste bins at the back of Charles Yelland's villa, she had been the aggressor. In all of the mental and physical stress that followed that moment, she had needed him, but it had always been left unsaid.

"Mike, I will come to Spain, but you have to trust me – otherwise what's the point?"

"I trust you."

"What's all of this about? By which I mean Eduardo and your main project. I know this is against the rules but if you don't tell me, I am wasting my time?"

"They are not connected. They are in no way connected but I will tell you all you need to know about both. Let me tell you what I think. You know some of this already."

She looked out of the window as they started to drive at speed along the A40 and she gave Wazz her short honest assessment.

"Firstly, Eduardo is mentally unstable, from a wealthy family and has gone missing. His brother has been kidnapped and his mother is being pressured to sell a division of her business empire. These people also tried to kill Eduardo by blowing him up in my cabin. They were clearly tracking his phone. He has his own weird agenda which revolves around his Basque heritage and his new best friend, Jim. Secondly, I am part of a large Agency team that has been tracking a drug smuggling business for nearly six months. They are moving vast quantities of cocaine from Colombia to the UK. We thought we had them a few weeks ago when a ship was impounded at Southampton docks and one hundred and forty containers were searched. The drugs were meant to be in containers of soya bean curd which is used as cattle feed. Nothing was found. The rest of my colleagues have moved on after an investigation by an in-house team who questioned some of the original intel, I have not moved on. I know I was right and, I know in my heart that those drugs are on that ship every month. There. That's it. Welcome to my life."

"Wow, and I think that I have problems with two drunk pervs at three in the morning."

"What pisses me off is that I am being diverted from my project to find some rich family's son when I know that I should be following all the leads on that ship."

"When is it due back in the UK?"

"Tuesday, into Southampton … but don't get excited, no authority will check it out again. I blew our chance."

"But you haven't given up?"

She turned to look at him. "That'll be a no, then," he said as an ambulance went past and he moved back into the outside lane.

"The week before my cabin exploded, I was exploring some ideas about how the drugs get into the UK. I can go on doing that anywhere … including Bilbao."

"I had better pack my suitcase. I was not expecting to go back so soon. It's like the old days, escorting women around Spain."

He assumed that she was smiling without actually turning towards her to check if that was true.

CHAPTER SEVENTEEN

The wake-up alarm went off at 5.30am on Saturday morning.

Mike got out of bed nervously as she checked the status of her back; it seemed fine, if bruised. She went to the bathroom and rattled the door handle to find that Wazz was already in there. He emerged with a dark brown towel wrapped around his waist and a big smile on his face.

"God, I hate people who are lively in the morning," Mike was wearing the white and green pyjamas that she had bought with Sally in High Wycombe.

He bit his tongue but asked, as she passed him, if she wanted coffee. Apparently this was a stupid question.

He went to the kitchen and set things in motion – the kettle, the coffee maker and the toaster.

Maybe fifteen minutes later, they converged in the kitchen where he had already drunk the coffee and eaten the toast.

"Ready to go?"

"After a coffee," she replied.

He put a new capsule in the machine and to the sound of muted machine gun fire, he retreated to his bedroom to finish getting ready.

Eventually they left the flat and began the twenty-minute drive to Heathrow.

"I can see why you bought the flat – it's so convenient for the airport," she said.

"My world used to revolve around London and flights to Spain ... and not much else."

This triggered something in her.

"After the accident, my world only settled down when I rented the cabin and now, sadly, that's gone."

"We are both moving on."

Their eyes met until he looked back at the motorway ahead of him.

Despite being a Saturday, the M25 was busy even that early in the morning. Wazz turned off onto the relative quiet of the slip road that would take them to Heathrow Terminal 5. He parked in the long stay car park, and they caught the shuttle bus which took them to Departures.

They could have been any couple on their way to Spain for a holiday as they checked in at the BA desk where they were given directions to the Business Lounge. Here, they sat in two armchairs but had no time to enjoy the experience. Barely had they eaten a croissant and drunk a cup of coffee, when they had to head off to the gate. Although Wazz was pulling both of the suitcases, he had to slow his pace to match Mike who was protecting her back while limping slightly from her damaged calf. The frustration on her face was enough to dissuade him from making any quips.

Wazz had never flown business class so the whole trip was a new experience. For Mike, one of her last flights had been on Charles Yelland's private jet and that was going to be hard to top.

Business class was called first to board the plane, another new experience for Wazz. This applied to only twenty passengers and in minutes they were walking along the tunnel of the air bridge. Stepping through the plane door, again he was not used to being immediately at his seat, even on EasyJet to Spain where he had always sat at the back. He lifted their hand luggage into the overhead lockers. Smiling at the air crew, they sat down on the black leather of 2A and 2C; between them a seat had been folded down to provide a drinks tray. A grey curtain separated them from Economy a few rows behind.

So far all was well, and they took off on time.

Before they were over Paris, Mike was showing signs that she was bored or, at least, looking for distraction; she could not focus on her phone or laptop and the view out of the window was of grey clouds. Wazz had already put his head back and closed his eyes. He had learnt in prison, in Spain and while working at the strip club that you grab your sleep when it is available whether that is during the day or the night, for twelve hours or ten minutes.

"I'm surprised that you can get on planes. Don't they trigger your claustrophobia?"

"No, the cabin's big enough that I don't get anxious ... and I'm excited to be travelling."

"Definitely not like when you were locked up in gaol?"

Perhaps unsurprisingly, this hit him low down. Why did she feel the need to keep mentioning his time in prison. He stayed silent, breathing in and putting his head back. After a long pause he opened his eyes and turned to her.

"Mike, do you have any filter? That's *any* filter?"

"This is not where I make jokes about cigarettes, is it?"

He exhaled, "No, Mike, for once it is not. Give me a break, please."

She turned quickly towards the window and felt an internal cramp that told her she had mislaid the compassion card.

"Sorry ... I mean, sorry."

"It's OK," he said but it clearly was not. Why begin a relationship, by which he meant why even think of beginning another relationship, with a woman who would most likely drive you to distraction.

———

Jim and Eduardo were having lunch on the covered rooftop of their hotel opposite the Guggenheim Museum. The silver metallic curves and stone walls in front of them were catching the light of the midday sun viewed over low clipped box hedges in black containers next to their table. It was the perfect temperature under the canopies before they ventured out into the heat of the day.

"I feel I am home," Eduardo was almost drunk with the thought that he was in the Basque lands for the first time. "I never felt home in the USA or in the UK. This is home."

Jim was picking up on his friend's fragile and volatile mental state; he was beginning to be slightly concerned.

Like most people who came up to this bar, Eduardo took a selfie on his phone with the museum in the background. He checked the time. "How long is the drive tomorrow?"

"It is only forty minutes, and you will meet many of your cousins and second cousins and distant relatives. If you genuinely wish to disappear, here is the place. You can say goodbye to Chuck Kilminster and Eduardo Ortiz, from this moment on you are Eduardo Vergara."

Jim poured some orange juice into each of their glasses and topped them up with champagne from the silver ice bucket next to him.

He proposed a toast, "To Eduardo Vergara and Iago Ibarra!" Eduardo repeated it and they clinked glasses.

"I must remember to call you Iago or your family will not know who I am talking about."

"They know me as Jim as well, so don't worry. The Basques have always been an international race."

"We have so much to do. I cannot wait to go to the Guggenheim, to visit our families and to head off on the route to Santiago de Compostela."

"To Saint James! To Santiago!" Jim proposed another toast to the patron saint of the Basques after whom he was named.

―――

The Airbus A320 landed at Bilbao airport and taxied towards the terminal and control tower designed by another Santiago – Santiago Calatrava.

It had been such a short flight that there had barely been enough time for the cabin crew to move the drinks trolley the length of the plane before it was necessary for the captain to begin the descent.

Mike and Wazz were among the first to leave the aircraft, but this merely meant that they had longer to wait at the luggage carousel. The warning alarm sounded, a red light flashed, and the belt began to move. All eyes turned towards the emerging baggage. The system worked and the suitcases of the business class passengers came out first. Wazz pulled theirs across the hall and out of the Terminal in the direction of the taxi rank.

"It's seems longer getting to the strip club from Ickenham than flying out here."

"I could get used to business class," Mike replied, being in a relatively good mood as the journey had not thrown any more curved balls at her.

Twenty minutes after getting into a taxi, they passed the futuristic Guggenheim Museum with its over-sized sculptures of watches at the front and, a few yards further on, pulled up.

They were stood outside looking around at the setting when Mike was telephoned by Leonard.

"How's the holiday?" he asked.

"I'm lounging on a sunbed drinking a cocktail."

"What? You ... you operatives or whatever your job description says, you're all the same ... anyway, it doesn't matter ... I need to update you. Pathfinder has traced the phones in use at Willow Tree Cottage and correlated them with those at Bristol airport and in Bilbao. I will send you Chuck's new number and a selfie he took there. He is obviously in a hotel right opposite the Museum. You know, the one that looks like a row of garbage cans? If you see Top Cat and Officer Dibble, say Hi from me."

"You're not into art, then?" She had no idea what he was talking about.

"Art's for people with limited mental capacity who cannot understand the complexities of sport."

"What?" she didn't bother to discuss this eccentric view, instead she reverted to the reality of the situation, "We've just arrived at some hotels in the block opposite the Guggenheim so, relax, we'll check which is his in a few minutes. We will stay there, if we can."

Mike had not booked accommodation for them both; she had no idea where Eduardo was staying until now. She had assumed that all she needed was a base for a couple of nights while she tried to make contact with him and warn him that his life was in danger and that he should return home to the protection of his mother. The selfie he had taken did not test her analyst's skill too much. He was patently a couple of buildings to the left of where she was standing; she could identify the exact one by assessing the angles and looking for the glass wall and box hedges on the roof garden.

For once, something had fallen into place and luck had been on her side; finding him had been relatively straightforward. He was obviously staying at the Nervión Real hotel which turned out to be a rather boring brown building with windows highlighted in white. She checked in for both of them. Inside, the décor consisted of everything that could be done with thin wooden slats; they were everywhere – on the walls and ceilings, behind reception and up the stairs. It reminded Mike of her cabin which prompted her to look for the fire extinguishers and exits.

Their adjoining rooms were on the second floor and gave oblique views of the Guggenheim behind a forty feet high sculpture by Jeff Koons of a sitting puppy made up of thousands of packed red, green and white pot plants. It made the dog look as if it had a skin disease. Her first act was to turn off the television that was playing some tourist film of the city below a 'Welcome Michaela Kingdom' message. Her second was to set up her laptop and gizmos in order that she might track Eduardo's phone.

His phone was currently turned off probably with the battery removed; he was being very careful, but she had no doubt that he would turn it on at some point later. Mike refreshed herself in front of the mirror over the washbasin, stepped into the corridor and walked the six paces to tap Wazz's door. He opened it immediately.

"His phone is turned off. Let's go and check out the hotel. He may be around somewhere."

"What's your plan of action?"

"I don't want to tip him off. I want to corner him in person or else he will disappear again. My thinking is that I won't leave him a note or call him."

"I think that we should do a reconnaissance and then, drink in the bar and eat in the restaurant tonight. He's probably going to come back here at a reasonable hour. I don't think he is going to spend his time in a nightclub 'til dawn. He's a nervous nerd."

With that, they walked around the hotel where they checked out the public rooms and took the lift to the rooftop restaurant and cocktail bar. There was no sign of him anywhere, but they had not really expected their luck to be that good. Mike reserved a table for 8.00pm and they went back down to the coffee bar that adjoined reception and ordered café con leche and *Etxeko bixkotxa* as recommended by the waiter; it turned out to be a type of Basque gâteau.

"I hope we get time to go around the Guggenheim once we have found Eduardo," she said nodding to the building that blocked the entire view out of the window across the road and square.

"You don't think that he is here because he is as obsessed with his work project as you are?"

Mike looked at him askance and in silence.

"I mean it is odd that he is working on art fraud," Wazz had lowered his voice even more, "and here we are opposite one of the most famous art galleries in the world."

"You're a sharp cookie, aren't you?"

"You're meant to say, 'not just a pretty face'."

"Hmm."

"Eduardo did have a copy in his bedroom of the huge Jeff Koons sculpture of tulips that's over there in the gallery."

"He kept banging on about tulips, didn't he?"

"True. I really want to take a look at the sculpture, round the back next to the river. I've seen photographs. It's a bunch of seven shiny, brightly-coloured tulips about fifteen feet long."

"Tulips drop their petals after five minutes, I thought."

"These are made of mirror-polished stainless steel."

"He's not normal."

"Jeff Koons or Eduardo?"

Leonard had just finished the call to Mike in Bilbao when his own phone rang.

"Bob, great to hear from you."

"I thought that I would give you a call as we don't seem to have made a lot of progress. Anything new from your end?"

"Actually, some news just in. Eduardo has flown out to Bilbao with a friend called Jim. We don't think that this is anything too weird. It seems the disturbed boy has suddenly discovered his Basque roots."

"The word Basque always bothers me."

"Me too, but I think that this might be for real. Who knows?"

"Do you have a team tracking him?"

"I do. Even better, we have identified his new phone and have access to his location, messages and photos. At the moment he is in a hotel opposite that art museum that looks like a scrap yard."

"Well, that takes a lot of weight off my shoulders but doesn't help me solve the problem of who blew up Mike's cabin and why I haven't arrested them yet."

"Eduardo's off British soil therefore you can leave him to me and the Agency. He was never a suspect anyway."

CHAPTER EIGHTEEN

Conrad was on the phone to Valentina Ortiz.

"Any news?!" she cut across his pleasantries.

"Yes, Val. Nothing on Diego, sadly, even though Doug's pestering the Swiss day and night, but the Agency and the Brits have tracked Eduardo to Bilbao. We have a team out there. I'm sure they'll find him soon."

"Oh, that's something. Thank God ... but why go there?"

"He's gone there with a British friend who is a Basque. I don't know anything more."

"Is it that girl who he went to see?"

"I don't know, Val. I'm passing on the news that the Agency have tracked him there."

"Have they got his phone number?"

Here, the President needed to tell a white lie. Thomas, his Director of National Security, had told him that Valentina must not ring her son. This would, in all likelihood, drive him away. The boy had obviously suffered a mental breakdown.

"I don't think so. They traced him via his passport, I think. Do you have any idea what he is doing there or where he might stay?" Conrad gently swerved the conversation.

"None. He has never been to Bilbao or Spain."

"But his father was Basque?"

"Yes, you know that. When Agustin originally set up the company, he based it in Bilbao. That's why the undersea cables to the UK and Portugal start there. That's why, having established the route and infrastructure, we are there on Wednesday to announce the contract."

"Does Eduardo know anything about the business, about the cable contract?"

"Nothing. He cannot remember Agustin. He only knows America and the UK. To him Paco was his father ... and he was Puerto Rican."

"Seems odd to me that he's gone to Bilbao at the same time that we are going there."

"It doesn't affect anything. I, you, we all need this darn thing signed otherwise the Chinese will find another way in."

"That's not going to happen on my watch."

The average person with a mobile phone or laptop, if asked, would be surprised to know that 95% of internet and communication traffic does not go via satellite or through the ether. It goes via a network of undersea cables, and these are mostly privately owned by a half dozen companies that are household names in computers, phones, shopping and delivery. There are over 750,000 miles of them and the longest is 25,000 miles long connecting thirty-three countries.

Agustin Vergara had been one of the first to see the potential and had been instrumental in laying some of the early cables from Bilbao to Highbridge in Somerset and to Seixal in Portugal. His company had grown and evolved to what Valentina now controlled. She was in charge of the largest western cable-laying company.

A new trans-Atlantic cable was proposed and desperately needed; it would cost $800 million and would start at Virginia Beach in the USA cross to Bude in the southwest of England and head south around the Cornish and Brittany peninsulas down to Bilbao in Spain. Agustin would have been so proud.

Raising the finance was surprisingly not the problem; each cable was funded by a consortium of the world's largest companies. The problem lay in the security of the communication traffic. In 2020, President Donald Trump had signed an Executive Order stopping any cable directly connecting the USA with China.

There was a new 'Cold War'- control of the installation of future undersea cables. In the late 90s, the $600 million contract to build the SeaWeMe-6 cable from Japan and China to the UK and Belgium looked as if it would go to the Chinese who made up three of the ten funders in the consortium. The USA used every means possible to prevent the Chinese from laying the 25,000-mile cable, even though they were, perhaps, $100 million cheaper. There were threats of sanctions against companies along the route, there were substantial 'training grants' to countries through whose territorial waters the cable passed provided by the US Trade and Development Agency and diplomatic pressure was applied everywhere. Two Chinese funders pulled out to be replaced by the Malaysians and Singaporeans.

The consortium decided to award the contract to USA and France.

Now, a new cable from Bilbao to the USA was being proposed and Chinese companies were in the frame to make the cable and lay it. Except that the USA did not want this, and, of equal importance, the President's main financial sponsor owned the largest cable-laying company in the world. This was a win/win situation for Conrad.

Hence he was flying to Bilbao to announce that Val's company had been awarded the contract for the next new generation, four-core-fiber cable from Bilbao to Virginia Beach via Bude, effectively providing another link between continental Europe, the UK and North America.

THE MONGOOSE AND THE COBRA

"Val, Agustin would have wanted you to do this, and Diego's kidnap should not deflect you. Fly out with me on Air Force One from Heathrow to Bilbao on Wednesday."

"You would rather have me under CIA and White House control?"

"We have known each other too long. I know that your heart is telling you to hire an army and a fleet of aircraft, all of which you can afford, but, as a friend, let me ask you to trust the Agency, Leonard and his team and ask you not to interfere and make the situation worse. Fly on AF1 with me."

"And what am I meant to do in the meantime?"

"How about planning how you are going to deliver an $800 million contract?"

"Hah ... I will and can you find out which hotel Eduardo is staying in?"

———

It was 7.30pm on a Saturday and Bilbao was surprisingly busy. The holiday season was in full swing. The bars were full, and the restaurants would become busier later: the Spanish did not eat early, especially in mid-summer.

Mike was drinking a Margarita, enjoying the salt on the rim of the glass.

"I had you down as a Piña Colada girl," Wazz drank the last mouthful of his beer.

"It would curdle."

They were at the hotel on the rooftop enjoying their cocktails but keeping an eye out for Eduardo. It was a beautiful evening. The sun had dropped and any heat in the building was being radiated upwards and away. The bar had small high tables and trendy barstools that looked like wine glasses made of a see-through plastic – some looked as if they were half filled with red wine, others with white. Mike could not make up her mind if sitting with your ass in a 'pool' of Rioja was fun or not.

At that moment, there was an ear-splitting bang. Mike, with memories of her cabin exploding, ducked level with the table as everyone else appeared to jump up. Somewhere a glass fell onto the stone floor and shattered. Wazz went into 'security' mode, looking around the bar at the two exits.

A single rocket exploded in the shape of a perfect orange chrysanthemum above their heads.

To a background of cheering, hugging and kissing, the waiter delivered another beer to Wazz excitedly saying, "That's *txupinazo*. The firework that marks the start of *Biboko Aste Nagusia*, 'The Great Week'. Now we have nine days of partying." They were speaking in Spanish.

"That scared me. What is the festival celebrating?" Mike asked the waiter.

"Everything Basque: bull fighting, boxing, singing, dancing, drinking. It always starts on the first Saturday after the Assumption of Our Lady on the 15th of August. That's today. The rocket is released from the balcony of the Teatro Arriaga. It starts the festival." He turned to serve other customers.

"That did nothing for my heart," she took an extra-large gulp of the cocktail as if a mouthful of tequila and Cointreau might not be equally bad for her.

"Do you think that Eduardo is here for the festival. You know … having discovered his Basque roots?"

"I really hope so but I'm worried that he's gone crazy, I mean real loopy and might be susceptible to every nutjob who discovers he's worth millions."

Her phone rang.

"Oh, hi Rosa … no problem, I'm with Wazz." She listened, saying the occasional word of encouragement. Wazz sat quietly trying to second-guess her reason for calling, interpreting every smile and frown on Mike's face.

"Rosa, do you think that Jim, Jacob and, possibly, Eduardo have gone to Spain for the Great Week festival?" Mike was carefully trying not to reveal that they were in Bilbao.

After a few more seconds, the call ended.

"She's never heard of the festival. I think she is a Brit and has only a passing interest in her Basque connections. It is Jim who is the keen one."

"Why did she phone?"

"She was giving me an update having spoken to her friends and family, none of whom have really heard of an Eduardo Vergara. There were two boys on the Habana with that surname. An aunt thought that Agustin Vergara, who we know was on the boat, had a child in America called Eduardo but that he had died. That's it. So, nothing we didn't already know."

"Was Rosa suspicious of anything ... including us?"

"I don't think so."

"She, genuinely, believes that her brother is walking the Pilgrim's Way with a friend called Jacob who she has never met."

"And you buy that?"

"I think that I do ... and I did a PhD in Cynicism."

"Surely not."

"You sound like you did one as well."

"Did you get it?"

Mike began to laugh at the thought, "Yes, but I felt that I never needed to attend a tutorial, and I was suspicious of the professors."

"Was being suspicious of the professors part of the course?"

"Ha, definitely. Maybe I really should do one?"

"Great idea. But I'm not sure that I believe they are here on a walking trip. How often does the word *Basque* usually turn up in your work?"

"Slightly less than in yours, I expect."

He looked confused.

"What? You must see them all the time," she goaded him.

"The girls have taken them off by the time I walk through to use the toilet."

"Great excuse."

"Where do you think Jim and Eduardo have gone?" he changed the subject.

"No idea but I thought that they might be back before dark. Of course, they might be in the streets enjoying the start of the festival. It sounds noisy down below."

"Your plan?"

"I'll message Leonard to see if there's any more information on Eduardo, then sit in the restaurant watching for his return."

"Another drink?"

"No, let's have some wine with the meal. Wait a second while I send Leonard a quick message. Eduardo's turned off his phone and could be on a flight to Thailand by now and we wouldn't know."

Eduardo, while having difficulty separating reality from fantasy, retained enough of his training to keep his phone turned off. He didn't need it, anyway. His new best friend Jim was in control.

They had spent all afternoon high up in the mountains where the air had been fresh and the peace overwhelming. To stand in the village where his grandfather had been born was almost too much to bear. When he thought of him leaving with the others aged five to go on a boat to England, it almost took Eduardo over the edge.

He had met so many distant relatives that it had become a joke when any one of them tried to find the right term. Were they second cousins twice removed and was this great uncle Luis or …? It didn't matter. They were all family, and he felt unconditional love for the first time. And he relaxed. No security, no pretence, no fear and, most importantly, no false name. He was

Eduardo Vergara. His only regret was that he had to speak Spanish and not Euskadi; this he would rectify quickly.

His grandfather's village only had 250 inhabitants but had most of its thirteenth century walls still intact as well as the church of the Immaculate Conception and a medieval stone tower. Above the village, forests stretched up to the rocky mountain peaks, below there were regimented rows of vines. Lunch involved fifteen people and a lot of wine; all he remembered afterwards was the honking of six geese who patrolled in a haughty manner around the garden.

The journey back to the coast was uneventful but equally stimulating. The mountains, the sloping fields and the sheep were all new to him. Being chauffeur-driven in central London was a luxury but it meant absolutely nothing to him, and it came at such a high price.

And he felt safe; no one knew where he was, no one was tracking him and trying to blow him up. Every time he thought about how close he had come to being killed at the cabin, he shuddered. He deeply regretted going there. By not thinking straight, he had almost got an innocent friend killed as well. Mike was one of the very few people with whom he felt a connection.

When Diego's kidnap had been revealed, it was a confirmation of what he expected. He was not being neurotic; his life really needed to change. He knew that he was in danger. If he did not disappear, it would be a matter of time.

Up in the mountains, Eduardo felt that he was getting back to some sort of balanced mental state for the first time in months.

"OK, we should be heading back," Jim was keen to get them back to the hotel before midnight. It had been a long, exciting day.

"I could stay here forever."

"In a few days, you can come back for as long as you like.

Let's get back to Bilbao. Tomorrow at 11.00am we are going to the Guggenheim and hopefully Jacob will join us."

"I cannot wait. What about the festival?"

"It has started and will go on for nine days. Don't worry, we will go to some of the events.

CHAPTER NINETEEN

Valentina was being served dinner at her Highgate house in London.

She was feeling ever more disturbed, and this was likely to get worse. Her days and nights were consumed by threats and challenges to her plans, her private life and her businesses; her billions were meant to protect her from all this. Apart from her fitness instructor and hairdresser no one paid her any attention or interacted with her.

Diego was her rock having become indispensable and her constant companion. She had presumed that he would take over the whole business empire and drive it forward, but would there even be a business to take over? She found herself in a vacuum where she was floating with all of her money but with her private life never quite as she wanted it.

While she was bemoaning her life, someone topped up her glass. There was no connection, no pleasure from this, no recognition.

The neo-Gothic surroundings had never depressed her before but now the building and interior seemed dark and unfriendly, the black furniture over-sized and stark.

She took another drink and attempted to shake off her negative mood, but these were dominated by wondering when and whether she would ever gather her sons together again. She thought that she had it all planned out.

It was at this low point while sipping from her glass that her phone rang.

The caller was brief. She had heard his voice once before. He simply said that they knew Eduardo was in Bilbao and that she had the simplest of choices – the cable contract or they would pursue her youngest son. They were ramping up the pressure.

While she had said little on the phone, her mood changed instantly. She stood up and walked to a window where she made sure that the heavy curtains were closed tight. Her mind was already made up. Back in her chair, she took off her bracelet and placed it on the side table next to her. It had been a present from a friend, a friend she was now about to call.

"I cannot think of anybody on earth I would rather have disturb my post-prandial sherry," a male voice answered in Spanish.

"I expect you are celebrating yet another win by your team?" She was referring to the Premier League football club that he owned, having guessed that they had played that Saturday afternoon. Soccer was of no interest to her.

"What else can I spend my money on?"

There was a pause, "I need you to spend a little on me."

"You only have to ask but, first, I am so sorry to hear about Diego. I hope that you got my message?"

"I did and thank you. Felipe, this is serious. Really serious."

"Then I will take it seriously. I owe you so much."

"If you sort this out, you will owe me nothing." Only he could understand what this meant. He was indebted to her beyond words and would be still running a building supplies business in San Sebastian if she had not 'cleared the path before him' as he liked to refer to it.

"You've heard about Diego, that they tried to bomb Eduardo and now they are threatening to try again to kill him. They know he is in Bilbao with a friend at the Nervión Real hotel using the name Eduardo Vergara." She waited for him to laugh.

"Oh, really?"

"He has discovered his Basque roots."

"I have never forgotten mine or Agustin's."

"I know. I know. Felipe, protect him. Do what needs to be done. I will never ask for anything again."

"My friends will be there in one hour. "

"I will fly in on Wednesday with Conrad on Air Force One, but I want to keep everything separate ... you understand?"

"I heard that the President was coming over here. It helps to have friends in high places."

"Not always."

"Well, if you need friends in low places, just ask."

"I just did."

"Send me an up-to-date photograph of Eduardo. It will be useful."

They ended the conversation, and she sent the picture before settling back down in her armchair.

There was one last thing playing on her mind. How did her enemies know that Eduardo was in Bilbao? She believed that only Conrad, Thomas the Director of National Security, Leonard de Vries in London and his team knew about this.

Any leak must have come from one of them.

Eduardo had not appeared back at the hotel by the time Mike went to bed. She presumed that he was out late enjoying the festival with Jim. There was nothing more she could do until Leonard communicated Eduardo's exact location to her; a team was tracking his phone 24/7. Eduardo was somewhere in Bilbao, and it was highly unlikely that anyone else could know this; he was safe for the time being.

The firework displays were random throughout the whole of the evening, illuminating the tall clouds that had built up unseen in the inky blackness. Jim had chosen a great hotel in which to introduce Eduardo to Bilbao, whatever they were doing that evening.

After a few cocktails spread over many hours she had relaxed and had begun to enjoy her time with Wazz. The bar and city were noisy, and they felt able to talk relatively freely about what was really bothering her.

"The stuff is on that boat. I know, I absolutely know," she was voicing her frustration while slurring slightly, "and it arrives Tuesday."

"Surely, it is in one of the other thousand containers. You only checked those with that cattle feed, didn't you?"

"The conversations I listened to all mentioned the curd. It has been used this way before and even turned up on some Somerset farm when the smugglers messed up and let the wrong container out of the docks."

"Were these people deliberately mentioning the curd in order to distract you? Are they doing what you thought they would do?"

This implicit criticism, on another day, may have elicited a sharper response but this evening she was relaxed – a rare event.

"That's possible, I suppose."

"What about the other containers?"

Mike lifted her phone from the table and scrolled through her photographs.

"Here, look," she zoomed a little to show the sheer scale of the *Carlos Sanguinem*, "It's over a thousand feet long and nearly two hundred feet high. There are two thousand containers on board."

"Wow."

"We are talking needles and haystacks, here," she said using her favourite way to describe her job.

"It doesn't look like that many, though." He was trying to count.

"You do realise that there are more in the hull than you can see on top? It's a completely hollow shell."

"Where do they find room for the crew? How many are there on board?"

"There are only twenty-two. They live here in cabins under the bridge – that's a hundred feet above the sea."

"That's a long way up, or of more interest to me, a long way down. Actually, I don't mind heights, it's confined spaces that I don't like, as you know."

"You wouldn't like the lifeboats, in that case. They can each hold the whole crew and are launched from up there," she pointed at an orange dot on the side of the ship.

"What?! That is really not a job for me. Twenty-two people crammed in a tiny lifeboat."

"It's a waterproof capsule that floats."

"I've swallowed bigger capsules."

"This type of ship, itself, is pretty reliable. Their main problem is that the containers right at the top tend to fall off in bad seas. Up to one thousand three hundred a year by one estimate."

"No, not a job for me. I'll stick to escorting women around Spain or stopping men causing aggro at the strip club."

They went on chatting for hours before she gave her phone one last check to see if Leonard had updated her. "Let's call it a day." She stood up, feeling unsteady from the tequila. She stretched her back and bent over slightly to rub her left calf, this she instantly regretted but tried to pass it all off as physical pain rather than anything self-induced.

She walked down some stairs with Wazz following. He smiled to himself as he listened to her chatter away about nothing while clinging to the handrail. Walking in a straight line down the corridor proved to be even more challenging but he kept quiet. They entered their adjoining rooms.

———

Mike did not go to bed; in fact, she did not even undress and wash. She pulled a table over to a small armchair that was against the wall. She set up her computer equipment with her mind on overload. Before she could enter anything on her keyboard, she stood up, walked across the room and picked up the bottle of water next to her bed; this she swallowed completely.

Back in front of her laptop she was ready to follow a thousand ideas, but this didn't happen. Instead, she put her head back against the wall and fell asleep.

She woke with a jolt and with no idea of the time or where she was. It was 1.30am.

There was a message from Leonard: *Ed back in hotel at 11.30pm. Catch him tomorrow morning first thing and call me.*

With so many conflicting thoughts, sleep was now not an option. The coffee machine beckoned, and she was happy to respond to its call; a cup of espresso later and five or six hours of searching and analysing was a tempting possibility; this was also an offer that she could not refuse. She settled down in front of her screen.

Had she and her colleagues been played? This question had been on her mind even before Wazz had voiced his opinions. The thought that the drugs would be in the cattle food containers on this next voyage drove her to distraction. It gnawed at her deep inside, especially as there was no way that those containers would be searched on Tuesday or Wednesday; no authority would support the idea or sanction it – especially Leonard.

And would the smugglers risk it? This was not a game; this was a billion-dollar enterprise that had been running for a long time. Now that the authorities were aware of the cattle fodder container method, would they stick with it? Clearly they hadn't used it the last time as she had discovered to her intense embarrassment. Perhaps, they had abandoned it months ago but still referred to it as 'cattle fodder' in their supposedly confidential communications.

She and her colleagues in Langley had access to several phones in Colombia and Mexico that indicated the shipments were continuing on a monthly basis. The drugs had left Cartagena on the *Carlos Sanguinem*. How did they get them off in Southampton?

For an hour, she wrestled with the problem. If they were in other containers, the authorities would have to come at this from a different angle – probably by preventing the supply in the first place or catching the distributor in the UK and mainland Europe. She parked all of this, or should that be moored, and tried to think laterally. Like when she was searching for individuals, she always liked a photo on her screen, so it was with this ship.

Search engines threw up dozens of images and even a video of it leaving Cartagena months earlier. She watched it as she let her mind wander.

The room had warmed up and she turned the air-conditioning back on.

If the drugs weren't in the containers they must be in the control and accommodation block. That would mean the Master or Captain, she wasn't sure of his title, would need to be involved and probably the First Mate and some of the other crew. She called up her photos taken at Southampton docks. In one, the Master could be seen remonstrating with John about the delay; the conversation had gone on for about ten minutes. She enlarged the photo and, using her fingers on the touchscreen, panned towards the ship that dominated the righthand half of the picture.

It was something that Wazz had said which set her off on a new line of thinking.

Replaying the Cartagena video, she waited for the ship to turn as it headed out into the Caribbean. There were four lifeboats, two on each side high up adjacent to the accommodation and near the bridge. In her Southampton photo, there was only one on the port side.

The coffee machine caught her attention once more and she made a second cup while she put her ideas in some sort of order.

First she needed to check how many lifeboats were required on a container ship; was four a usual number? It transpired that there must be two with either one of them capable of taking 125% of the crew numbers. If the ship could theoretically take thirty crew, it looked like there would need to be two on each side. Where was the one missing in her Southampton photo?

The next fifteen minutes was spent reading about lifeboats. It was as if they were spaceships from a sci-fi film – bullet-shaped capsules that were fully enclosed and waterproof, capable of being launched from a great height. Some were lowered by cranes or davits, and some slid down a ramp. Inside they have water, supplies and the latest communication equipment. On the outside they are bright orange with the ship's call sign loudly displayed. There are many fatalities every year from the lifeboats hitting the water with too much force for the crew to withstand.

What if? Mike had too many *What ifs?*

She started with the simplest: What if the drugs were in a lifeboat and jettisoned at sea somewhere near the British coast?

The ability to temper her enthusiasm had never been one of Mike's strengths but she was more than aware that she could not raise any of her questions through Leonard; she needed to be much surer of her facts before that. There was only one person she knew who could give her the answers and, perhaps, do something about it without involving the CIA and British secret services. It was very early Sunday morning, and the *Carlos Sanguinem* docked on Tuesday at midday.

She texted John attaching her photograph of the ship at Southampton:

Should we be looking for the missing lifeboat?

I would love to come down on Tuesday, but I am on holiday in Bilbao. Call me when you get this.

Mike

CHAPTER TWENTY

The pale blue sky over Bilbao that Sunday morning was streaked with the contrails of planes heading to the Mediterranean and beyond from northern Europe. Mike had slept for about three hours before showering and making it for a 7.00am breakfast with Wazz. She was conscious that Eduardo may have risen early if he was going anywhere with Jim. Unbeknownst to her, in this she was unfortunately correct; they had already left at 6.00am to visit some monks in a Convento high in the mountains before joining them for a special Sunday Mass.

Mike was buzzing with excitement, and caffeine, waiting for Wazz to arrive. She could not wait to tell him all that she had discovered overnight.

"You look ... as if you have been up all night."

"I'll let that compliment pass," she had more important things on her mind than how she looked, "I have made a major discovery. Look." She showed him the photograph with the missing lifeboat.

"So, it's meant to have two on each side?"

"Yes, here's a screenshot from a video where the ship has two. You can clearly see."

He did not look impressed, but suggested, "It might have failed a safety check and been removed, or it might have been transferred to be used on another ship?"

It was her turn not to look impressed.

"That's not very helpful."

"OK, let's go with your idea, or what I think is your idea." He looked around the restaurant but there was no one near, "Where is the lifeboat now? How did they get the ... stuff out of the lifeboat? Surely not in Southampton Water?"

"No, of course not, but what if they launched the lifeboat in the ocean a hundred miles from the UK. Who would notice?"

"You mean apart from the twenty or thirty crew? You think that they are all involved?"

A waiter came over and they paused for Wazz to order Eggs Benedict, tea and croissants. Mike glowered at Wazz.

"I'm just being a *critical friend* as my mentor at the Open University says all of the time."

"How about some constructive criticism or preferably some constructive help?"

"OK, here are my thoughts. I don't believe it involves the whole crew; that's too risky. My bet is that it is only the officers and probably only the Master and First Mate. They would have to slow the ship down probably, don't you think? Did they lock up the crew for an hour while they reduced the speed and jettisoned the lifeboat?"

"I was thinking along those lines. It all appeared a lot more certain last night, now I'm not so sure."

"Is that Eduardo?"

She turned around quickly but it wasn't him. They went on chatting until the eggs arrived.

"If he doesn't come for breakfast, I'm going to get the hotel to push a note under his door. I've had enough of this; I'm not sitting in Bilbao for a week trying to second guess his itinerary.

He's a grown man, some people want to kill him, but nobody knows he's here. Big deal!"

"They must be hard to sink?"

"What *are* you talking about?"

"Lifeboats."

Her phone buzzed and she moved the basket of toast to one side in order to pick it up.

"What? Hi, John, thanks for calling back."

Wazz was trying to scrape some of the egg yolk onto his fork and listening to one side of the conversation with its frequent pauses.

"Yes ... me too ... I know. No, we all need a holiday, I'm having breakfast looking at the Guggenheim."

Wazz felt a tinge of jealousy as she continued in a voice as close to flirty as she would ever get.

"Oh, great ... that's good to know ... of course ... so, you'll check? ... I didn't know that ... thank you so much ... yes, you are right, I cannot ask for that through official channels."

Wazz needed distraction; using his knife, he managed to extract the last drop of marmalade from the small jar onto his croissant.

"That was John."

"I guessed that and what does he think about your lifeboat idea? Does it float?"

She sensed the tension but was not able to interpret it.

"He is going to check on Tuesday. He thinks it's unlikely to be the way they transport it, but he didn't laugh at it ... like you."

"Good. Would you like some more tea?" he lifted the white teapot and tilted it towards her cup.

———

After an hour and a half of winding up the mountains of the Cordillera Cantábrica, Eduardo was feeling a little queasy with his head still throbbing from the drink the previous afternoon and evening. Everyone had been so excited to see him and so welcoming. Despite arriving back very late at the hotel, Jim had been adamant that they must get up early to visit the monks during the week of the festival and celebrate Mass at the Sanctuary of Our Lady of Artxanda.

While he was discovering his roots and enjoying his life away from London, the formal religious side of it all left him a little cold. Roman Catholicism in Spain merely echoed the restrictions that his mother had placed on him for his whole life. She had even arranged that he be reborn like Jesus. Except, he did not want to establish a religion or acquire a worldwide following, all he wanted was a quiet, safe life among his extended Basque family deep in the land of his ancestors.

Jim had other ideas which meant that Eduardo was spending his first Sunday of freedom, the first week of his new life, kneeling in a four-hundred-year-old church listening to monks praising Santa Maria as the morning sun came through a large circular stained-glass window. For a few minutes, living in Kensington and playing games online had a certain appeal.

Despite the culture shock, everyone was so friendly and did not give a damn who he was, who his mother was or how high his family were in the Forbes Rich List.

After much hugging and back-slapping they had made their way to Jim's car for the return journey through the mountains and down to the coast. They had a booking at 11.00am for the Guggenheim Museum which, for Eduardo, would be the highlight of his week so far.

The scenery was breathtaking, and the descent was easy and traffic-free, in fact they made such good progress that Jim suggested they stop for a coffee at a café in a picturesque town dominated by the bell tower from which a bell began to ring out.

"I've had enough religion for one day," Eduardo adjusted his chair to avoid the direct sunlight.

"It's good for your soul."

"So is art. I cannot wait."

Jim's phone rang.

"Hi Rosa. Oh sorry, I forgot," he screwed up his face and stared at Eduardo, "Well, Happy Birthday for yesterday."

Eduardo put on a smile, but it soon dissolved as he thought of his missing brother.

"We're still in Bilbao but will be off to Santiago de Compostela tomorrow or the day after," Jim continued, "What? Who was asking?" There was a long gap while she explained something to him. "Has she been in contact since?"

Eduardo gazed around the paved area in front of the church, his eye drawn to a row of closed-up wooden sheds used to sell market produce and tourist paraphernalia during the week. In the distance the neat fields of vines covered the foothills surrounding the village.

"Call me if she makes contact again. Happy Birthday for next year in case I forget. Love you." He hung up.

"You forgot your sister's birthday?"

"I did. I am useless at dates." Inside, Jim was weighing up whether to tell Eduardo that Mike Kingdom had been down to see his sister, asking questions; he decided against it. He did not want to put any stress on his friend who was beginning to relax and, he was so pleased to see, gradually regaining control of his emotions. The crazed look that had been never far away was now being replaced by genuine smiles.

They paid and resumed their journey; the visit to the Guggenheim Museum lay ahead.

Driving along the river in Bilbao between the high-rise apartments and past Calatrava's Zubizuri bridge, the unmistakeable silhouette of the museum appeared. Eduardo rocked gently in his seat restrained by the seatbelt.

Mike, having finished her breakfast, had walked over to Reception and asked for a pen, paper and envelope to leave Eduardo a message. She could not risk that he might check out of the hotel and head off somewhere; she was losing patience. But what to write so that she didn't spook him? Mike returned to the breakfast table to join Wazz.

"Right, Superbrain, what do you think I should put?"

"That you were worried about him and came out here to check that he's OK. Give him your phone number and ask him to call."

"I'm not good at this. I don't do this sugar-coated stuff."

"Tell him you are here off your own bat and won't say anything to his mother or Leonard. Once you know that he's really fine, you will fly home."

"What does *off your own bat* mean?"

"Tell him that you are here on your own initiative, he'll understand."

She put her tongue between her lips while she wrote the simple message:

Eduardo,

I am here in Bilbao because I am worried about you as a friend. Your mother and Leonard don't know I am here. I found you by talking to Jim's sister, Rosa. Please trust me and call me when you get this message. I just want to make sure that you are safe and happy. After that I'll go home (Well, I would if I had one). You know what I mean. Call me.

Mike (the one in the red wig)

She added her phone number and sealed the envelope. At Reception, they said that they could not reveal his room number, but it would be put under his door. She thanked them and returned to Wazz.

"Let's go. I need a walk. He either phones or he doesn't."

Wazz jumped up and let her lead the way to the door.

The heat hit them as soon as they stepped outside of the hotel and crossed over towards the shiny titanium-clad museum with the trees on the opposite bank of the river providing a backdrop. They passed the enormous sculpture of the West Highland terrier puppy dominating their foreground view until they meandered along the riverbank looking down on a yacht towing an inflatable tender downstream.

Wazz raised a hand to shield his eyes, "That's a Moody 42," he said.

"What?"

"I have spent too much time in Marbella looking at the yachts. Sorry. You have to look at something while the women in your charge are nattering away about Louis Vuitton and Manolo Blahnik over their coffees."

"Why's it called that?"

"Because it's made by Moody and is forty-two feet long."

"D'uh!"

They sat on a concrete bench overlooking the river; Mike was wearing her forage cap. The yacht towing the inflatable was disappearing from view, but it had triggered something in her mind.

"Will you bear with me," she was getting her defence in first, "could a container ship tow something across the Atlantic?"

He smiled but could see that she was serious and wanted to think through every angle, "Of course, it could tow an enormous barge without having the slightest impact ... but it would all be a bit visible, don't you think? And how do you get the stuff from this barge to the land without the Coastguard spotting it?"

"That's the problem with the lifeboat as well, isn't it?"

"Yes ... but at least the lifeboat would be hidden in plain sight for ten days until the ship hits British waters."

"Then what?"

"Well, I would slow down the container ship and launch the lifeboat fifty miles from the UK sending the coordinates to someone in a yacht like that one. Actually," he corrected himself, "I would rendezvous with a Moody 42 who already knew the rough handover point. The lifeboat could have something bespoke which transmits a signal. The yacht transfers the drugs and sails back to its home port. The *Carlos Sanguinem* docks in Southampton with nothing illegal on board."

"Won't the yacht be checked? You know, have to go through Customs or whatever?"

"I don't think so. Not if it has sailed out for a few days and not visited another country but I don't know."

"Would the drugs fit on a yacht like that one?"

"I would think so. What are we talking about? The weight of three or four human beings?"

"Probably."

"They'd have to sink the lifeboat but that's not impossible. You couldn't risk it being discovered and identified."

She smiled as he was obviously warming to the idea. "If you had a Moody 42, what would you call it?"

"How about Royal Yacht?"

"What? That would get you into so much trouble." She was laughing as she spoke.

"But it would be taken seriously when you radioed for help. You are lucky, you wouldn't need to change the name – Moody 42 seems perfect for you."

"I'm not forty-two!" The 'moody' element had obviously been taken for granted.

Three hundred yards behind them, two young men were chatting animatedly. One in particular was beyond excited to be visiting the Guggenheim at last.

―――

Xavier paced up and down his study wearing a checked shirt with the sleeves rolled up. He was alone and contemplating the consequence of the contract not being fulfilled. Eventually, he came to a standstill and leant his elbow against the wall with his hand on his forehead; he was barely controlling his rage.

He had recently finished a call that had left him in no doubt; the nephews needed to finish what they had so spectacularly failed to achieve at the cabin.

While he had a senior role in the international consortium, he was simply one cog and others, much more powerful than him would not tolerate failure. Governments and ministers were behind this, and they depended on him playing his role.

He dialled Alain's number and made it clear that this was the last phone call. He passed on as much information as he had been given and suggested that he explained to his nephews that failure was not an option, and their uncle would pay dearly if they failed.

CHAPTER TWENTY-ONE

For every time that someone bumps unexpectedly into that vaguely remembered friend on a beach in Majorca twenty years after they both left their school, there are the five hundred times when similar paths almost crossed but did not. There is no record, there are no consequences.

Eduardo had walked from the car towards the Guggenheim Museum not paying any attention to the couple on the bench staring at the river. He was so excited that he never saw the woman in the forage cap or her partner. As he was twenty minutes early, he decided to go back to his hotel room and freshen up before enjoying the highlight of the trip – the museum. Every day he relaxed more, every day he began to enjoy his life more.

Pushing open the heavy door, he almost stepped on an envelope – not the bill, surely?

He opened it while crossing to the bathroom but stopped in his tracks when he read the message.

"What?"

It threw him out of kilter. What should he do? Crazy

thoughts came back to the surface, and he sat down. "Relax, relax," he said to himself, "she's a friend. She won't harm you."

But if she could work out where he was, others might as well?

An odd smile broke out on his face. He had to respect her for finding him. By the way, how had she done that? He was impressed and couldn't think how he would have gone about it.

"Mike, you're good. You're good."

Should he tell Jim? Should he phone her number? He could not think straight but he was fascinated by how she had tracked him.

Out of the window, there was a perfect oblique view of the Guggenheim shining in the late morning sun.

"No, no," he chided himself, "I'll go to see the tulips first."

With that, he put the message in his pocketbook, freshened himself in the bathroom and went back down to join his friend.

"You look as if you've seen a ghost," Jim stood up as Eduardo crossed the hotel foyer.

"Just me in the mirror," Eduardo laughed as he tried to hide his thoughts.

"I've got the tickets ready," he waved his phone at Eduardo, "Let's go."

There was minimal traffic, and they crossed the road and began to walk across the vast paved area at the front of the building.

Whether Eduardo spotted Mike first or it was the other way around, neither would know but their eyes met. Neither reacted by shouting or waving, instead Eduardo grabbed Jim's arm and said that he needed to get out of the sun.

―――

Mike whispered, "There's Eduardo with Jim." She began walking and quickened her pace, this only serving to emphasise her slight limp.

"Did they see you?"

"Yes, I think Eduardo did. They're going to the museum." At which point, both men disappeared from view behind a wing of the building.

"How many entrances are there?"

"What? I don't know."

"Sorry, it's my job. Well, my old job."

By the time that the glass doors at the main entrance appeared before them, Eduardo and Jim had either entered or, perhaps, headed down the side of the building towards the river.

"Oh, great." They were faced with a queue.

"Isn't this where you pull out a badge and run up shouting 'Out of the way, CIA!'?"

"Which films do you watch? No, dammit, we join this fricking queue. You Brits love doing that anyways."

There were about forty people forming a line down to the entrance; these were visitors not having pre-booked tickets.

"The tulips will have wilted by the time we get there."

"I will have wilted if we don't get out of the sun soon."

"Why don't you stay in line, and I'll check down the side. I'll call if I spot them otherwise I'll come back in five minutes." He walked as fast as possible without drawing attention to himself and went down a long gentle ramp to the lower level. On the way he could see a line of fountains, a park with trees and a café. Here, there were fifty or more people sitting at tables; he passed by while approaching the river with, to his left, the skyline dominated by a blue skyscraper, thirty or more storeys high. There was no sign of either of them. He rested under a tree and let his eyes wander, casually checking everyone. His attention was taken by people walking up a ramp to a glass door. Was this another entrance? An exit?

There was only one way to find out. He walked up the ramp and saw that it did lead to an entrance. At his side there was a very shallow formal lake in which some tall metallic sculptures were reflected. Beyond that there was a platform on which he could see the bright colours of the infamous tulips.

He jogged back down the ramp and retraced his steps around the side of the building past some street performers who were setting up their equipment. Two minutes later he was back with Mike in the queue.

"There's another entrance but there's no sign of him."

"We're almost in. I suggest that you go upstairs, and I will go straight to the tulips. I have a funny feeling that's why he's here."

"And what do I do if I find him?"

"No idea. Call me. I don't know what I am going to say either. I want to assess his state of mind."

"We don't know how Jim is going to react, do we?"

"I'm hoping he's not got ulterior motives and will keep out of the way. I want to get Eduardo alone, I don't know, for a coffee or something."

They entered the building and soon approached the ticket desk.

It seemed a shame to visit such a stunning building with such amazing and impressive pieces of art and not take time to appreciate it all; unfortunately, this was not possible. Mike and Wazz split up and made their way through the rooms and around the clusters of people. She was walking under an enormous, knitted installation that spread like a series of brain synapses up and around the atria and walkways. He was taking his time upstairs looking in some dark rooms resembling an Ibizan club with flashing light displays that were not helpful to him as he tried to scan faces.

Ahead through a glass door, Mike could see the vibrant colours of the shiny metallic tulips pointing towards the reflecting pool and the river; the individual flower heads were bigger than she had expected but looked so lightweight. She stepped out into the sunlight with the background sounds of the city.

Their eyes met almost immediately as they had done twenty-five minutes earlier.

It was impossible to gauge his thoughts; he did not move and said nothing to Jim who was photographing the sculpture nearby. At least he had not run off. She mimed holding a saucer and drinking from a cup while inclining her head indoors. Mike had no idea where this idea came from. He was staring a little oddly but nodded in consent, or it looked like he nodded, before turning to Jim and suggesting something like he was going to the bathroom.

Mike turned to lead the way occasionally turning to check that Eduardo was following. Under a flight of stairs and away from the main pedestrian traffic, she stopped and waited for him to catch up. It gave her about five seconds to choose her opening line which would probably decide how this entire encounter developed.

"The tulips are bigger than I was expecting," is what came out of her mouth – it could go either way.

"They're beautiful," he said, looking away with a sad expression, "Why are you here?"

"Because I'm your friend. I want to check that you are safe and well ... and to tell you not to worry about my cabin. Both of us survived."

"Is the Giacometti damaged?"

"He's not going to enter the London Marathon this year but after physio, he'll be fine."

He smiled and breathed in, "Awesome, that's awesome."

"Are you OK?"

"I'm good. I'm with a friend."

"You had to get away, I guess?"

"Yes. It's all over. I'm not going back to London." Some important thought passed slowly through his mind, "You're not here because of my mother, are you?"

"No, definitely not ... but I expect that she is worried. She's already has one son kidnapped ... and I'm so sorry that you have to deal with that as well."

"I'm doing fine. It's a great relief to be away from her and London. She can afford to pay any ransom – Diego will be released. I want to live out here hidden away in the mountains." He let all of his thoughts pour out of him.

"I know, I know. I worked that out and I am not here to stop you. People are worried about you but that's to be expected."

"Please don't say anything to anyone but I'm going on the Pilgrim's Trail to Santiago de Compostela."

"I won't, trust me," she changed tack, "Did you get my note? I left in under your door at the hotel."

"Yes, I saw it."

"It has my phone number on it."

"I saw, thank you."

"Ch ... Eduardo, please call it if you need a friend. Promise me that you will?"

"I will. I knew that you were like me. I'm so sorry that they blew up your cabin. They are after me. It's why I need to hide away. I will be safe among my Basque family."

"I understand."

He dipped his eyes.

She was so absorbed in her role that a crazy thought popped into her head, "You couldn't help me for twenty-four hours, could you?"

"What? Doing what?" Her bizarre question did not faze him in the slightest.

"My main project is ... well, I would like to explain here but let's say that I messed up my main chance, and I think that I now have one last way to crack it."

"What can I do?"

"I need an analyst to help me. There's too much data. Help me ... and I will help cover up your tracks so that you disappear completely to where you want to be."

"I don't understand."

"Out here ... in Bilbao ... in my hotel room, will you help me nail my project before you disappear off? One last piece of analysis."

His shoulders dropped and his big black eyebrows knitted, "Mike, please tell me that you are not working for my mother. Please?"

"I am definitely not working for your mother. This is separate. Something where you can help me – you owe me. I am breaking all of the rules, but you know what it is like when you are so close after six months."

He looked directly at her but had clearly not made up his mind.

"I will shut all of the doors behind you. You can disappear."

"What shall I tell Jim?"

Mike knew that she had won and felt like leaping up and shouting with joy but kept it under control.

"You obviously trust Jim so why not tell him the truth?"

"Really?"

"Why not? If he really is a friend, why not? Tell him that I'm a friend who will help hide the tracks. Don't tell him about my project, obviously."

"OK," he had decided in a second, "I must go back." His demeanour was surprisingly calm. It looked like his trip to the Basque lands had enabled him to establish some sort of equilibrium.

"Ring me when you are back in the hotel this afternoon. I'm staying there, too. Then, bring your laptop over to my room, 206, and I will explain what I need you to do."

"OK," he turned and walked back into the crowds.

She took out her phone and rang Wazz.

"See you at the main entrance."

She pushed her way between people mostly unaware of the quality of the art that they were looking at and filming it with their phones to view it back home in their flat in Osaka or their dacha outside of Sochi. She was also not looking at the art but, at least, she would have appreciated it but not today where other things took priority; she was on autopilot and replaying her conversation with Eduardo in her head. She could clearly see that he was not normal and that would be evident to anyone but what was bothering her was that neither was she. Was he any madder than her?

Wazz joined her at the door but said nothing as he approached; they walked out together.

"Where is he?"

"He's gone back to Jim. He's nervous but he's agreed to help me."

"Help you what?" they were crossing the vast paved area in the direction of their hotel.

"On my project." She turned to him, "I had an idea ... suddenly, that he could help me on the container ship project."

"What?" Wazz was completely at a loss, these analysts were a breed apart.

"I will negotiate with Leonard. I will deliver Eduardo ... willingly, if Leonard gives me access to certain things so that I can smash that drugs ring."

"You've thought this through, have you?"

"No, but I will make it happen."

"And Eduardo has bought into this?"

"The first bit."

"You're mad."

They marched in silence until they entered the cool of the hotel reception.

"I need to call Leonard. See you in the bar at six."

"I hope that I am disturbing you?" she asked with just the right amount of venom.

"You are ... and thank you. I was trying to sort out how to keep the big boss alive while he attends three events in two hours travelling across London," Leonard did not sound at his most relaxed.

"I've found Eduardo."

"Wow, that's one box ticked. Hoorah, I need some good news."

"At the end of this call I need you to tick another box, then we have a full set."

Leonard was too experienced to ask for specific details. He preferred to let it all play out before he commented on any contentious elements. Keep it simple was his byword.

"How is he?"

"Calmer than the last time I saw him, which is not saying much as it was ten minutes before someone tried to take him out with a bomb, but we had half of a normal conversation. Leonard, the first thing to say is that he is safe, I'm guessing that this should please your boss, but he is not ready to run back to mummy. She has been smothering him all of his life. Without discussing anything with you, I have done a deal with him. It is not negotiable." She stopped while she thought through the consequences of this ultimatum.

"If he is safe and stays safe, nobody will give a hoot about the details."

"He is safe, and I can guarantee that he will stay safe." She didn't elaborate further.

"I fancy there's a *but only if this happens* about to enter this conversation?"

"Well spotted. He has got involved in my project and, like me, can see what needs to be done. We don't have all the details yet, but we need specific access to some satellite coverage."

"You wouldn't be using our friend as a bargaining chip, would you?"

"Who me? Look, he's excited to be involved in it, which I am hoping should be resolved by Tuesday."

"Please tell me that you are not going to ask me to arrange a search like last time only I'll be thrown out of kindergarten."

"Time you left there and put on some long pants."

CHAPTER TWENTY-TWO

When she heard a knock on her hotel door later that Sunday, Mike could not describe the warm feeling that she felt inside that everything would now go swimmingly. Eduardo had phoned earlier to say that, although he was still scared for his life, he had reassured Jim about her and was ready to help if, in return, she helped him to disappear for ever; the fear of being bombed again was too much for him. She opened the door to find him standing there in a red Hawaiian shirt and surfer shorts carrying his laptop.

Without having Eduardo as a bargaining chip this would not have happened, Leonard would never have entertained allowing her to pursue her main project in any meaningful way. He would have only paid lip-service to it.

"Pull up a chair and I will tell you what I need you to do."

Together they rearranged the furniture to create a work area on the desk; one chair on one side, one on the other. The latter had come from Wazz's room where he had been asked to stay in order not to frighten or distract Eduardo. In fact, it did not take long for the question to come up.

"Who was the guy you were with?"

"He's a friend but he's not from our world; he's not cleared for any of this."

"Your boyfriend?"

"Sort of." She stole one of Leonard's favourite expressions when avoiding a direct answer.

Mike plugged in a piece of hardware and connected both their laptops to it.

"Right, it's 'hunt the ship time'. We have restricted access to some special satellite coverage – I mean restricted as in not normally available and restricted in area and time period. The first bit's from almost a month ago and I would like you to work backwards from when the ship, the *Carlos Sanguinem*, arrived in Southampton docks. It came originally from Cartagena in Colombia. I'm looking for a point where it slowed down and launched a lifeboat. I am guessing that this will be the day before docking and that should be somewhere off the southern coast of Ireland."

"This is easy. You don't need me," he looked at her as if she was mad, "You know that all ships are tracked, don't you? I can find the ship's number in seconds and call up its current position and all of its previous trips."

Mike bit her tongue – not something that she usually did.

"The smugglers know that as well. Don't you think that they may have done something to hide their actions?"

"Such as what?"

"Once out of Cartagena harbour, they could have turned off or jammed the AIS – the automatic identification system – that uses the permanently installed electronic transponder device. This would hide the unique identification number assigned to it –its MMSI – Maritime Mobile Service Identity … or they could have used manual override and typed in a false route or location? Or they could have carried a second transponder with them and pretended to be a different ship? Who would care halfway across the Atlantic?"

Eduardo's mind was obviously stimulated considering these possibilities.

"What ... and change back to the real one once they had ditched the lifeboat?"

"Possibly. The advantage of using another number is that there would be a working system on board. That means they can see other ships and other ships can see them which is quite important as these ships are massive and can't slow down or change course very quickly."

"I expect there's another false transponder in the lifeboat so that the boat that picks up the drugs can find it in the open sea?"

"I'd already thought of that but, irrespective of whether they left the real transponder working or not, we need to search the satellite coverage of the whole trip to spot when they launched the lifeboat. They will probably have slowed down but not necessarily as, I'm guessing, there were no humans on the lifeboat, and it wouldn't sink even if they dropped it from a great height; that's what it's designed to do."

"Perhaps there *was* a person on board it? They could steer it towards the rendezvous or, at least, hold its position."

"True ... but then you have a human being to hide or dispose of."

They were both taking stock.

"Now you see why I need you?" she continued, "We only have two fixed points in space and time for the last voyage – the moment it left Cartagena and the moment it arrived in Southampton. Once we know where they launched the lifeboat we can check when the ship is going to reach that point on its current voyage, and I am guessing that will be today or tomorrow. So, time is pressing."

She went on to fill him in on some more details and to set up the starting point for him on his laptop. This search could take one hour or five; she had no idea. For her part, Mike began searching for the *Carlos Sanguinem* on its journey last month sailing from Cartagena at 8.30am on 21st July.

The first twenty minutes consisted of silence broken only by the tapping of keys and the occasional expletive as they both found the most efficient way to scan the US satellite imagery of the journey starting either from the departure point in Colombia or the docks in the UK. If they moved too fast they might lose or confuse the ship with others but, generally, they found that the pattern of the containers viewed from above was akin to a fingerprint that enabled them to have confidence that they were following the right ship. Mike knew straight away that it was impossible from the satellite view, vertically from above, to see the orange lifeboats. They would need to see it launched or in the water.

Eduardo stopped tapping and put his head back, staring at the ceiling. He was motionless for over a minute.

Finally, he looked across the laptops. "I don't buy this 'turning off transponders' idea. Why do it? It would just potentially draw attention to a perfectly normal container ship on a perfectly normal route. Owners of the containers need to track the ship. It would only take one person to spot that the transponder was off or changed and all attention would be on the ship. Why not sail normally, launch the lifeboat and sail on?" and he added, "I bet the individual containers have trackers, anyway."

Mike frowned but did not bite back.

"Hmm. I think that you may be right." She went on digesting what he had said.

"I think that you are over-complicating things. All we need to do is follow that ship on the aerial coverage. It's simply going to take time."

"You are right," she conceded, "I don't know what I was thinking."

This did not sound like the Mike of old.

"On my screen, the ship is south of Cornwall in the English Channel, I'm now following it backwards in time towards Ireland."

A casual observer might have noticed two people completely in their element despite all of the protestations, sighs and throwing back of heads. After an hour they were even beginning to rib each other about whether it was easier to track forward or track backwards. Neither of them had been so expressive when working in the same large office in London where they had barely exchanged a handful of words.

Mike was the first to break away and offer anything from the minibar and snack drawer; this was almost entirely selfish as she used food and drink as a structure to help her cope.

"Coke, please, and chips."

She brought over two cans and some packets, and they paused their searching while staring at each other across their laptops.

"How far have you got?"

"I'm due south of the tip of Cornwall; it's called Land's End."

"Well, I'm about seven days across the Atlantic near no dry land. I've assumed that they wouldn't launch it until they were nearer to the UK."

Keen to resume their tasks, they tapped their keyboards and muttered to no one in particular for another hour as they refined their techniques, trying to speed up the process.

It was Eduardo who shouted out first.

"It's slowed. Well, now it's actually speeding up, but it had slowed down, if you know what I mean." They were talking their own language.

"Great!" she walked around to look at his screen.

He moved back in time thirty minutes, called up the satellite image and zoomed into the *Carlos Sanguinem*.

"Here, it's just beginning to slow down. I've gone too far back." He moved forward in time ten minutes.

He searched the satellite image for what seemed like ages before he reached what he felt was the point at which the ship was moving at its slowest somewhere south-west of the Isles of Scilly. Mostly to mark the moment, he lifted the silvery can to his lips but found that it was empty.

"Brilliant!" Mike was now torn between returning to her own laptop to begin looking at how far away from this point the ship was today or stay with Eduardo and try to see where they launched the lifeboat a month ago and what happened next; for her, this moment was sheer pleasure.

It was thirty-five minutes later that Eduardo made the breakthrough.

"The orange lifeboat is in the water!"

"I knew it! I knew that I am right. Give me the coordinates."

He sent them across to her machine and she called up the view on her screen. It took another seven minutes to find the point where the lifeboat went down the ramp and splashed into the sea. She made a note of the location.

"Right, now we move to the next phase. Watch that lifeboat and see who comes to collect it."

Emmanuel was pacing the room like a caged bear; his frustration was palpable. He did not like failure, but he disliked criticism even more. His older brother did not even bother to try to calm him down – hopefully he would get himself under control by the time that they got to check-in at Heathrow.

They had joined the French Foreign Legion, although this was never part of any plan for the two delinquent boys from

Montpellier who, as teenagers, made a handsome living stealing tourists' bags and watches on the streets of Perpignan; the elder brother rode the scooter while the younger, on the pillion, snatched whatever he could.

Unfortunately, their luck ran out in Collioure and they were caught. Despite their violence towards the police as they were arrested, they were accepted into the Foreign Legion in lieu of a custodial sentence. This was to change their lives.

As per the statutes of the Foreign Legion, they changed their names to Henri and Emmanuel, names they decided to keep when they left. Their parents were pieds-noirs, that is of French stock but born in Algeria, and the sons wanted to remove any stigma from the past.

However, even when they were in the French Foreign Legion, Emmanuel could not control his temper and was eventually released after five years; he was in the GCP, the parachute commandos, where he served in France, French Guiana, and several countries in Africa. Henri stayed another year although he was in a different regiment, his was the motorized infantry 2e REI, deployed all over the world and never, surprisingly, stationed at any time in the same place as his brother.

It began well as the discipline gave some structure to their lives but for Emmanuel, in particular, the suppressed need for violence and complete detachment while using it began to come to the notice of his commanding officers. After one incident in the Republic of Congo where seven locals were killed, he was sent back to France for re-assessment. This did not go well, and he was given what should have been a safe position in the Caribbean on the tiny island of Martinique. The regiment's duties were not onerous mainly connected to training local forces and providing guards of honour to visiting French dignitaries. Emmanuel still managed to become involved in the killing of a local man although the details were hazy enough that he was not charged. However, it was enough for the Legion, and he was discharged back into civil society.

His uncle Alain took him under his wing and began to use him for his dirty work all over Europe. A year later Henri joined the team, and, together, they became a successful assassination unit. Emmanuel was emotionless and conducted the killings without expending too much thought. Henri was tasked with keeping him on the rails, under control and making sure that his brother did not get caught up in the violence such that their cover was blown.

He was having to handle his brother with kid gloves as they made their way to Spain that Sunday evening. They were loading their bags into the back of the Vivaro ready for their Uncle Alain to drive them in the van to Heathrow Terminal 5, twenty-five minutes away. Unfortunately, they had to leave the guns, explosives and other ordinance at his garage, unable to take any of it on the plane. Before they left the house outside of Slough, they had said their emotional goodbyes with much kissing and hugging; it was highly unlikely that they would return to England for a year or two. Having failed once at the cabin in Oxfordshire, they would have one more chance in Bilbao, after which they would make their way by train back to Montpellier via Barcelona to await their next job.

The consequences of failure in Bilbao were not really contemplated – they would succeed. Whatever it took, they had to achieve their objective; it was their uncle's neck that was on the line if they were in any way to cock this up. Xavier had made it beyond explicit that they had no more than twenty-four hours to hit the mark, and every hour was critical. This time they not only had a photograph of their target and a phone number but also information about a hotel in Bilbao. Xavier had been waiting for a new location and had passed this on to Alain as soon as he had received it in a WhatsApp message from his main source.

There was not actually the name of a hotel contained in the message, rather there were some photographs of the Guggenheim Museum taken from the rooftop restaurant of an hotel. They rightly identified it as the Nervión Real and made their way to check it out. Emmanuel, who had calmed down on the flight, began to get excited again. Henri had his work cut out keeping him on an even keel.

CHAPTER TWENTY-THREE

Early evening on that Sunday, Xavier had returned from a village function that he had felt obliged to attend. He had paid for the marquee, donated the main prize and subsidized the bar. The children's charity was a worthy cause, but he could not simply send a sizeable donation, despite trying to do this. He was, of course, buying respectability using what, to him, was not even petty cash; this meant he had to deal with committees of people who had not the slightest idea of how he made his money. They had accepted the backstory which had him as a Spanish banker working in London.

Having performed his role as generous village benefactor, he was sitting alone in his favourite red leather armchair warming a glass of rum in the palms of his hands. All around him was a room decorated entirely to his tastes and not readily accessible by anyone else. This lounge was in his half of the house; the eastern end was where his wife and children lived. Rather than divorce, they had come to an amicable agreement made all the easier when you have so many rooms, cottages and barns.

With his jacket thrown over the back of a sofa and the sleeves rolled up on his white shirt, he was leaning back contemplating his life; almost everything was under control or would be very soon. He had taken a huge risk by jumping the gun and having three million dollars transferred to his offshore accounts. This had been activated using the cut dollar bills that had been delivered to him by personal courier. Each piece was worth ten thousand dollars once it had been matched with its other half. It was a simple system that avoided the transference of suitcases of money from country to country. Someone whose name he did not know, and he had never met, was acting as a banker in Europe for his business connections. As long as Xavier displayed his half of a note in a WhatsApp message, the banker would transfer the funds. It was not Xavier's concern how this banker was reimbursed or from where. Each note with its unique number could only be used once. It was a foolproof system.

Xavier's job was to import the drugs and hand them on to a series of distributors who used a version of the payment system, only in reverse, to pay the cartel – they always had to pay in advance.

This was the first time that he had cashed in his notes before performing his side of the agreement. There was only one consequence of not delivering on his side of the bargain – a slow and painful death. It was a big risk. He swallowed the last mouthful of rum and made his way upstairs for an early night.

"This is what I love," Eduardo was totally absorbed with the problems of tracking a drugs shipment on the *Carlos Sanguinem*. Time had passed by so quickly that it was already mid-evening. Most of his Sunday afternoon and beyond having been spent on his laptop in Mike's room.

At the desk, Mike was looking at him across their laptops trying to understand his mental state. Was he stable? Had he come out to Bilbao because he really, really wanted to spend the rest of his life amongst his Basque extended family. Could he live on lamb stew, goats' cheese and cider? After a fortnight would he miss having staff to arrange his life, cook for him and drive him everywhere?

He was excited, animated and had a light in his eyes. His one focus was following an orange lifeboat and watching on his screen who approached it and when. He was totally caught up watching the series of video sequences.

Mike was bothered that he had suffered some sort of breakdown and had jumped on board this Basque heritage idea as a life raft to get safely to shore or to any port in a storm, perhaps.

"Me, too, "she paused, "Is anybody near? By which I mean, is the ship away over the horizon?"

"Yes, the *Carlos Sanguinem* has gone but nothing else is near the lifeboat yet."

"Whatever ship, boat or submarine turns up, it will be small so that it doesn't stand out, I'm guessing, and privately owned by that I mean that it cannot be another commercial ship, or they would face the same Customs dilemma."

"But it's got to be big enough to carry the drugs. Actually, it could be a fishing vessel?"

"True, I hadn't thought of that. I wonder how packed the lifeboat is? If it's full, then it wouldn't fit on a tiny yacht, would it?"

It dawned on her that Eduardo was conversing normally without any odd non-sequiturs or strained facial expressions.

"The lifeboat can take over thirty people – that's over two thousand kilos. They will only bring in a fraction of that, surely? Even if they bring in three hundred kilos each time, that's £360 million in one year ... and three hundred kilos is only the equivalent of a few men. That means it would fit on a medium sized yacht, wouldn't it?"

"Hopefully you'll find out soon."

While Mike was establishing how far the *Carlos Sanguinem*

was today from the point where it had launched the lifeboat last month, Eduardo continued to watch out for any vessel that came near.

"Ha!" he shouted, twenty minutes later, "We are right. It's a yacht."

"Does it have an identifying number?"

"No, they are not stupid. That means I have to follow it back to its home port."

Mike's phone buzzed; it was Wazz asking if all was well. She replied with a Thumbs Up emoji and wrote 'see you at breakfast'. It reminded her about Eduardo's situation.

"Do you want to phone Jim? I don't want him to worry about you."

"I will in a minute," he sounded reluctant, "His friend, Jacob, is arriving soon, then we head off. It's only that with my life being threatened all of the time, I can't relax, and I don't get to enjoy doing things like this with you. I haven't felt so happy and safe for such a long time."

"Eduardo, trust me, you can relax. You are as safe as houses here with me. No one is going to hurt you, and no one knows where you are."

A few miles away, Emmanuel and Henri had arrived in Bilbao on an EasyJet flight.

They had selected a rather non-descript hotel about two blocks away from the Guggenheim, down a side street. They chose a twin-bedded room on the second floor, where they changed into lighter clothes leaving their suitcases packed in case they needed to leave in a hurry.

Their main problems were that they did not have a detailed plan and did not know how long they actually had. To this list could be added the fact that they had no weapons.

"What are we going to do?" Emmanuel asked.

"First, our escape route. Whatever happens, we fly to Barcelona and catch the train to Montpellier. There are seven flights a day and it only takes just over an hour. The train to home is three hours. If we get separated, we should still travel along this route."

Emmanuel nodded.

"Secondly, I think that one of us should check out the layout of their hotel. The other can hang around outside of the Guggenheim, we might get lucky and spot them. They are probably going there, anyway."

"I need to go down to the docks. Pierre has made the call, and I can pick up a gun from one of his sailor mates called Benoit. He has paid him up front."

"Do we need a Plan B? Uncle Alain won't tolerate failure. What if the gun jams? I think that I should get a knife from a kitchenware shop, we might need to be opportunistic. They might catch the underground train, one of those green and grey trams or cross that weird bridge. Having an accident might be a possibility. We need to keep alert to the possibilities. If not, I'll use the knife. It gets crowded in Bilbao at this time of year during the festival."

"Sure. First we cannot keep entering the hotel and it's not a great place to kill anybody is it?."

"No, inside a building is too confined and too traceable."

"OK, let's go and get the things and look around outside of the hotel. One of us needs to be on watch all day."

There was a hint of turbulence as the private jet passed through the thunderclouds building over west London. By the time that it had passed over Reading, the night sky was illuminated by the occasional lightning flash, and the pilot banked to the south and headed for the English Channel.

Valentina unfastened her belt and made her way to the sofa mid-way down the plane. In her hand was a file of papers that was half-read. She was using the two hours of flying time to Bilbao as an opportunity to catch up on some reports.

While the offer from Conrad to join him on Air Force One flying out of London on Wednesday was generous and tempting, she couldn't wait that long. She needed to be in total control.

As the coast of France appeared through the cloud, a wave of tiredness swept over her. Things had been going to plan until Eduardo had decided to visit a work colleague. Why had he done that? She was always torn between selfishly wanting to bring Eduardo back into her world and wanting to hide him away to protect his life; one bombing was enough. The next time, they may get him. From now on, she decided, she would keep him with her at all times – this would be easier.

The loneliness was also tinged with regret. While Agustin may have set up the businesses, it was she who had really driven them forward and expanded the empire exponentially. To do this, she had become involved in some dubious areas and with some unpleasant individuals. She had been a little too headstrong and should have waited, she was already wealthy without needing to dirty her hands. It had left her exposed and a target. Her life, moving between her different houses in different countries, was becoming a chore not a pleasure.

Balanced against this was the protection she received from those in high places. Conrad, while he remained President, was her ultimate shield but, here too, she had been too eager in retrospect and allowing the relationship to progress beyond business had been another mistake.

Valentina rarely regretted anything and never showed her emotions anyway. She looked down at her hands and rotated a ring. By the time her eyes had returned to the view of the streetlights of a French town out of the plane window, she had confirmed to herself what she already knew deep down – it was time to sell most of the businesses and pay whatever it took to gain freedom for her family. Her sons could not be left on their own. Whether her sons wanted this or not did not enter her mind.

Her interest in the various parts of her empire had dissipated, even the award of the $800 million undersea cable contract from Bilbao to the USA via the UK no longer overly excited her. Once signed on Wednesday, she would let others have the problem of building it; she would take the money and run. She should have done it five years ago.

Her entire focus now would be on her family and their protection.

As her steward asked if she wanted a drink, her thoughts drifted to: firstly, who knew Eduardo was alive? Secondly, who had discovered his protected alias in London? But, much, much more relevant, who knew that he was in Bilbao – she went through everyone she believed to be on what was a very short list.

Having exhausted these topics, her mind wandered to the upcoming vote in August where Puerto Ricans would have the choice between four alternatives: annexation to the United States, independence, sovereignty in free association, and a free state associated with the United States. It had been in September 2023 that legislation providing for a two-round consultation process to decide the territorial status of Puerto Rico had been reintroduced in the United States Congress; she had been an active participant behind the scenes, pressing for limited independence but with free association with the USA; this would suit her worldwide pharmaceutical business which was based in Puerto Rico. This would be one company whose control she would retain – it was too lucrative post-pandemic.

In what seemed a matter of minutes, Valentina landed at

Bilbao airport very late on that Sunday evening; the pilot came to a stop on the apron reserved for private jets. A car was on its way to pick her up before the door had opened and the steps deployed. She descended under the high, downward facing floodlights which created strong shadows and a stage-like atmosphere. The rear door was opened for her, and she was driven in a large arc across the tarmac to the terminal.

Earlier, somewhere over Nouvelle-Aquitaine, she had received a call from Felipe telling her that his men had spotted Eduardo and followed him to the Nervión Real hotel. The men could not hang around all night without being spotted but were at her disposal; they were ten minutes away. She had thanked him and had unfastened the seatbelt with her face displaying anger, although as so frequently with her, who or what was the cause was not discernible.

CHAPTER TWENTY-FOUR

It was Monday morning and Mike was having a coffee with Wazz.

"Shall I ask for some toothpicks so that you can keep your eyes open?" he asked.

"I get carried away and the time flies by ... but we made good progress."

Mike and Eduardo had been up half of the night tracking what had happened a month ago. It was as she had predicted. They had watched a yacht approach the lifeboat but, unlike the *Carlos Sanguinem*, it had turned off or disabled its AIS which meant that it could not be identified, and neither could its journey history or home port. Mike and Eduardo were forced to manually follow it using the high-grade military satellite coverage to which Leonard had given them access. They had given up searching for the night after the yacht approached the Isles of Scilly; they would pick it up again in the morning.

Eduardo had said that he would come across to her room at 9.00am, and before that Mike needed to ring John and tip him off.

"Hello John, sorry to disturb you."

"I'm driving to work. How's sunny Spain?"

"I haven't seen much of it; I've been tracking our container ship."

"It's due in at 11.30 tomorrow unless anything's changed overnight."

"I have been checking what happened a month ago and the lifeboat was launched as I guessed just south of Ireland. A yacht pulled alongside to collect everything. It went back to the Isles of Scilly."

"Wow! Have you identified the yacht?"

"No, not yet. After this call, I'm going to follow the yacht to wherever it goes. After I've done that, I will swap over to live footage and watch the ship today in real time. I bet that it will launch the lifeboat at the same point or nearby."

"Have you told Leonard?"

"Not yet, he has other things on his mind this week; today the President is coming to the UK and then, here to Spain."

"Leave it with me. I will see what I can do but whatever happens, I will see if one of the lifeboats is missing."

"Is that enough for you to keep the ship and crew at Southampton?"

"I doubt it. They legally only need two lifeboats as they have a reduced crew. I checked and the ship typically carries four lifeboats as it could theoretically have a complement of over thirty. If one of these is missing, that's not illegal ... and there won't be any drugs on board to find if your theory is right."

"Oh for... Damn! What about the yacht?"

"Well, unless it sails into the Solent and Southampton, it's not in my patch but I will let my colleagues in Border Force, National Crime Agency and Joint Maritime Security Centre know once you have either the name or the destination. It could sail to France or Holland for all we know. Well done, by the way." He sounded impressed. She rang off.

Wazz was eating a plate of cheese, cold meats and rough

bread listening to the conversation. His face was slightly red having caught some sun; this only served to highlight his blue eyes and pale eyelashes.

"Isn't using a yacht a bit … well, let's call it small-scale?" he asked.

"No, you have it all wrong. If that yacht successfully brings in two and a half tons a year, it is supplying two percent of the British demand for cocaine."

"Isn't most coming in on a more industrial scale in containers?"

"It was, it was … but it's changing. Take Rotterdam, for instance, where fourteen million containers come in each year. Only one per cent is scanned and from that, only sixty tons were found. But now, the port authorities are changing the way container release codes are generated and are about to start scanning every container as well as using AI to target those most likely to contain drugs. This will mean that the cartels will need to move to other less high-tech ports or find more bespoke methods … like the lifeboat/yacht idea."

"Because they avoid all scanning?"

"Exactly. They could already be using other ships, other yachts and other ports like Felixstowe, Tilbury, Bristol, Grangemouth – there are so many."

"How do they get it ashore?" Wazz had returned to the practicalities.

"I don't know the details, but I expect that it is not a rushed operation. Perhaps they leave the stuff in the yacht and two or three people bring it ashore in their bags and rucksacks over a number of weeks. There would be a constant flow, but I cannot believe anyone would notice in some sleepy yacht harbour."

"Any thoughts on which harbour?"

"Hey, you're British, I've no idea. Eduardo and I need to get back tracking the yacht. I am guessing that we will know this morning unless it sails halfway around the UK, which sounds unlikely."

"I suppose that this yacht has to be emptied and be back ready to pick up another load in a month?"

"Exactly, so I am not expecting them to sail to Scotland."

"I'll sit out on our bench and enjoy the morning sunshine. Call me when you have found the harbour ... or wherever it stops."

"Put on some sun cream."

"Yes, Mum."

―――――

Five weeks earlier in late July, Manuel and Barbara Diaz had set off from Gloucestershire on the two-and-a-half hours' drive to Devon where they kept their yacht. Their son, Ricky, had set off separately from Salisbury to join them at the marina.

Manuel and his brother had over the previous year been developing another way to import cocaine into Europe. The current method of using containers full of cattle fodder was working well but they never wanted to be complacent, and they didn't like all of their eggs in one basket. Manuel loved sailing and this had been how he had met Barbara in the first place thirty-five years ago; he was South American, she was from Bristol. They now lived in a seven-bedroomed, brick and glass hacienda-style property with far-reaching views down a valley near Stroud; their neighbours were minor royals.

This was ostensibly their main residence, however, they owned an estate in Costa Rica near the Parque Nacional de Santa Rosa on the Pacific coast adjoining the Gulf of Papagayo; nobody who met them in Gloucestershire or Devon knew anything about the Central American retreat.

Their son, Ricky, had gone straight into the Royal Navy from school and at the age of thirty-three was now settled in Salisbury where he ran a courier business.

They had already sailed to the Isles of Scilly on a reconnaissance trip two weeks earlier but on this day they would set off in earnest with the aim of intersecting with the *Carlos Sanguinem* off the south-east coast of Ireland.

After a slow drive down, their dark blue Lexus had pulled into the multi-storey carpark neatly hidden in an old quarry in Brixham, South Devon; this is where the yacht owners parked while sailing from the nearby marina. They were an unremarkable middle-aged couple dressed in weatherproof gear who had emerged from the car with a Jack Russell terrier on a lead and had carried their assorted holdalls and bags the short distance down Berry Head Road. It had been a grey morning with a light breeze from the east. At the entrance, they had entered the code at the security gate that gave them access and they had chatted as they walked along the footbridge and down to the floating jetty. Their yacht was moored right at the end because it was slightly larger than all of the others; it had been bobbing gently with its sails furled; it was a royal blue Oyster 53 named *Hyperion III*.

Half an hour later, Ricky, a stocky man had arrived in a Volvo estate, parked and made his way out to the same yacht. He had been wearing a Musto jacket with a rucksack on his back, in his hands he had been carrying a yellow holdall and a cool box. It looked as if it was he who had been tasked with bringing most of the food and drink for the trip. This was not the case; the cool box was full of explosives.

"Where you off to, this time, Ricky?" A man re-varnishing the deck of his boat had asked.

"We are going to the Scillies for a week or so. Depends on the weather."

"The forecast is perfect, I think."

"I think so."

"Your mum and dad are already on board."

"Good. They obviously have made better progress than me." With that, Ricky had continued along the jetty and had stepped aboard the *Hyperion III*.

―――

There was a gentle knock on Mike's door. It was precisely 9.00am which was no surprise as Eduardo was an obsessive timekeeper.

"Have you started?" he asked as he unloaded his gear.

"About five minutes ago. I needed breakfast."

He again took up his position opposite Mike and they resumed their painstaking search.

"How's Jim?" she wanted to make sure that everything was good with him.

"He's fine. He knows loads of people here and has been catching up with them. We are meeting Jacob at 2.00pm today. I told him that you and I would be searching all morning as a minimum."

"Have you met Jacob before?"

"No, he's Jim's friend. They planned this trip together. I've hitched a ride."

They continued to chat while they tapped and scrolled.

"Are they near the Isles of Scilly?" she was trying to get an idea where the yacht was.

"No, they look to me as if they are keeping away from them. The islands don't look very big. Why go there? They would still have to get it to the mainland." Eduardo was completely engaged in the project.

"Are they keeping a constant course now?"

"Yes, pretty much."

He paused to unzip his rucksack and take out a croissant wrapped in a paper napkin. She said nothing about this but was trying to equate in her mind his previously pampered life with his breakfast choice today. Mike updated him on her search.

"I've been trying to estimate where they might be today, I mean right now, assuming that they all repeat the exercise using the same coordinates, routes etc. A month ago they were moored off of southern Ireland about twenty-five miles away from the rendezvous point. I cannot find them, but they might have varied their route a little to avoid anyone accidently picking up on the repetition."

"Whammo!" he shouted spraying bits of his croissant everywhere.

"What?"

"They've turned on their AIS. Wait a minute. Here we go ... it's the *Hyperion III* out of Brixham. Where's Brixham?"

"Ha! They needed to turn it on, or the Coastguard would get suspicious as they neared the land. I'll check out the boat, you go on tracking them. They might not have gone to Brixham, they could stop in any port."

Mike's hand movements sweeping across the keyboard and touching the screen were a sight to behold; she could have been her mother playing a Beethoven sonata on the cello at some concert in Oregon. There was an elegance, a beauty to her movements.

"I've got the owners. They're Manuel and Barbara Diaz. Now, there's a good Spanish name. Give me a second, give me a second."

In fact, it did not take long for her to discover their home address near Stroud and that they had owned the yacht for six years.

"It's them! It's got to be them." There was relief showing through her voice; a vindication of all that she had done over the last six months. "So did they go back to Brixham last month?" she couldn't wait and couldn't make up her mind what to do next.

"They're heading that way."

"Right, I'm going to track them on the new trip. I'll start in Brixham."

"No need. We have the log. You will be able to follow them until they turn off the AIS past Land's End. When did they leave Brixham?" He was multi-tasking both tracking them on the satellite images and reading the log. "They left four days ago. Here." He waited for her to join him on his side of the table.

"There's going to be another consignment," she said, unable to remove the smile from her face.

"I don't need to track them anymore on their trip last month, the log says that they arrived at Brixham on 2nd August. I wonder if Brixham Marina has CCTV? I bet they do. Do you want me to hack in?"

"Why not? I didn't expect us to make so much progress. I need to phone Leonard and give him the good news."

"Don't mention me. Please don't mention me."

———

"Good morning, Leonard. How are things in the farmyard?" Bob was calling for an update.

"Up to my neck in bullshit, as usual."

"Me too, probably for the same reasons as you. When your President is about to fly in, everyone gets tense."

"As if I don't have enough with everything else ... including keeping Eduardo alive. That will be the first thing POTUS asks me about."

"Are Eduardo ... and Jim OK? Are they still in Spain?"

"Yes, hopefully he's safe, nobody knows he's there and he is off my patch, hopefully not visiting too many cabins in nearby forests."

"Talking of forests, we are continuing to eliminate vehicles that turned up and lingered within five miles of the cabin before the explosion. There were not many ... about fifty, I think. My colleagues are checking which ones fit the bill. Once we have traced them all and checked them out, I will let you know. The bombers must have had a vehicle and parked not too far away. They would not have hung around once they had triggered the bomb.

It would take the team until mid-afternoon on that Monday to identify all of the vehicles; a Vauxhall Vivaro was one of the last. It would take another two hours to collate any mobile telephone numbers associated with the known locations of the van. By 6.00pm UK time, Henri's phone had been identified and the fact that he had been near the cabin for almost an hour before the explosion; his current location had been established as Bilbao.

Mike was obviously the target, there could be no doubt; this had nothing to do with Eduardo. Unfortunately for her, this information would not reach Leonard until too late.

CHAPTER TWENTY-FIVE

"Damn you! Why isn't he answering?" Mike was shouting at her phone while Eduardo was keeping his head down and trying to block out her aggressive tone; he stayed silent.

"Leonard! Damn you." She ended the attempt to call him which gave her time to think. "I'll leave a WhatsApp message."

Using her two thumbs, she tapped in a quick update about the yacht and the rendezvous point. She finished with 'Call me'. "Well, he can't be at lunch, it's only 10.00am. Though anything's possible with him. I'm surprised that he doesn't have a microwave in his office so that he can heat meals himself."

"His daughter is a chef in Montgomery," Eduardo did not even look up as he continued to hack into the marina security system.

"What?"

"Leonard. Leonard's daughter is a chef in Alabama?"

Mike did not know where to start.

"I didn't know that. I didn't even know that he was married. How did you find out?"

"She called him while I was in his office."

"Where's his wife? What else do you know about his family?"

"Nothing. I just overheard him talking to his daughter."

Mike was so frustrated. Why hadn't this call happened while she was in his office? Not once had Leonard ever mentioned his private life before. He only talked about work and even then he spoke sparingly.

"I'm guessing that he is divorced. His wife cannot be living in London, surely?"

"They were talking about a new grandkid, I think."

"Hard to see Leonard with a bouncing baby on his knee."

"There they are!" Eduardo screamed.

"What?"

"I'm still following the yacht last month as it enters the harbour at Brixham. There's the *Hyperion III*. It's arriving exactly as per the log."

Over the next few minutes, he fast forwarded the CCTV footage until people appeared on the deck as they moored. Mike walked around to see it for herself on his screen.

"Two men?" she asked.

"Looks like it but who is at the wheel?"

Eduardo fast forwarded the footage again until a woman in a dark blue fleece could be seen and the three of them went about their tasks in an unhurried manner, tying up additional lines, closing hatches and connecting an electricity cable from the charging point. He took screenshots of the individuals although their faces were not that clear.

"You are good at this," she said.

"So are you," he was almost whispering.

"Will you miss this?"

"A bit. Actually, a lot. It's the only thing I'm good at."

"I would miss it."

"I know."

"If you ever change your mind, send me a bunch of tulips. I'll sort it for you."

"OK, I will," he smiled, and they both went quiet, continuing their searches.

"Are they carrying anything off the boat?" Mike thought that it was wise to change the subject by asking a prosaic question.

"The big guy has a bag and, is that a square cool box or toolbox? ... oh, and a rucksack. He's walking off on his own along the jetty." Eduardo was transfixed, "They all look heavy."

Mike stood up and began pacing the length of the room, wiggling her fingers trying to release the tension and thinking what to do next.

"If only Leonard would ring back. The Agency should be involved in this. Damn. There's nothing I can do except follow the *Hyperion III* in real time. You continue watching what they did last time. How many trips they make to their vehicle and how many bags they carry in total. Perhaps, one of them stays on board for a few days?"

"I've lost him. The CCTV coverage doesn't extend far beyond the building. No, wait. Wait," he paused, "There are other feeds for a multi-storey carpark."

He went on tracking the man while at the same time checking the yacht to see what the remaining man and woman did.

"God, this is frustrating." Mike was back at her keyboard staring at her screen following them on the current journey. "I am at the point where they turned off the AIS. This is a right pain in the butt. Now I've got to follow the damn boat across the sea south of Ireland."

"You could put in the coordinates where they launched the lifeboat last time and see if the yacht's nearby? That might be quicker? You know which direction the yacht's coming from, don't you?."

"Who's a smartass?"

He didn't answer as he had not picked up on her compliment and instead said, "It is quite distinctive with that black inflatable in tow."

Surprisingly, she did not glare at him but smiled; there was a recognition in her eyes that things had fallen into place – that's if only Leonard would phone back.

The ceiling with its stuccoed frieze was high above everyone's head, perhaps making what was a very large room seem more like a corridor than a salon; it was on the second floor of a Regency building in west London and Conrad, who had recently landed in AF1, was in full flow discussing with the British Prime Minister an emerging trade deal between the two countries post-Brexit – an event of momentous importance. Leonard de Vries was happy to be occupying one of the chairs against the wall behind the key players who were sat at the large oval table. He was not directly involved until later on the agenda.

There were about sixteen people in the room, and the President was speaking generally about the main areas left to be negotiated; they were not meeting to haggle as there would be specific one-to-ones and team discussions later. The meeting between the President and the Prime Minister was largely symbolic. Leonard's thoughts wandered off as the issue of chlorinated chicken was raised and he checked his phones that were on silent. He read Mike's message.

Fifteen minutes later, the trade teams left and only six people remained. The focus of the meeting changed to counterterrorism. When this discussion ended, Conrad asked the Prime Minister if he could have two minutes with Leonard while the others around the table took a comfort break.

They moved over to a tall window framed by curtains of burgundy velvet, held back by gold ropes.

"Where's Eduardo? Safe?" Conrad asked Leonard.

"Mr President, he's in a hotel room in Bilbao with another of my agents who he likes. It's all under control. She'll get him back here soon but the kid's not all there, as you know." He tapped the side of his head while rolling his eyes.

"What can I tell Val? I don't want her flying out there."

"Tell her he's safe but fragile. Things are under control. Ask her to trust me."

"She's not somebody who sits back and waits."

"I know, I know, but it is all very sensitive right now. In fact, a few seconds ago I received a message from the agent with him. After this meeting, I need to organise something and then we can get him on a plane."

"Val can send her plane out there."

"Can she wait twenty-four hours? Can she have her plane on standby and I will call her."

"OK, I'll tell her. Do you need to leave this meeting?"

"Unless there is anything else, Mr President?"

"No, you go and sort this out, Thomas and Morton can deal with the last few matters."

With that, Leonard excused himself from the meeting, nodding out of respect to the Prime Minister. Along a corridor, he entered a lift and emerged in the foyer. He avoided anyone he recognised and headed out into the street looking for a bar. On the corner, tucked down a side street he saw the sign hanging outside of The Six Bells. Inside, it was cool and dark with walls covered in etched mirrors and framed film posters; it had only opened a few minutes earlier. With a cold beer in his hand, he sat in the corner as far away from the bar as possible. There was repetitive electronic music playing from the speaker above his head.

After taking a large mouthful of beer, he dialled Mike's number.

"Just got your message. I was tied up in a meeting with the big boss who's in town."

"At last. You understand what I put in the message?"

"Yeah, you think they're using a yacht to pick up the you-know what that's in a lifeboat ditched from the ship."

"I don't 'think', I know that this is how it's being done. I have tracked it last month and could even see them transferring the damn stuff at sea. They sail the yacht back to Brixham harbour in Devon."

"Mike, you were certain last time."

"I know but let me send you the footage of the lifeboat leaving the ship, the transfer with the yacht and them beginning to unload it at Brixham."

"You are asking me to put my butt on the line right after it was kicked last time."

"Leonard, the Agency has been after this Cenote cartel for years. I was right that they had been using containers into Southampton docks, but I wasn't to know that they had changed the system to this lifeboat idea."

There was silence at the other end of the line as he took a drink.

She filled the gap in the conversation, "This Manual Diaz is probably quite senior in the organisation, he should lead us to whoever is controlling the European end. It could even be him. But Leonard ... this is urgent. They are transferring the stuff out at sea today about now."

"How long before they will be back in Brixham?" he pronounced it 'Bricks ham'.

"Last month it took them four days. What I'm doing right now is checking for the rendezvous on this trip and then I can follow them back to port and get an exact fix."

"OK, OK. I'll make the call. If you are wrong, it will be you and me going down with the ship, you understand?"

"I do ... and thank you."

"Before I go, the big boss just asked me about the safety of our friend. How is he and when is he coming home? That was the deal, right?"

Eduardo was sat opposite her and listening while checking

the car registration numbers of vehicles leaving the multi-storey car park at the harbour.

"Yes, OK ... um ... difficult to give you an answer to that at this precise minute."

"Why?" he took a second, "Oh, you mean that he's with you?"

"Yes, spot on. So glad our projects are back on track."

"Send me a message about him. His mother will be keeping a plane waiting in London to fly out to pick him up. I told the big boss that it will probably be needed in twenty-four hours. Capiche?" Leonard and, indeed, Conrad had no idea that Valentina was already in Bilbao.

"I hear you. Thanks again. I will go on tracking the yacht and send you updates. Enjoy the rest of your beer."

"You should not automatically assume that I'm in a pub having a glass of cold beer."

"Sorry, didn't realise that you had piped acid jazz, or whatever it is, in your office now."

He didn't answer immediately but his mind had wandered, "Be careful, won't you?"

———

The sea was grey with a broad swell through which the *Hyperion III* was cutting a swathe. They were making good time but had allowed half a day as a safety measure in case of bad weather or adverse sea conditions. They were sailing along at seven knots; there was no other sound apart from the wind once the herring gulls had been left behind somewhere between the Isles of Scilly and the coast of Ireland. Ricky was down in the galley, balancing with one hand while boiling a kettle on the gimballed stove. Occasionally, there was a slap on the hull or a splash on the long window but generally this was plain sailing.

Barbara, in a large waterproof jacket, was stood up top in

front of the large wheel, gripping it lightly while staring ahead; she was a superb helmswoman having sailed since she could walk. A small screen was showing her their position and their destination. Occasionally, she would reach for a satellite phone on the shelf in front of her to check if there were any updates. Manuel was arranging the bags on the seats nearby ready for when they made contact with the lifeboat.

Ricky's head emerged from the galley and handed the mugs of tea one at a time up to his father. There were smiles all round. This was the third trip out here – the first a practice and the second for real, and it was so much easier to repeat everything, having tested it. Even in August the wind was still cool, so they drank their tea quickly and Manuel handed the mugs back down to Ricky.

They were less than ten miles away from the lifeboat.

The sea became choppier and there was a bank of threatening dark grey cloud in the distance to the west. The sound of repetitive 'pings' grew louder, and Barbara steered against the mild current to keep them on track. The wind was following and filling the sails. Time passed slowly. Ricky's head appeared again, this time eating a Mars bar.

"How long?" he asked.

"About an hour and a half," his mother answered, "come and help look for it."

He heaved himself up the ladder and, together, they began to scan the horizon. This was a silly game they had played since Ricky was very young. Nothing was going to appear for some time.

Even with all of the latest technology, including the transponder on board the bright orange lifeboat, it was so easy to miss something that small in the vastness of the ocean. It was Barbara who spotted it first and she let out a happy and relieved shout. There was no sign of any other shipping including the *Carlos Sanguinem*, long gone on its way to Southampton.

CHAPTER TWENTY-SIX

There were two explosions at almost the same moment.

One happened several hundred miles to the south of the *Hyperion III* across the Bay of Biscay. In a nondescript grey building on a small industrial estate outside of Bilbao, four men had breached the security and placed a remotely activated bomb that had destroyed not only the internet cable but also the power supply; it would take weeks to repair.

The second happened off the town of Bude in north Cornwall where another explosion happened at one-hundred feet below sea level. This cable which carried a large proportion of the internet traffic between southern Europe, the UK and the USA was severed by a device that had been attached by two divers. With a colleague at the helm, they had been searching for the target site using a fishing boat over a period of a couple of days. The boat had only been on station for forty minutes when they had located the cable, where most of that time was spent by the divers adjusting to the pressure on the way up and down. Apart from a line of planes from the Americas beginning their descent to London airports high above and, ironically, the Royal National Lifeboat Association practising with three hard-bottomed ribbed inflatables in the bay, there was no other activity. A solitary vessel fishing here was in no way suspicious.

Although internet traffic and data transfer across the Atlantic switched almost seamlessly to other cables, the system was at maximum load and there were occasional outages.

One person unaffected by this was Valentina who was on a call from her hotel in Bilbao to Conrad in London.

"Oh, Val, I was hoping that you would travel with me to Spain. Are you safe? Have you met up with Eduardo yet?"

"Don't worry, I have my security with me, and no one knows that I am here. As to Eduardo, I have checked into his hotel and will see him in a few minutes. I wanted to tell you that I am worried sick about the attempt to kill him with that bomb; it has obviously tipped him over the edge. I am really bothered about how anyone knew that he was here? If the CIA could track him, then so can the bombers ... whoever they are. He has messed up all of my plans. Why did he have to visit that damn work colleague in that cabin?"

"What are you going to do when you meet him?"

"Get him away from here ... and from Europe. We will go somewhere else, somewhere safe."

"Val, I gotta go. I have a busy day in London. I will see you in Bilbao for the formal announcement on my way to Madrid."

She put down her phone and picked up her handbag; it was time to confront Eduardo.

Emmanuel walked into the hotel room he shared with his brother and threw a canvas bag onto his bed; Henri was a few hundred yards away monitoring the hotel Nervión Real from across the road. The room was hot as the air-conditioning had turned off automatically once they had both left earlier. Emmanuel had taken a taxi around the low wooded ridge to the docks following the river as it flowed to the Bay of Biscay. His destination was a barely three-star hotel that catered for dockworkers and sailors. His friend Pierre in Montpellier had made the necessary arrangements having called in a number of favours; an untraceable gun and a box of bullets would be waiting. Payment had already been made, all Emmanuel needed to do was turn up at a set time, say the word 'Montpellier' and he would be given a package.

As the taxi driver slowed, Emmanuel asked him to pull over onto a piece of wasteland in the distance and wait; he did not expect to be long. When the driver asked for payment, Emmanuel showed him a picture of the taxi he had taken on his phone when he had walked up to it outside of his hotel. No more words were necessary, a combination of his scarred face, a menacing look and the communication that he could find the taxi if necessary was more than enough.

The road had modern warehouses on the land side but undeveloped expanses of bare earth on the seaward side behind fences. Several articulated lorries were parked up having, presumably, arrived early for some sailing the next day. Any cars lining the road displayed unfolded silver foil reflectors inside their windscreens to combat the fierce sun. The hotel was new and brightly coloured with some unconventional cladding shapes and colours, none of which disguised the fact that this was really rows of prefabricated concrete units on top of each other. If anything it made it look specifically like a container ship – probably the last thing its guests were interested in seeing before weeks at sea.

He walked, as he had been instructed, across the road to an empty industrial shed that had no windows but two blue five metre high sliding doors. Leaning against a large yellow plastic refuse bin, he lit a Gauloises and stared across at the skyline of cranes. There were no security cameras evident, and Emmanuel felt that he was dealing with professionals.

As a cawing black-backed gull appeared on the gable end above him, so a wiry old man with a weather-beaten face came around the corner and approached, exactly on time. He asked if Emmanuel was looking for somewhere and when he replied *'Montpellier'*, he handed over the canvas bag and walked on down the street. Whether this was Benoit or not did not matter.

Emmanuel put the bag over his shoulder and headed for the waste ground. The taxi driver watched him approach and opened the rear door; neither party spoke apart from the instruction to return to the hotel. The journey back to the city centre was uneventful and took twenty-five minutes.

After drinking some water, Emmanuel sat on his bed and checked the gun; there was no time or place to test it. He loaded it and put it into a small, brown leather bag which was slung over his shoulder. It was time to re-join his brother.

He sat down on the bench and whispered to Henri that everything had worked well, asking if there had been any developments or sightings. He had assumed not as otherwise he would have received a coded text message. Now it was Henri's turn to walk off and buy a boning knife from a kitchen shop two streets away, paying in cash. The packaging was deposited in a waste bin down the side of a tapas bar, and he slid the thin knife into his waistband on his hip. Twenty minutes later they were back together walking around the piazza in front of the Guggenheim ostensibly two tourists wondering what to do once they had visited the museum. Their attention, however, never left the entrance to the Nervión Real hotel; time was pressing.

"What did the Brits say?" Mike was back on the phone to Leonard.

"Give me a break. I called them, they are on the case. Just tell me that our mutual friend is safe and missing his mother."

"The kid's fed up with being attached by the umbilical cord. He needs a break."

"But he's safe?"

"Relax, he was very happy half an hour ago. He's having lunch with Jim."

"Is this Jim kosher?"

"I am meeting them both after lunch ... relax. Eduardo has calmed down and is enjoying himself."

"Lucky him. I still have the big boss for another couple of nights here so no relaxing. Why did you call?"

"I am sending you the satellite sequence of them loading the yacht and blowing up the lifeboat. It also give you the yacht's latest location."

"I'll pass it on to the Brits," there was a slight hesitation before he said, "and, well done."

"Oh," she also hesitated, "thank you."

Their father-daughter relationship had never been more evident. Perhaps, Leonard had substituted Mike for his own daughter four thousand miles away and, equally, she had looked up to him as a replacement for her own father who was distant and always away playing in jazz bands on tours around the USA or on cruise ships.

"So now, you need to fulfil your side of the bargain and get Eduardo back with his mother. He needs her protection, and I need the big boss off my back."

"I'll talk to him today when I can get him away from Jim who will try to get him to stay out here in the hills."

"Great. Tell him he can have his old job back ... though, I don't need him, and he hardly needs the money."

"Leonard, he is actually a brilliant analyst. I mean really good, and he enjoys it."

"Whatever. Get him home and we can sort details like that out."

They had arranged to meet in the bar of the hotel. It was hot and so busy outside with the festival in full swing.

Eduardo had regained some sort of balance and knew, deep down, that she could trust Mike. It was time for her to meet Jim and for him to meet her friend, Wazz. No harm would be done and, whatever happened, after they met Jacob that afternoon, they would leave for the trip to Santiago de Compostela and the walled city of Lugo in Galicia.

Mike and Wazz arrived first, and they chose a large table with a padded bench along a wall.

Jim and Eduardo walked into the bar looking like twins – scraggly dark hair, long noses and big ears. Eduardo was smiling which revealed the gap between his front teeth. Jim, wearing a coral patterned shirt, looked nervous and was playing with his watch. Mike stood up and made the first move by shaking Jim's hand.

"It's great to meet you at last, Jim. I bet you were wondering what Eduardo and I were doing?"

"No, he explained that you were working together. It's no problem."

"Hi, I'm Wazz, good to meet you. I was left on my own as well while these two were working. We should have gone for a beer." He shook Jim's hand.

"Great idea."

The ice had been broken and they sat down around the table.

"Jim, I know that you are helping Eduardo find his Basque roots and I want you to know that I have no hidden agenda. I simply wanted to check that he's safe and well after what happened when he visited my cabin, and it was blown up." She heard herself telling a lie and realised that she was becoming an operative. Analysts never needed to lie.

"Thank you, we had already planned for him to escape out

THE MONGOOSE AND THE COBRA

here with me even before someone tried to kill him at your place." He looked across at his friend.

"I had lost the plot ... I was scared and needed to talk to someone. I don't know why I called in to see you. Sorry."

"Don't be sorry. We are all safe and happy. My cabin will be replaced."

"Are you going back to Burford, Jim, after your road trip?" Wazz asked.

"Yes, I live there but I come out here quite often. I run a jewellery shop in the High Street."

"Is that shell earring one of yours?" Mike was curious.

"Yes, it's a symbol here in the Basque lands."

"We are meeting Jim's friend, Jacob, at 2.00pm up at the sign and we're setting off along the Pilgrim's Trail immediately."

"What sign?" Mike frowned.

"The one up on the hill ... reached by the funicular railway. Have you been there? It's like the Hollywood sign but in red."

"No, I haven't," Mike and Wazz said, almost in unison.

A waitress came over to take their drinks order. Wazz asked for an orange juice, and this prompted the other three to follow suit with various fruit juices. She repeated the order and walked off towards the bar.

"What do you do, Wazz?" Jim was keen to check out everyone that might mess up all of his detailed planning.

"I'm a bouncer at a strip club in London." With Wazz, there was no saccharine coating or white lies. "I'm working nights while I complete my degree," he continued.

"And how do you know Mike?"

"We've worked together ... in the past ... not at a strip club," he smiled at her. But there was no time to gauge her reaction.

At this moment, a middle-aged woman wearing black-framed glasses and dripping in gold and diamond jewellery approached the table from behind Jim.

"Eduardo," Valentina held out her arms to hug her son.

"Mother!" he stood up and awkwardly reached towards her, "What are you doing here?"

"Making sure that you are safe. People are obviously trying to kill you. They tell me that you escaped a bomb by the skin of your teeth. You were lucky. Do you know the lengths I go to in order to protect you?" It was as if there was no one else at the table.

Mike was twitchy. She stood up and put out a hand, "You must be Valentina. I'm Mike."

"Hello," was all that was said in reply before her eyes returned to her son, "Which one of these is Jim?"

"It was my place that was bombed when Eduardo paid me a visit." Mike had taken an instant dislike to this woman and was not allowing the conversation to move on.

"I'm sorry to hear that ... which of you is Jim?"

"I'm Jim." He stood up and offered his hand.

Eduardo at this point started shaking and went pale. He glanced at Mike as if she had betrayed him. "I trusted you."

"What? I've got nothing to do with this. Ask your mother."

But there was no time for a reply as he screamed to Valentina that he and Jim were meeting Jacob at 2.00pm at the viewpoint, leaving on a road trip and that she would never see him again. He stormed off past Tadeo who had been standing a few yards away.

"Eduardo!" his mother shouted but he did not turn around.

"I'll go and make sure he's alright." Jim leapt up and disappeared in the direction of the lifts.

"He has always been such a difficult child."

In retrospect, it would probably have been for the best if Mike had held her counsel and drunk her juice, but this line of action was not in her playbook.

"He's not a child. He's a grown man."

"He's my child and always will be," Valentina glowered at

Mike and turned on a heel walking off in pursuit of her son; Tadeo followed behind without a word said.

"That went well," Wazz leant back against the padded bench.

"God, I feel sorry for Eduardo. What a horrible ... woman. No wonder he wants to run away."

"Does he think that you told her he was here?"

"Probably, but I'm guessing that it was Leonard and the Agency who told her. She carries a lot of power."

"... and jewels. Did you see the size of that diamond?"

"I was too busy fuming."

"What happens next? Do we go home? You found him and have handed him over to his mother ... and you cracked your project. What's left to do?"

She was staring into space somewhere above a framed outfit of a toreador high on the wall.

"Something's not right, I feel it."

"You mean that his life is still in danger?"

"Yes ... and no. There is something that doesn't fit together."

"You operatives are all the same."

"Don't you start. Leonard is bad enough."

"Had you better tell Leonard?"

"He probably knows. He probably told Valentina ... but you're right." She lifted her forage cap and rubbed her bare scalp.

CHAPTER TWENTY-SEVEN

The link up was going well, better than the first time, in fact.

The sea was calmer, and it was easier for Barbara to pull alongside. She was standing at the wheel with one hand steering and one on the throttle. The sails were down. However easy it seemed as one approached, it was always the last few yards that put the manoeuvring into sharp relief. The swell seemed greater and any wind stronger.

Manuel was so pent-up that he had leapt into action, if only to release some of the tension. He had already moved the teardrop fenders along the rail to protect the yacht while Ricky was using a boathook to hold the lifeboat in position while his father secured a line. Teamwork at sea was everything and this was a well-practised unit. Given their experience, they were all thinking that this would be a lot more difficult in autumn or winter battered by bad weather. How could the transfer be improved? Accidents were bound to happen and there might be an occasion where it was not possible to board the lifeboat let alone transfer heavy sacks to the yacht; this was something for Manuel to discuss with his brother. They needed to bear in mind that hardly any cocaine had been discovered by the authorities at the ports and harbours but was this because they kept changing their system? Perhaps it would be better to go back to using the cattle feed containers for a few months over winter?

Ricky tied and re-tied the lines that were now attached to the lifeboat until he was completely satisfied. There was no point spending days sailing to this rendezvous only to blow it because of a rope that became jagged or a knot that slipped. Timing it to perfection, he jumped across the gap, judging the relative movements of the boats. He re-positioned his orange lifejacket and steadied himself against the housing. He looked around the horizon but there was absolutely no sign of life. With the experience of a month ago when the sea had been rougher, he now knew how to open the hatch, lock it in position and where the extra transponder was located.

He climbed down inside to be greeted, as before, by the sight of the white plastic sacks stacked under a net on the floor so that they wouldn't move when the lifeboat hit the water at speed. The fact that there were twenty-two of them each weighing twenty pounds rather than sixteen as on the trip before was the only surprise. The lifeboat could have contained hundreds more, but the *Hyperion III* realistically could not; it would sit too low in the water and draw attention to itself.

His first task had been to turn off the transponder; it was unlikely that anyone would track it but there was no point leaving it on – it was no longer needed and represented an unnecessary risk. After this, he cut the net which had been knotted to the seat supports with his knife. The sacks had been wrapped around with shiny, white tape as an added protection which made them even more slippery. He grabbed the first one and retreated back up the steps and out into the daylight.

It was tiring work lifting them from the rocking floor, manoeuvring them up the metal non-slip steps out of the hatch to the side of the lifeboat and passing them across the yacht's rail to his father. At each hand over, he said out aloud the running total of sacks – it seemed to make the whole task easier. The twelfth sack, however, slipped out of his father's hands and sank instantly down into the depths. Manuel cursed but moved on from the loss in seconds telling Ricky to hurry up and not stand still. The fact that God knows how much money was sinking to the bottom of the ocean was a minor inconvenience; he and his family were so wealthy. Of course, his brother would accuse him of stealing it but only in a good-natured way. Manuel's response to any criticism was always, "Well, you sail out and get the stuff yourself."

They were particularly careful with the remaining transfers, but there were no further mishaps.

The last sack was safely stacked in the forward cabin of the *Hyperion III*. They had been distributed throughout the boat to keep an even keel, some were also on the side bunk behind a curtain and some either side of the main double bed.

Manuel handed his son the cool box containing the explosives. This was manhandled down the steps into the lifeboat, now emptied of contraband. This time, Ricky slightly adjusted where he placed the linked explosive charges to have a more targeted effect. He set the two devices – one to blow a hole in the keel and another to blast the roof so that it could not trap air and float ashore. There were ten black sacks of sand already specifically loaded in Colombia to add weight to the craft. This would help it sink in case the detonation misfired in some way; the intention was not that it was blown to smithereens. After the first trip, there were some smallish pieces of dense glass-reinforced plastic left but these would have soon dispersed. All identifying marks, numbers and names had been removed in Cartagena so there was no risk that any of it could be traced to the *Carlos Sanguinem*.

Together they uncoupled the two boats and pushed off.

Their heavy work was not quite over until they had raised some sail to catch the now light southerly wind. When they were five hundred yards away, Ricky detonated the explosives. There were two almost simultaneous dull thuds that echoed across the water, this was all about minimal noise and smoke not an entertaining pyrotechnical display. He watched the results through binoculars as, this time, the lifeboat sank more quickly and there was less fragmentation; what little smoke there was began to drift down wind.

Manuel headed down into the galley – he was exhausted. He had done the last two night shifts on the way over from Brixham and it had taken its toll.

He may have been drained but he was exhilarated in equal measure; the system was working perfectly, and it was so difficult for the authorities to spot. He flopped back into one of the four small, blue leather armchairs that was fixed to the floor of the main cabin but swivelled on its central chrome pillar. After raising the sails, Ricky joined him for a quick celebration, and he opened a bottle of Pussers navy rum, and they toasted the success of the project. They shouted up to Barbara who was on the wheel with sails billowing, allowing them to skip across the swell in a series of accelerating lunges as they surged over the surface towards the Isles of Scilly.

She declined a drink but licked the salt from her lips as she looked down at the compass and at the bright horizon.

There was not a vessel in sight and to all intents and purposes they were alone in the ocean. Above them, there was a white line spreading ever wider from a Geneva to New York aircraft and to the side, a lone gull was making its way back to the coast of southern Ireland. They were, however, not doing this unseen. It was true that eight hundred miles to the south-south-west in Bilbao, Mike and Eduardo were no longer watching them in real time, but in Langley, London and Cheltenham, there were people actively viewing the satellite images.

The disappearance of Eduardo, Jim and Val from the bar followed by Tadeo had a slight soap opera feel to it. Mike and Wazz had chatted for a while, sipping their drinks while they digested what was happening. When Mike was sure that no one could hear, she dialled Leonard's number.

"Have you been talking in your sleep?" she had not calmed down entirely or, indeed, at all.

Wazz was smiling to himself.

She was trying to find out if Leonard had told Valentina about Eduardo.

"Possibly, I had a nightmare last night, I dreamt that I was the CIA Director in London, and no one respected me. I woke up to find that it was actually my real life. I'm guessing that you are not going to tell me that it was all a bad dream?"

"No, sadly not. Valentina, you remember her, she turned up here ten minutes ago with her entourage and confronted Eduardo. It wasn't all hugs and kisses. She sucked most of the oxygen out of the room. God, what a dragon."

"She has that effect."

"So you told her that Eduardo was here? Or you told your boss who told her that he was here?"

"Possibly." Leonard had not been expecting this. "Hmm, I thought that she was flying out to Bilbao in AF1 with the boss."

"No, she's here ... very loud and clear. I have no idea where Eduardo is, he was shaking and may well have had another breakdown. It wouldn't surprise me if he disappears again."

"The woman's a nightmare. Please hang on to Eduardo or I'll be put through the ringer. Changing the subject, have you heard about the explosions affecting some undersea cables?"

"No, where?"

"One at the landing point in Bilbao and another off Cornwall. It's messing up the internet. I think it is a threat and connected to the boss's visit to Bilbao on the way to Madrid."

"You mean that someone is sending a message to Valentina as well as kidnapping Diego?"

"It could be. We are checking. It's not looking good for Diego. There has been no more contact."

"Well, Eduardo says he is leaving with Jim on their road trip when his friend Jacob turns up this afternoon. I have no idea if Valentina will try and stop him."

"She'll be even more paranoid that someone's out to get him. I almost feel sorry for the kid."

"He just wants to be left alone ... and not blown up or shot."

"Don't we all?"

It would, in fact, take several months for the authorities from four countries to establish who was behind the acts of sabotage.

These were not random attacks; they had been planned and coordinated to have maximum effect when the undersea cable contract was about to be announced. Three South Africans had flown into London and had made their way down to near Padstow in Cornwall after collecting explosive devices from a colleague in Ealing; two were divers and one was to be the boat captain. All had served previously as Attack Divers in the special forces amphibious unit based in Langebaan, north of Cape Town.

They had booked an Airbnb and had acted like tourists for a while visiting local sights in the August sunshine. After asking around, they had chartered a forty foot boat to go diving, ostensibly to explore the wrecks of a Canadian corvette sunk by a U-boat in 1944. In order to back up their cover story, they spent the first day actually going down to not only the HMCS Regina, a screw-driven steam vessel, but the Ezra Weston which was part of the same convoy torpedoed by U-667 off Trevose Head.

The following day they had set off north-east to undertake their real task.

Despite having precise coordinates, it had taken them four dives over two days to locate the Augusta King cable, named after the mathematician and computer pioneer Augusta Ada King, Countess of Lovelace, who died in 1852, and to attach the charges with their sophisticated timers. The waters had been murky and the currents surprisingly strong. However, once the cable had been located, it had not taken them long.

Twenty-four hours later they were aboard a British Airways plane out of Heathrow on their way back home to South Africa. When the charges attached to the cable detonated, they were somewhere over Egypt at thirty-eight thousand feet enjoying beers and watching films.

A team of two Dutch and two South Africans belonging to the same mercenary group were also heading home having left Bilbao for Barcelona. They had arrived separately, one pair driving from Rotterdam in the Netherlands in order to bring the explosives and guns, and the other flying in via Madrid to provide more firepower and back-up, should that be necessary. When they had completed their task, one of the Dutch mercenaries drove the car under new, false registration plates to Barcelona depositing the South Africans at the airport. The Dutch pair drove on to a villa at Sitges on the Mediterranean belonging to a contact; here they would ditch the car and make their way back to Rotterdam flying from Barcelona to Amsterdam.

Earlier, they had rented a villa to avoid using a hotel where there would be prying eyes and CCTV. It was eight miles from their target which was a secure unit in an industrial estate giving no indication that it was the landing point for another leg of the Augusta King cable. It was adjacent to an undeveloped plot of land and a cold storage facility. Next to nothing happened at the secure unit and the single on-site security guard had little to occupy him which presented the saboteurs with an opportunity. The shift was changed every eight hours; one man arrived in a van and swapped places with his colleague who drove the vehicle back to the office a few miles away. This was a weak system and allowed the assault team to effectively hijack the van once the gate had opened and gain access as the other guard came out ready to go home.

At the 8.00pm changeover that evening, neither the arriving nor departing guard was paying enough attention; they did not survive.

With access to the facility, it took three of the team seconds to attach the explosives to key control and connector points. Once outside, they jumped into the car where Henk, the main driver, was waiting to whisk them back to the villa. They heard the explosions but did not see the devastation that they had caused. Little of the unit was left standing and even the side wall of the refrigerated cold storage facility next door had been blown away.

At the villa, they collected their bags, and Henk changed the registration plates. It was a long six hour drive via Zaragoza, but it avoided the first places that the police would check like Bilbao airport and the nearby border with France. Their plans were successful, and they had timed it to coincide with the underwater explosions off Cornwall; they were never caught.

CHAPTER TWENTY-EIGHT

"Give me a break," Conrad was not happy, "I'm not going to Bilbao to get blown up."

The American President, unlike his recent predecessors, was notorious for not flying to places that posed any threat to him; this was most of the world ... and half of the USA for that matter. It made meeting world leaders and attending summits a mountain of a task for his White House team. He did, however, like flying to London to see Victor, the Prime Minister, something he had done several times.

"I can announce the contract award in Madrid. It's still Spain. Who cares? Val can fly down, it will only take her an hour, won't it?" he was in full flow, and everyone wisely kept quiet, including Leonard.

"So, who blew up this cable and landing station? Do we know?"

There were seven people in the meeting at the American Embassy located at Nine Elms in southwest London, some attendees came from the over one thousand staff who worked there and some had accompanied the President on his trip to the UK and Spain.

"It's normally the Russians who do this sort of thing, but we are beginning to think that this is Chinese backed. We have tracked the dive boat in Cornwall and have some names, probably false. We're liaising with the Spaniards on who blew up the landing station."

"It could be that the Chinese are pissed that you are going to give the contract to an American company," the man to the left of Conrad explained.

"I'm guessing the actual people who did this are long gone? The President asked.

"Yes, they will be Turks or Albanians hired in for the job and untraceable."

"How long will it take for all this to be repaired?" POTUS was trying to gauge the impact.

"A couple of weeks for the cable here in the UK and up to a month to fix the landing station near Bilbao, by which I mean a temporary fix so that it works again."

"Gee, we sure need the new cable," he changed tack, "Is anybody going to throw their toys out of the pram if I don't go to Bilbao?"

"No, not really. A few Basques but that doesn't matter. We'll use the explosion as an excuse. You are going to Madrid which is much more important."

"Against my advice, Valentina's already in Spain. She decided to go straight to Bilbao, but she will fly down to Madrid for the announcement. Any update on her son? Leonard?"

"She's met him at his hotel. I haven't heard anything since. It's in her hands now. I am sure she will put him somewhere safe."

"Oh, that's great news. I was worried that this was all connected to my trip to Spain. Well done, Leonard, your team has done a great job. I will speak to Val later. Can I go back to the explosions," he was moving all over the agenda, "When will the Spanish know about who is behind all of this?"

"My guess is days if not weeks. They have to track phones and check CCTV. After that they have to do the airport/ border thing and do the vehicle check on their car ..."

The conversation went on with no hope of any resolution at this stage.

"Get up here!"

There was nothing that Barbara could do apart from scream down to Manuel and Ricky. She had been standing at the wheel for hours making steady progress towards the Cornish coast; her legs were aching from the continual bracing against the rolling, following sea. The weather ahead to the east was brighter and there was no threat of rain. She had been listening to the shipping forecast and they were now in sea area 'Sole' on the way to sea area 'Plymouth'. They had entered British Territorial waters ten miles south of the Isles of Scilly a few minutes earlier.

She was sailing as if on her own autopilot, half asleep and with only one eye on the swell as she rode down the slopes of the waves which crept up behind her and suddenly launched her forward down a slope. Something took her eye. On her radar, a vessel could be seen steaming straight towards them at speed. She watched it for a minute to make sure that it was nothing important. The boat continued on its course and was probably heading to France or beyond having to pass around the Brittany peninsula and Cape Finisterre.

After a few more minutes, it was still heading directly at the *Hyperion III* and had, more relevantly, adjusted its course to intersect with hers.

She presumed the worst.

"Manuel! Get up here!"

Ricky was nearer to the steps and was out of the hatch first, his father not far behind.

THE MONGOOSE AND THE COBRA

"Jesus!" Manuel shouted, "How long have they been on that course?"

"They are coming straight at us."

The distant sound of a helicopter could be barely heard over the wind and the splashes from the bow.

"Only one boat goes that fast and accompanied by a helicopter."

"Let's ditch the stuff!" Ricky was the first to think that the game was up.

"There's no time. There are too many sacks, and they are too heavy. They will be here in minutes and are probably filming us already." Manuel had gone very pale.

"What can we do?" Ricky felt helpless.

"It's over," his mother spoke in a normal tone, "It's over."

"OK, OK, you are probably right but not necessarily, let's bluff it out until they actually board us and go into the cabins. They may be after someone else or … I don't know, think that we are people smuggling from France. Don't look guilty and stick to our story." Manuel was holding on to the rail to counter the swell.

"I have enough explosive left to scuttle the *Hyperion*. We could get into the tender and say we were having engine problems," Ricky was trying to find a way out.

"No, no. If they are after us, it's because someone has told them what we are doing or somehow they have tracked us. Scuttling the *Hyperion* will not get us off the hook, "I need to send a message that we are not going to make it to Brixham."

Manuel disappeared back down the hatch.

"Why not take the tender and head for the Scillies? Your father and I will stay here and face the music. It's less than ten miles away," Barbara was thinking only of her son.

"Why don't we all go?"

"No, if they find an empty boat they will start searching the area. If we are here, they might not search for you. Ricky, take the grab bag and go! Now!!"

He reached over the top of the hatch and took hold of the grab bag. It is kept within easy reach up top for emergencies when there is no time, or it is impossible, to go back inside – the last thing you grab as the boat goes down. He hugged his mother, told her he loved her and hurried along the rail to the stern. She followed him aft to release the line holding the black rubber tender. By the time she reached the taffrail, he had pulled it in close to the stern and was climbing down onto the ledge. She pulled on the line to bring it even nearer, tying a knot to keep it secure for as long as possible. He jumped and rolled into the bottom of the tender, pulling himself up to sit on the side. He unlocked the engine and tilted it down from its horizontal position; it began on the second pull. He knew it would, he had checked it in Brixham before they left.

Manuel, having finished his call, re-emerged to find the wheel locked and Barbara at the stern. By the time he made it down the side to join her, there was only time to shout across the water to his son. Ricky turned the throttle, and the boat sped across the waves towards the north. The approaching cutter was still two miles away.

———

After the encounter with his mother, Eduardo had headed for the lifts in Reception with Jim following silently behind. The two of them had gone back to their rooms to pack; only having rucksacks and hand luggage meant that this did not take long. Eduardo had reached his limit and had made it clear to Jim that they were leaving. He said that he would check out for both of them and, while he settled the bills at reception with cash, Jim had walked off to get the hire car.

Tadeo was standing in the lobby with his arms folded quietly observing everything and waiting for Valentina to come down. She did not need to pack her bags, she had not done that for thirty years and she did not need to check out, her PA would do that. It was not the mindset of the ordinary person; if there was a problem she could buy the hotel ... or the chain ... or all of the buildings in the street. Having only spent a few hours there, she would be glad to leave, it was not up to her usual standard. She had only taken the room in case she needed to touch up her make up or use the washroom. She had made plans to sleep elsewhere at a private twenty room villa up in the mountains near Lezama. There had been only one purpose for visiting the Nervión Real and that was to see Eduardo and check that he was safe after the bombing.

Outside, the chauffeur had already brought the Mercedes to the front of the hotel, occupying the prime spot.

Everyone appeared to be ignoring each other in some sort of stand-off until Eduardo crossed to the main door, not even glancing at Tadeo, and stepped outside into the heat of the day.

Jim pulled up behind the chauffeur-driven Mercedes and Eduardo opened the passenger door and jumped in.

All of this was happening in front of Henri who was sat nearby on a concrete bench opposite in the shade of a tree, partially hidden by an advertising hoarding. Having been watching the hotel all morning, it was while Emmanuel had gone to buy some filled baguettes that all this activity was occurring.

Wazz and Mike also came out onto the pavement, raising their hands to shield themselves from the sun. Awkwardly, Valentina and her entourage emerged a few seconds later. She looked rather dismissively at Mike and nodding towards the viewpoint on the hill, said, "I suppose that you will go up there? There really is no need now that I am here. I will take over."

There was no time for Mike to answer as the back door to her limousine was opened for her by Tadeo who then took his position in the passenger seat alongside the driver. They purred over the cobbles and joined the tarmac of the road.

"What a bitch." Mike was dumbfounded.

"If that's what having billions does to you, I think I'll stay poor." Wazz took out a handkerchief to clean his sunglasses.

She looked at her watch, "We have forty minutes to get up to the viewpoint. Let's go before I explode."

They crossed over and began walking along the Nervión river towards the Zubizuri bridge. Unlike almost all other bridges, it was not built in a straight line across the water but in a gentle, horizontal curve. There was no time to appreciate the thirty-nine white steel cables that held it up like a cat's cradle or the see-through glass tiles now covered by a non-slip carpet put down after numerous accidents. They had been further distracted by a frisky brown dog which had joined them and taken a liking to Wazz; it now scooted alongside as if its back left leg had cramp.

The route to the Funicular de Artxanda railway was clearly marked; it was a popular attraction in itself as well as the main recreation area with its displays of large sculptures up on the wooded ridge.

Across the river, a high stone retaining wall came into view at the base of the hillside. The dog was in a routine: it continued to run ahead, drop onto its front legs and wait for Wazz to catch up. Luckily it didn't follow them as they entered through the grey marble portico under a red arch celebrating the funicular's centenary 1915 – 2015.

It was dark and a little cooler inside the ticket office, and Wazz pushed his sunglasses up onto his short, blonde hair. Mike paid for the two return tickets with her phone, and they made their way towards the boarding point.

The train, if that is what it is called, comprised a single, steeply sloping carriage made up of five very small cabins, each with its own door and accessed by its own mini-platform. Wazz and Mike chose the rear cabin and were joined by two Swedish backpackers who, once the carriage moved off, turned to look backwards at the track with its counter-balanced cable system.

When everyone was leaving the hotel, Henri had only seconds to make a decision – he could stay and wait for his brother and risk losing contact or follow them. He had overheard the conversation and Valentina say *I suppose that you will go up there?* and he had worked out that they were all heading for the sculpture park with the best views of Bilbao and, particularly, down onto the Guggenheim Museum by the river.

The fact that they now appeared to be a group of six with support staff was going to make his task even more difficult. Although Henri had initially run down a side road looking for his brother, there was no alternative, and by the time that Emmanuel had returned, he had set off. He was about two hundred yards behind Mike and her boyfriend; he rightly guessed that like him, they would take the funicular up to the park.

It was while crossing the bridge and watching an excitable dog run back and forth pestering Wazz, that he messaged his brother and told him to take a taxi up to the viewpoint where they could meet up.

CHAPTER TWENTY-NINE

Jim drove the hired car, a white Seat Ibiza, to the north side of the river and followed the circuitous route to get up to the viewing point in the park. He found himself heading east through Galdakao and Gerletxe before turning north and back west up the BI-3741 to the wooded ridge and the famous Artxanda begiratokia, the viewpoint on the mountain. His passenger had said nothing for the entire fifteen-minute journey having settled on staring through the windscreen at the rear end of a coach also on its way up. Near the top, and seeking shade, Jim parked under some trees.

"At last, my friend, we are here, and we can begin our journey proper. Let's go and meet Jacob, I know that you will like him. Forget about your mother. She is well-meaning."

Eduardo, however, had regressed to a less stable mental state and was trying to focus on the middle distance. "I'm ... what? I'm not sure ..."

"Let's get you out of the car. Trust me, you will feel better once you meet Jacob and we all toast our trip looking down on the rooftops of Bilbao." Jim was speaking quietly and reassuringly.

He walked around to the passenger's door to help and encourage his friend to leave the car. Eduardo stood up stiffly and looked around without fully taking in where he was and why there were so many tourists milling around.

"Let's walk over to the drop and wait for him." He put an arm around Eduardo and helped him to cross the road.

They made their way in the sun to the sign comprising the large red letters of 'Bilbao' repeated and reflected several times and thrown into sharp relief; it was so much more attractive than a fence or other type of barrier. Although not as iconic as the Hollywood sign, it did feature in most tourists' photographs and, especially, selfies taken of the city. They rested their arms on two letters: Jim on a letter 'o' and Eduardo on a letter 'a'. Jim used his phone to take his own picture and a selfie of the two of them, this would be his record of their achievement. In the background, the view across the rooftops and tower blocks to the mountains was dramatic but Eduardo did not show any reaction or say anything.

Jim's phone buzzed and he read a message that Jacob had arrived and would be two minutes.

"He is parking the car. Would you like some water?" he offered a plastic bottle but there was no response. Eduardo was somewhere deep within himself sheltering inside his skull, avoiding looking out.

Jim tried to reassure his friend, "You are safe here, no one is going to hurt you. You are with me. There will be no bombs."

A vulture was circling high up using the thermals on its way from the Pyrenees to the Picos de Europa. At ground level, a host of sparrows was chattering near the trees sharing a dust bath. Groups of tourists came and went, also chattering in a mixture of languages.

Jim and Eduardo stood in silence as the world moved around them. Time seemed to slow until Jim spotted the third member of their party striding towards them wearing a pink striped shirt, white shorts and a Panama hat.

———

"How's the claustrophobia?" Mike asked.

"Fine, thank you, I don't mind it so much if there are big windows." Wazz was holding on firmly.

The bright red and grey funicular had only taken three minutes to travel up to the top and the views back down the steep rail were more likely to induce vertigo than anything else, especially as the carriage swapped rails halfway up with the one coming down. There had been a group intake of breath – no one on board was expecting that to happen.

One of the Swedes had not stopped filming out of the back window for the entire journey.

At the top, the five doors slid open in unison and about thirty passengers disembarked onto their small platforms.

The day was so hot that everyone sought any and every area of shade on the short walk up past a variety of sculptures and displays to the viewpoint. Under trees, next to a large rusty metal latticework representing a fingerprint, Mike and Wazz drew breath and swigged from their water bottles. Everyone was sweating and red-faced. She took off a white cap that Wazz had bought her from a street vendor, it had BOSS written on it in large letters although whether this was the manufacturer or a comment on their relationship was debatable. She wiped her palm over her scalp, making a mental note to buy a wide selection of thin hats as soon as she got home.

"Why exactly are we here?" he had not dared ask this question before, even though there had been plenty of opportunities to probe as she had been unusually untalkative on the way up from the hotel.

Her frown was not as deep as he had expected. Perhaps,

because she had successfully dragged him up to this park, having already successfully dragged him out to Spain.

"To meet Jacob." This begged further questions.

"Why is this important to you? I can see it is important to Jim and Eduardo."

"Because something is wrong. Something doesn't add up and I am meant to be protecting him and delivering him safely back to Leonard."

Wazz could not see her logic. "Sorry, you've lost me. Eduardo needs to escape from his life in London and with his friend, Jim, they decide to run off to northern Spain. Jim's friend Jacob is joining them here in Bilbao and they are going on a road trip, a walking trip, I don't know which. What's odd about that?"

"His mother," was all that she said, although what this added by way of explanation was not evident.

After a few moments of unproductive thought Wazz voiced his opinion, "His mother is a pain, but she has said her piece and is probably at this moment on her private Boeing 777 deciding which country to buy next."

"No, I don't believe it, that's not how the cookie crumbles."

He looked confused but never got the opportunity to delve deeper because Mike spotted Eduardo and Jim leaning against the big red letters.

"There they are!"

Wazz rubbed his hands over the metal of the lattice-like sculpture to remove the sweat, "What are you intending to do? Go over?"

"No, I want to watch from here. I have this bad feeling in my gut."

"Do you trust Jim and Jacob?"

"I don't know what is in their minds. Who is this Jacob? I haven't had time to check him out, that's why I'm here, and Jim seemed a bit nervous when Valentina turned up."

"Everybody was nervous when she turned up. I don't think that is a rare occurrence."

"She's nasty. I didn't like her or the way that she treated Eduardo."

"She was worried that one son has been kidnapped and the other has survived a bomb attempt on his life but run off to Spain with a friend. How do you expect her to react? And she has limitless money so she can pay to sort anything out."

"No, something is not fitting together. I'm worried for Eduardo."

"He looks as if he's out of it. That boy needs help. I hope that he doesn't jump over the cliff."

"Or gets pushed over the cliff."

"Shall we go over?"

"No, let's wait until ... is that Jacob in the Panama hat?"

Manuel had managed to throw the cool box containing unused explosive and equipment overboard. There was no time, and he did not have the strength to jettison the sacks of cocaine. His main objective was to conceal the method of smuggling using the *Carlos Sanguinem* and to protect his brother and the network. The others could all live to fight another day or escape to somewhere where they could hide for a time. He had also moved Ricky's bag, clothes and washbag into the master cabin. He was praying that his only son would make it to safety. Unfortunately, his and Barbara's luck had run out.

In minutes, the helicopter had arrived overhead but the Border Force cutter, HMC Vigilant, kept its distance, stopping three hundred yards away. It was 128 feet long and capable of almost thirty knots – there was no way to outrun it. It dispatched a thirty-two feet long, black, rigid hull inflatable boat or RHIB from its stern slipway with six men mostly in assault gear on board that skimmed across the water towards the yacht; it was capable of the even faster speed of thirty-two knots.

As it neared, one of the officers spoke to Manuel and Barbara through a megaphone. There was no resistance, and, on board the yacht, they raised their arms without being asked. The helicopter, from RNAS Culdrose on the Lizard peninsula, approached closer dispatching a Marine down a rope. Landing near on the bow, he unfastened himself and made his way to the stern as the RHIB arrived alongside.

"Is there anyone else on board?" he asked in a calm West Country accent as some of the others came aboard.

"No," Manuel and Barbara had said in unison.

"Sit there with your hands on your head." They obliged and watched two of the men dressed in black wearing caps, go down inside the cabin.

It did not take long to establish that there was no one else on board and that there was an enormous haul of drugs in sacks below. One of the men came back up saying that all was clear. After a minute or so, the most senior of the boarding team, who was called Forrester, approached Manuel and Barbara, "I'm arresting you on suspicion of importing drugs contrary to section 3 of the Misuse of Drugs Act 1971 and section 170 of the Customs and Excise Management Act 1979." He proceeded to read them their rights and asked them if they wished to say anything. They both lowered their eyes and declined.

The man who had remained down in the cabins appeared and beckoned to Forrester. A whispered conversation took place.

"Who was sleeping in the cabin at the bow?" Forrester asked.

"Nobody," Manuel answered.

"It looks like it has been used on this trip."

There was no reply and Barbara looked at the deck.

"Your tender is missing, isn't it," he said to no one in particular, not expecting an answer, as if it had just come into his mind.

"We don't have a tender," Manuel sounded South American for the first time.

Forrester lifted his cap by the peak, brushed his curly brown hair back and replaced it. He turned and took a few paces along the rail towards the bow, peering down through the narrow windows to the galley below. Out of earshot, he proceeded to speak on his radio to someone aboard the cutter suggesting to them that the helicopter undertake a sweep of the area looking for the missing tender.

He explained to Manuel and Barbara that they were going to be transferred to the cutter after which the *Hyperion III* would be towed to Plymouth.

Manuel stared intensely at Forrester while Barbara looked over her shoulder towards the Isles of Scilly watching the helicopter peel off and begin to quarter the area like a marsh harrier.

On board the HMC Vigilant, it was noisy despite the fact that they were only travelling at a slow rate of knots with the *Hyperion III* in tow; two men had remained on the yacht. There were ten crew members on board the cutter including the commander who was called Frost. He was talking to Forrester in private.

"How much?"

"There were twenty-one sacks, each about twenty pounds."

"Wow. Have they said anything?"

"No ... nothing important. They say they are a married couple who sail out of Brixham and have kept a yacht in the marina for years and are well-known there. He seems to be Spanish and she's West Country."

"... and the drugs?"

"They say that they have been blackmailed into carrying them, but they are not saying anything else. She will break in due course but he's a tough nut."

"Have you called it in?"

"Yes, I did from when I was on the yacht. Everyone's quite excited."

They went on discussing the boarding and arrest while Manuel and Barbara were being held in separate cabins. It was while taking a call from London that the news came in that the helicopter had found the third member of the yacht crew in a rib heading for St Mary's on the Isles of Scilly.

The RHIB had set off again from the cutter towards the coordinates given by the helicopter. Half an hour later or so, they had picked up a man who had given his name as Ricky Diaz from near Salisbury but apart from the fact that he was the son of the two being held on board the Vigilant, he had not said anything else. A Marine took the inflatable tender from the yacht the seven miles to St Mary's where the helicopter landed at the airport to pick him up. None of the tourists arriving in the harbour had any idea what was happening all around them. The authorities took the tender into their safekeeping in case it was evidence in any future legal proceedings.

Manuel and Barbara were not told that Ricky was now on board in a separate cabin at the other end of the cutter.

CHAPTER THIRTY

Eduardo, in his head, was replaying a version of the meeting with his mother at the hotel. He had for the first time in years fought back, telling her to concentrate on getting Diego back and to leave him alone. By turning up in Bilbao she had merely highlighted to the bombers where he was; she needed to accept that he had escaped by his own devices and wanted to build his own life in northern Spain with his father's extended Basque family.

He came back to reality to hear Jim saying, "Here's Jacob."

Eduardo almost collapsed against the red letters and needed to steady himself.

"Diego? Diego?" he was having difficulty separating dreams from reality.

The man before him removed his Panama hat to reveal his wavy black hair and stepped forward with his arms outstretched.

"Ed," a smile revealed perfect teeth under a long nose, "Yes, brother, it's me ... don't worry, it's all good."

"I thought you were Jacob," he was not entirely convinced.

"I am ... well, in a way. Diego is a corruption of Jacob if you want to be precise ... which I know you like to be."

Diego hugged his brother who slowly raised his arms as questions formed.

"Why? How are you here?"

"I wanted to escape my life – like you did – and start again. I met Jim some time ago and asked him to help me," he broke off to give his brother another hug, "I know that you are suffering but I hope that this can be an end to our lives looking over our shoulders."

"They tried to blow me up."

"I know, I know."

"Jim ... you knew. You ..."

"Eduardo, I'm sorry, I couldn't tell you, but I knew it was for the best and that you would be happy once Diego had faked his kidnap."

"This is all too much," but the tension was gradually disappearing from Eduardo's face, "Are the three of us really going on the Pilgrim's Trail? No lies."

"No lies, brother. We are going all the way to Santiago de Compostela and, afterwards, when Jim has gone back to the UK, you and I will live here in the Basque country. No one will know who we are ... and don't worry about money, I have that more than sorted."

Eduardo's face finally broke into a weak smile, "I want this so much to be true. I cannot take any more. I cannot look over my shoulder."

The brothers hugged so tightly that Diego dropped his hat which Jim picked up.

"Let's take some photos so that we can remember this day. Jim, here's my phone."

Diego and Eduardo adopted various poses next to the letters and, afterwards, Jim took a couple of selfies with them.

"I thought you were kidnapped and, probably, dead." Eduardo was beginning to think rationally again but was still shaking gently.

"I'm sorry, I couldn't risk telling you ...I hope that you understand. It took a lot of planning."

"I don't care as long as you are alive."

"You realise that you almost blew it, literally, when you went off to that cabin and were followed. Jim told me that you were seconds from being blown up."

"That's why I've hardly let you out of my sight, Eduardo." Jim looked two inches taller now that the responsibility had been handed over to Diego who was tilting his head forwards to shade his eyes as he took in the panorama.

"I've never been up here. That's a fantastic view," he turned to his brother, "I won't miss all of the travelling, all of the living in this house for two days, then, off again to another house in another country ... or all of the pressure of running the companies. How much money does anyone need? I have hidden away a few million dollars ... so we won't be out on the streets."

"Jim, you asked me to take out twenty thousand dollars," Eduardo laughed.

"Well, I wanted it all to sound credible. That wouldn't have lasted long though, would it?"

"Which reminds me," Diego reached into his trouser pocket and took out a mobile phone handing it to Eduardo, "this is for you. It's best that you ditch the one you have. We still need to be sensible and stay safe."

Henri had watched all of this from the relative dark of the stand of trees.

At some distance, he had followed Wazz and Mike to the funicular railway, his guess had been confirmed that the group was heading for the viewpoint. He had no idea why they were going there or, indeed, who they all were. His eyes had quickly adjusted as he had entered the dark of the ticket office, almost tripping over a dog that had scooted along the wall outside of the door. Armed only with a knife, the chances of killing Mike and escaping with his own life were slim; Wazz would see to that. There was no hurry, he would wait for his brother. Not wanting to risk being spotted or drawing attention to himself, he had caught the next train fifteen minutes later.

The small cabin in the carriage had been hot and packed with tourists. He had almost held his breath for the three minutes until they had all reached the top. Out in the sunshine, it had been easy to blend in with the small groups of people making their way along the road. As he had reached the paved area, he had stopped and taken up a position leaning against the trunk of a tree. He could see everyone up ahead where most people were standing next to the large red letters taking selfies.

Earlier, when he had messaged his brother telling him to get a taxi and head for the viewpoint, he had told him to text when he arrived.

Emmanuel, on receiving the instructions, had shouted some expletives to himself and cursed the God who had chosen that brief moment while he was food shopping for them to leave the hotel.

His training had kicked in and he had focussed on the matter in hand; recrimination and analysis was for later. All that mattered was that they were out of the hotel at last and he could do his job. He would not fail this time. There had been a taxi across the road outside of another hotel. Emmanuel had run across and opened the rear door, jumping onto the rear seat where he had thrown the bag containing baguettes and cans of drink. The driver had turned to remonstrate but one look at his unwanted passenger's face had dissuaded him.

"To the viewpoint," Emmanuel had ordered, and he had taken out one hundred euros which he had waved at the driver who had sworn in Basque under his breath but had started the engine. This had been a good move on his behalf because

Emmanuel's next move would have involved violence and no financial transaction other than what the driver would need to spend at the hospital.

The journey had barely taken fifteen minutes but several times he had grabbed the passenger seat headrest and encouraged the driver to hurry up. There had been little either of them could do about the traffic and there had been no opportunities to overtake. At the station for the funicular at the top, the driver had pulled over and Emmanuel had handed him the note not requiring any change. He had grabbed his bag and jumped out.

Marching up the road, he had texted to find out exactly where Henri was standing – this had turned out to be on the right-hand side where some cars had been badly parked on the grass and bare earth under the tree canopy.

Emmanuel had been sweating and had stains under the armpits of his loose shirt; it was hanging over his jeans concealing the gun that was tucked into his waistband.

Henri had taken a pace forward so that he was more visible, and they had acknowledged each other in a low-key way.

"There are a lot of tourists around." Emmanuel was assessing the situation and weighing up options.

"That is a good thing, I think. There will be more chaos when you fire the shots."

"But it is harder to escape up here. It would have been easier near the hotel where we could have disappeared down the backstreets."

"If you select the right point from which to fire, no one will know that it is us, especially if you throw the gun away and we split up and meet back at the hotel."

"Remember that I do not have a rifle, I have a second-hand gun that I haven't fired yet. I would prefer to be within ten metres."

"Let's see how close we can get to her."

"I may have to shoot both of them, we cannot risk the other one chasing us."

"I will have the knife ready if things don't go according to plan."

They glanced at each other with a look that recognised the time had come. They would not fail this time and would make Uncle Alain very proud.

———

"That must be Jacob."

Mike had watched a man in a Panama hat approach Eduardo and Jim. She saw the various reactions; the hugging and the selfies being taken.

"You can relax," Wazz tried to reassure her, "everyone is friendly and happy. Your fears were misplaced. He is safe. All is well in the world."

"Jesus! That's Diego. I knew something wasn't right." While Wazz was speaking, she had been calling up the images of him she had saved on her phone from various business magazines. His photographs were all over the internet.

"What does that mean?"

"Well, he's not kidnapped, is he?"

"What are they planning?"

"I don't know. I'm going to call Leonard."

She dialled and leant back against the thick metal lattice, waiting for him to answer.

"de Vries."

"Leonard are you sitting comfortably?" she was lowering her voice although no one was within earshot.

"Yeah, thanks, the new cream is working a treat."

"Glad to hear it, actually, Leonard, this is serious. I am at the viewpoint overlooking Bilbao watching Jim and Eduardo. You will never guess who has just turned up ... Diego."

"Jeez," he was silent as he thought through the possibilities.

"Diego is Jacob. The three of them had it all planned."

"You're sure?" Leonard was catching up.

"I have checked his photo. It's him. No doubt."

"He must have faked the kidnap, or his mother has paid the ransom, whatever that was. She hasn't told me anything."

"What do you want me to do?"

"If he's safe and with his brother what more can we do? We are the CIA not a kindergarten and he really should be out of diapers by now."

"Where's his mother flown off to?"

"Haven't heard from her. No idea."

"Oh, you're joking ... Leonard, she's here."

"Who is where?"

"Valentina has just turned up with her minder."

"Sheesh, now who's playing games?"

"I'm going over," and to Wazz she said, "Hold my bag."

"Is that wise?" Wazz expressed his view. Mike made it clear from her face that, apparently, it was wise.

"Fill me in when you know what's happening. I've got a President to babysit." Leonard took his leave.

It was Jim who had caught Eduardo when he had fainted or, at least, had gone extremely light-headed.

"Have you told him yet?" Valentina was looking at Diego.

"No, not completely, he thinks that I planned it all."

"Well, you did ... most of it."

Jim was giving Eduardo a drink from his bottle of water. This seemed to partially revive him.

"Mother?"

"I know seeing me twice in one day is unusual but even you,

poor boy, should be able to work out what's happening, can't you?"

He said nothing which revealed that, obviously, he couldn't.

Diego took over, "We'll speak later but, Ed, Mother and I planned all of this. It's not only you and me who are disappearing for good, Mother is selling up as well. We will all get out of the spotlight and enjoy the rest of our lives."

Eduardo was not sure if he had won or lost, whether he should laugh or cry.

"Please do not run away again or speak to me like you did this morning. You do not realise the extent that I protect you," Valentina was attempting to lower her voice but not being wholly successful.

Diego was trying to reassure his brother that it was all for the best, "You, Jim and I will go to Santiago de Compostela as planned. Cheer up. I will fill you in on all of the details."

"Oh, good, I'd love to know the details, as well, given I've spent the last week finding Eduardo on behalf of Leonard and you know who, Valentina." Mike had joined the throng which included Tadeo in his dark glasses looking the least like a tourist as is possible to imagine.

"Miss Kingdom, thank you for your hard work and I will tell Leonard how competent you have been but there is no need for you to be involved any longer."

"Really?" Mike turned towards Valentina and stared her down. She looked back at Eduardo, "You have my number, give me a ring if this all turns out to be more of the same by which I mean you being hidden away in a big villa in Spain and waiting for someone to bomb you as opposed to living in London and ... you get the idea."

Unfortunately, she never got to hear his answer as several gunshots rang out.

CHAPTER THIRTY-ONE

In London it was 3.30pm, Commander Bob Trevelyan was being given the latest information by Leonard.

"Leonard, thanks for the update. I've heard no more on the vehicles, and I was wondering what to do next. It's great that you've found Eduardo in Spain, but I need to clear up the case. What has he said about the bombing?"

"Bob, he's said nothing to my knowledge. He's run away from home and doesn't want to come back and if you had met his mother, you might understand."

"Leonard, that's great news that you've found Eduardo but it's Mike Kingdom I'm very bothered about. If she hadn't left the cabin at that moment, we would be looking at murder."

"True, Bob, but they weren't after her, they were after Eduardo. They were trying to put the frighteners on the mother."

"Leonard, I am not buying a lot of this, sorry. People with bombs, even professionals, don't drive around the Home Counties on the off chance that they bump into their target. No one knew that Eduardo was going there, and he went by taxi, then walked through the woods. I doubt he knew he was going to turn up until a few hours before. He also had two burner phones so that he could hide his movements. How did the bombers know where he was? Even if they had found his new numbers and had traced a phone, they didn't have time to follow him into the woods of Oxfordshire. On top of which, his first phone was dead and out of battery. That's why he left it on Mike's table ... it was of no use to him or anyone else. The bombers did not use that phone to locate Eduardo in that cabin, I don't believe it."

"If you're right, who were they after?" He was distracted by something that had appeared on his screen about the President's visit.

"Leonard, the one person who was near certain to be there was Mike. I accept that this Wazz and the forester are possibilities, but I have ruled them out unless someone tells me otherwise. The bombers were after Mike, weren't they?"

Leonard went quiet while he digested what his friend, the Commander, was saying.

Bob continued, "Is she safe? Can you put her under some sort of protection?"

"Shit, Bob, she's in Bilbao tracking Eduardo and Jim."

"Jesus Christ."

"... with Wazz."

"Leonard, they are after one of them. This is a perfect storm."

There had been a lot of screaming. Every tourist had tried to hide or had started to run away down the hill.

There was a body lying on the gravel; it was not moving.

Tadeo had swivelled round looking for the gunman. He was in time to see Wazz run up behind the shooter and kidney punch him. As he collapsed, Wazz delivered a vicious two-handed blow to the side of his head while rolling forward and grabbing the gun. Emmanuel was unconscious. By the time that Henri reacted and pulled out his knife, he was faced with Wazz standing up with the gun pointing at him.

"Drop it!"

Henri let the knife fall to the ground and Wazz motioned to him with the gun, "Lie on the ground!" He repeated it in Spanish, but Henri had understood. Wazz kicked the knife away and stood behind the two prostrate brothers, regaining his breath.

From out of the panicking crowd a man in a red and white Athletic Bilbao football shirt emerged running towards Wazz and the source of the shooting. He looked like a body builder but, whatever his background, he was calm and unfazed.

"Let me help," he said in Spanish.

The man picked up the knife and knelt on Henri's legs. A powerful blow with his elbow pushed Henri's nose into the compacted earth. He sliced the back of Henri's shirt into strips and used one piece to tie his hands behind his back. He repeated this exercise on Emmanuel who was gradually coming to. He used the last piece of shirt to tie the brothers' legs together as if they were about to enter a three-legged race.

Another man in his thirties, a friend of the first, had joined them while everyone else was running away or trying to find somewhere safe to see what had occurred.

Wazz looked across to the group. He could not see what had happened.

"I need to check on my girlfriend," he explained as he handed the gun to the local football supporter.

They encouraged him to go, saying that they had the two killers under control. Wazz would never know but the two men would report back to Felipe later, his debts to Valentina discharged.

Wazz ran the short distance, perhaps twelve or thirteen paces, across the gravel; to him, this felt like it had taken hours. In his head, he was beating himself up. He had been a few seconds too late. After Mike had said she was going to speak to Valentina, he had leant back against the screen and surveyed the scene; personally, he would not have got involved. Family disagreements were not his bag, especially the family of a billionaire.

To begin with, his focus had been on Mike and Valentina but soon he had begun to scan the crowd, something that was in his DNA and refined after years of protecting people. Two men under the trees had caught his eye. They had been intently watching Valentina and her family. The larger of the two men was clearly ex-military and had stepped sideways to stand behind a small tree. This movement triggered something in Wazz as he imagined this man using the trunk to rest his arm while firing a gun. There was barely time to react.

Wazz had moved slowly but purposefully in an arc to end up in the trees behind the two men.

And this is what was gnawing away at him. He had positioned himself perfectly but ten seconds too late. Replaying the moments in his head, he could see the man take out the gun from the waistband under his long, creased shirt and line it up ready to fire. Two shots had rung out before Wazz had leapt forward and kidney punched the shooter.

If Mike was dead, he would never recover.

In all the years that he had escorted wealthy women around Marbella, an aggressive approach by a cheap watch seller, one of the 'Looky-Looky' men from north Africa, had been about the most threatening. When this had happened, Wazz had grabbed the man's arm and twisted it behind his back, spilling the fake Rolexes in the tray all over the floor outside of the coffee shop at the marina. It had not troubled him one bit and paled into insignificance compared to what had just happened.

Of course, when he was appointed by Charles Yelland to protect his Spanish villa, he had come under serious threat but could never have imagined what might happen and that he would end up meeting and working with Mike Kingdom.

But from the first day he had met her, he knew ...

———

While all of this was happening that Tuesday lunchtime high above Bilbao, Xavier was having a glass of rum with coke. He was alone, which was how he preferred to be, and was toasting another successful trip.

His brother, Manuel, had sent him a coded message that he had picked up the twenty-one sacks of cocaine from the lifeboat and was on his way back to Brixham. They would take a few days to make the return trip avoiding land and keeping a low profile. This haul was worth over thirty million dollars.

On its last visit to Southampton a month earlier, there had been no drugs on the *Carlos Sanguinem* for anyone to find; they had already been collected off the south coast of Ireland by Manuel. It had worked like a dream. Barbara, a very experienced sailor had been in charge of the yacht and Ricky had provided the muscle to transfer the sacks to the yacht and to deploy the explosive that destroyed the lifeboat and sent the pieces in every direction and to the bottom of the sea.

John, his undercover man at the docks in Southampton had been invaluable. He had been able to let all of the authorities search anywhere they liked. Of course, they had found nothing, there was nothing to be found. This made it highly unlikely that they would pick on this ship again. This was a massive result and was a virtual carte-blanche to import what they wanted.

On the previous seven journeys, the *Carlos Sanguinem* had carried sizeable amounts of cocaine concealed in containers of soya curd animal feed, but the authorities were getting suspicious, therefore Xavier changed how it was transported. A few weeks in advance, John had learnt about the work of the CIA and British agencies which would very likely result in a full search, and he had tipped off Xavier. If only this Mike Kingdom had accepted defeat, like her colleagues in the other authorities, when they had found nothing, then no further action would have been necessary – but she had persisted. For the next week and a half, she had pestered John with questions and ideas, some of which were getting too close for comfort. Without her, the case would have been closed and Xavier's business could have continued to flourish.

She had been a serious problem and had needed to be removed – urgently.

He had called Alain, someone he had used before to eliminate any individual who was obstructing his system. This had led to Alain's two nephews being given the task of eliminating this thorn in his side. John, who had proved invaluable, had provided her photograph, address and phone number; this was all they needed, and the next step should have been easy. However, blowing up her cabin had, apparently, failed.

It was tempting to revert to his old system using the cattle feed containers; this would have definitely worked for the next crossing, but he did not have much time to make that choice. At the Colombian end, they needed to know what and how they should load the *Carlos Sanguinem* in Cartagena for its return; he had decided to stick with the new system, the one that Mike was beginning to suspect.

She had raised these thoughts with John without realising that they would be conveyed immediately to Xavier. The WhatsApp messages warning that Mike Kingdom had now asked him about lifeboats had been the final straw. Less than a day after that message, a lifeboat containing a consignment of drugs would be launched into the sea at roughly the same spot as the month earlier. This could not be changed. They had been put on board nine days previously and were now far across the Atlantic Ocean. The lifeboat had to be launched before the *Carlos Sanguinem* properly entered the English Channel.

He made himself calm down by taking a sip of his rum and allowing his mind to run free. They were now hot on her heels in Bilbao or wherever she had gone on holiday with her boyfriend.

With the last mouthful of rum, he had relaxed and prepared to head out for a meeting. Before getting out of the chair he checked one last thing on his phone – the current position of the *Carlos Sanguinem*. He put its Maritime Mobile Service Identity number into a specialist tracking site. A smile passed his lips, it was predicted to arrive at Southampton docks in a little over one hour – later than expected. Nobody was going to check the containers but if they did, there was absolutely nothing on board.

A WhatsApp message in Spanish appeared on his phone from Manuel that stopped him in his tracks.

"Police coming towards us. No time to do anything. Run. All my love."

Xavier put down his glass. What had just happened? They were on their way back to Brixham having done the difficult bit, surely? How had the police or Border Force found out?

He told himself not to panic. He had time to get out of the house.

In his study, he opened the safe and took out the remaining dollars that had been cut in half, a wad of cash, his passports and some paperwork. In his bedroom, he packed his suitcase as if going on holiday except that he threw in some framed photos of his children. When would he see them again? He couldn't say goodbye, they were at swimming lessons although they were meant to have returned half an hour ago. Back downstairs, he put everything he needed from his study into his briefcase together with his laptop.

It had been going so well but, hey, he would disappear for a while and regroup. He had done it before.

With one last look around the room, he grabbed his car keys and headed down the corridor.

The sound of a car outside gave him hope that at least he could kiss the children before leaving. There was movement at the front door, and he opened it.

He was faced by a group of policemen, some in uniform, some armed.

"Mr Diaz? Mr Xavier Diaz?"

He nodded and said yes.

"You are under arrest on suspicion of ..." Xavier did not hear the rest of the sentence or anything else that the senior officer said but he did feel the handcuffs being put on his wrists behind his back.

"Is there anybody else in the house?"

"No, there is no one ... I'm alone."

Four policemen entered through the large front door and spread out through the house. Another officer collected the suitcase and briefcase inside the hall and took them out to one of the vehicles.

CHAPTER THIRTY-TWO

Wazz could not see Mike among the large group now standing or leaning over the victim. He grabbed two people out of the way, he had no idea who they were.

It looked as if one of the large red letters had melted – there was such an extensive pool of blood. Out of respect, someone had placed a thin, white cotton jacket over the victim's face, but the blood had seeped through.

Tadeo was stood upright while Diego was knelt over the body in a sort of silent prayer. Relief swept through Wazz. Guilt at feeling this was nowhere to be seen. The victim must be Valentina.

The sound of sirens was echoing from the city far below, but this may have been coincidence.

Any relief that Wazz had felt, however, was very short-lived. There was a second victim, and this was Mike. In another huddle, he could see Jim standing, bare from the waist up, having taken off his shirt and having used a sleeve to tie a tourniquet around Mike's upper arm. She was laid out on the ground in the sun, only her bald head was in the shade of the capital letter B.

"Mike!" Wazz was out of his mind.

"Are we safe?" Jim had paid no attention to what was happening behind him.

"Yes, they're out of action."

Wazz looked down at the woman who had crept into his life and taken over. There were no signs of life except for very shallow breaths that hardly caused her chest to move. Her eyes opened slowly.

"You took your time," she whispered.

He shook his head. No witty response immediately came to mind. Instead he dropped to his knees shading her upper body.

"You silly sod."

"What happened?" her voice was weak.

"You were shot ... as was Valentina, only she's dead." He was taking off his shirt to fold up and place under her head.

"I guess I was unlucky to be stood next to her?"

"No, she was unlucky to be stood next to you, I think."

"What?"

"I think that the gunmen were after you, that's my guess."

"No."

"Now, take it easy and stop talking until the ambulance gets here."

This was not likely to be long as the sound of the sirens was growing ever louder way below.

No one around Valentina's body at that moment, apart from Wazz, suspected that she was collateral damage. Publicly, she was the obvious target. It had always been assumed that she was being pursued by criminal, political and commercial enemies; more often than not, this was not the case. She had extended her neurotic behaviour to include the protection of Eduardo, whom she regarded as weak and vulnerable. No one had ever really threatened him, but this had not stopped her from engineering his fake death and creating his subsequent life in London under Leonard.

She had kept Diego close; he was different and would not have tolerated such interference. She controlled him in a different way by allowing him to progress up through the management of the companies but eventually he, too, began to resist her overbearing manipulation.

He had devised a way out for him and for Eduardo which had only taken off as an idea when he had met Jim at a random social event in London. He knew that his brother would never listen again to his mother or, even to him, but he might follow the dream of living in the Basque lands under his old name; he had fallen for the idea more than Diego could ever have hoped. But this was not solely for Eduardo, Diego would use the opportunity to escape as well ensuring that there was enough money for both of them.

Unfortunately, after that, the project had rather stalled. Diego had felt guilty that his mother would be utterly broken if she had 'lost' both of her sons at the same time. He could not let her suffer thinking that they were both dead. She would have been suicidal.

The answer, although he would have preferred not to go down this route, was to involve her. She was coming under increasing pressure to sell the businesses and did not appear to be enjoying her life as much as she once had. He had convinced her to stage an escape for the three of them but on Diego's terms. She could enjoy her money for the rest of her life. The plans were made, and his own kidnap staged in Switzerland; this element had worked perfectly, and he knew that he could never have performed this role if Valentina was not part of it.

Jim had played his role so well. Diego had generously funded him but, surprisingly, Jim and Eduardo had become good friends. Eduardo had bought straight into the Basque adventure. He was already halfway there with his obsession with his birth father and the Catholic saints.

Everything had gone swimmingly up until that fateful Saturday. Eduardo had left London and had headed to the Cotswolds. When it was actually becoming a reality, his crazy brother had begun to have one of his wobbles and had stopped on his journey to visit a work colleague. This was one of those things that only made sense inside Eduardo's head.

It was a complete shock when an attempt on his life was made by bombing the cabin. It rather endorsed what Valentina had been fearing and she became ever more convinced that it was time for the three of them to disappear and enjoy her fortune.

While Diego had been hiding across the border in France, Valentina was playing the distraught mother running her businesses and bankrolling Conrad's re-election campaign. She had been spooked by the attempted bombing of Eduardo and had decided to adjust the plan. She was not meant to come out to Bilbao until Jim, Eduardo and Diego had completed their road trip and Eduardo's state of mind had reset to normal or, at least, to what passed as normal with him.

After a day in Bilbao, Jim had secretly reported to Diego that Eduardo was a changed man; he was so happy meeting his extended Basque family, travelling around and visiting his beloved 'tulips' at the Guggenheim. He could not wait to follow the Pilgrim's Trail to Santiago de Compostela.

Jim had become worried when Mike had turned up. Why was she following him and who had sent her? After all, it was while visiting her that the bomb had exploded. Was she leading the bombers to him again?

After she had asked Eduardo to help with some of her analysis, he had become even more excited. Jim was concerned that she would entice him back to London and ruin the progress that had been made. All of this became irrelevant when Valentina suddenly turned up and Eduardo had flipped. He had told his mother to get out of his life and to leave him to do what he wanted. She was completely taken aback. He had never spoken to her like that.

Valentina was not somebody who rolled over easily and, even after the two explosions which disrupted the Augusta King cable offshore of Bude and on land at Bilbao, she calmly regrouped and reconfirmed in her mind that it was time to gather her sons back under her wing, probably in the backwoods of America.

And now she was dead ... even though, ironically, she was not the intended target.

It was the day after the shootings.

Bilbao, Spain and, indeed, the world's press and social media were speculating over who would murder one of the world's richest women. The fact that she was the American President's largest sponsor had not been missed nor that he was scheduled to be in Bilbao but was now to fly straight to Madrid. He had been advised, privately, not to announce the awarding of the cable contract to Valentina's company yet but to link her killing to the two explosions that had partially disrupted internet traffic between Europe and the USA even though his advisers knew that there was no direct connection between the events.

Instead, Conrad in a speech majored on the discovery by the CIA of the largest drug-smuggling operation from Colombia into Europe using container ships. He thanked the UK Border Force for their prompt action once the CIA in Langley and London had uncovered the system and individuals involved.

He didn't mention that the two killers, who lived in Montpellier, France, were in custody and being interviewed by the Spanish police and Interpol. Neither did he mention the fact that a young woman, an American tourist, had been injured in the shooting in Bilbao and was being treated in the Basurtuko Uniburtsitate Ospitalea, the main hospital.

Unaware of all this, that young woman was having a second blood infusion while complaining about her private room being too bright.

Wazz was next to her, and he had also warranted no mention at all in the media. He had joined Mike in the ambulance which had taken them both back into the city, across the river and past the Guggenheim to the hospital. They would never know the identity of Felipe's men who had handed Emmanuel and Henri over to the police.

"I need a new hat."

"We'll get you one."

"You keep staring at my head."

She was sitting in bed, bald-headed with a large, purple mark on her face where she had headbutted the letter B as she collapsed to the ground.

"I am staring at a bruise that is the size of a dinner plate on your forehead."

She dismissed this as irrelevant.

"All that money and now dead," Mike was finding it hard not to think about Valentina and her billions, "When we get home, I'm going to sell *The Running Man* and buy a house. What's the point of owning a million dollar sculpture and having nowhere to live?"

"You can stay in the flat as long as you want."

"Thank you. At the moment I don't know what I want apart from leaving Bilbao," she changed tack, "Any sign of Eduardo?"

"Jim and Diego are still looking for him. In all the confusion, nobody saw where he went. He took his rucksack with him and must have run off. When he calms down, he'll come home, I'm sure."

"I know that he didn't like her but seeing your mother killed in front of you would freak anyone out."

"I bet he's scared that he's next."

Her phone that was on a white side table buzzed. Wazz reached across and passed it to her.

"How you doing?" Leonard was calling from London.

"I'm in hospital ... having a blood transfusion."

"Glad to hear it ... but not too many details. I'm squeamish about that sort of thing. That's why I like my steaks well done," he got distracted for a second, "I thought you'd like an update."

"Great because I haven't a clue what's been happening."

"First, your yacht idea was on the money. They found tons of cocaine on board and the owners are under lock and key. The brother of the owner was the bigwig and he's helping the Brit police with their enquiries. He was the one who took out the contract on you. They failed when they tried to bomb you in your cabin and had a go at shooting you in Bilbao. You need to start looking after yourself better. Good operatives are hard to find."

With one arm resting on the bed receiving the transfusion and the other holding her phone to her ear, she was not in a position to react to several things he had said apart from to say, "What? Me? How did they find out about me?"

"The bigwig had a guy called John on his books ... you must have met him at Southampton. He gave him the details of your cabin. Oh, and John's also helping the police with their enquiries."

"What a jerk. I thought he was one of the good guys."

"You need to be pickier with your friends."

"How does Eduardo fit into all this?"

"He doesn't fit in anywhere, if you want my opinion. He just happened to call in to your place on his way to meet this Jim. Bad timing. Mind you, worse timing for Valentina ... standing next to you."

"Do you do empathy?"

"I can do empathy if the other person tells me to."

"Leonard!"

"Anyway, she's dead and Diego takes over the businesses. POTUS has already spoken to him. He'll get the cable contract. Don't worry about him, he knows now that Valentina imagined 90% of the threats. He's more grounded ... but it would be hard to be more neurotic than his mother."

"Who blew up the cables?"

"Our friends from China. They get jealous now and again. It'll pass. Is your boyfriend still with you?"

She didn't bother to rise to the bait, "Wazz is next to me."

"Good, tell him that you need protection. I don't think that they'll come after you again but it's possible."

"Oh, wonderful. I think that I need to disappear off the radar for a while."

"Nah, best to get straight back on the horse. Come back into the office. You're safe here."

"Is that empathy?"

"You could take over Chuck's art project. You like art."

"Nice try. Is the Agency looking for Eduardo?"

"Yeah, POTUS has reassured Diego that we are on the case. The Spanish police are searching for him, as well. Don't worry, he'll turn up. Nobody's after him. He's scared of his own shadow."

"Would you offer him his old job back, if he wanted it?"

He reflected for a second, "Is this one of those *Buy one, get one free* offers?"

"And if it was?"

"Who doesn't like a bargain?"

After the call, she sent a 'How are you?" message to Eduardo's phone. Half an hour later, he replied with five emojis of tulips: 🌷🌷🌷🌷🌷

ACKNOWLEDGMENTS

I would like to begin by declaring my debt to the late Gerald Pollinger who, with his father, was agent to Graham Greene among others. He represented me in the late 1990s and his support and advice were invaluable, particularly as I began to write the Mike Kingdom series; he never lived to see *The Tip of the Iceberg* completed.

Further thanks go to my wife, Natasha, my sister, Angela, and my friend, Amber, who have shouldered the burden of reading my first draft. Paul and Mandy have also given me great encouragement.

All four of the Mike Kingdom thrillers have been edited by Lindsay Corten and she still has not changed her name and moved abroad. I hear her voice in my ear even as I write this. She has been the most wonderful critical friend.

Jem Butcher has produced the stunning covers for the series picking up on all of the subtleties as only a gifted designer can.

My thanks go to Adrian Hobart and Rebecca Collins at Hobeck Books whose advice, support and friendship are what every writer needs. It only took me twenty-nine years to find them.

Finally, a big thank you to the reviewers and bloggers who have all been so generous and who have, unwittingly, given me the strength to follow Mike Kingdom wherever she takes me.

DAVID JARVIS

ABOUT THE AUTHOR

David Jarvis went to art college, and then ran his design and planning practice for forty years, working all over the world. He ended up planning countries. His canvases just got bigger and bigger.

HOBECK BOOKS – THE HOME OF GREAT STORIES

We hope you've enjoyed reading this novel by David Jarvis. To keep up to date on David's fiction writing please do follow him on Twitter/X, Bluesky or Instagram.

Hobeck Books offers a number of short stories and novellas, free for subscribers in the compilation *Crime Bites*.

- *Echo Rock* by Robert Daws
- *Old Dogs, Old Tricks* by AB Morgan
- *The Silence of the Rabbit* by Wendy Turbin
- *Never Mind the Baubles: An Anthology of Twisted Winter Tales* by the Hobeck Team (including many of the Hobeck authors and Hobeck's two publishers)
- *The Clarice Cliff Vase* by Linda Huber
- *Here She Lies* by Kerena Swan
- *The Macnab Principle* by R.D. Nixon
- *Fatal Beginnings* by Brian Price
- *A Defining Moment* by Lin Le Versha
- *Saviour* by Jennie Ensor
- *You Can't Trust Anyone These Days* by Maureen Myant

HOBECK BOOKS - THE HOME OF GREAT STORIES

Also please visit the Hobeck Books website for details of our other superb authors and their books, and if you would like to get in touch, we would love to hear from you.

Hobeck Books also presents a weekly podcast, the Hobcast, where founders Adrian Hobart and Rebecca Collins discuss all things book related, key issues from each week, including the ups and downs of running a creative business. Each episode includes an interview with one of the people who make Hobeck possible: the editors, the authors, the cover designers. These are the people who help Hobeck bring great stories to life. Without them, Hobeck wouldn't exist. The Hobcast can be listened to from all the usual platforms but it can also be found on the Hobeck website: **www.hobeck.net/hobcast**.

ALSO BY DAVID JARVIS

The Mike Kingdom Thrillers
The Tip of the Iceberg
This Is Not a Pipe
The Violin and Candlestick
The Mongoose and the Cobra
The Green Feathers

The Collation Unit

Buy online, from your local bookshop or from the Hobeck Books website.